The Slim Chance Tour

Shawn Michael Bitz

Advance Praise for *The Slim Chance Tour*

"The discovery of one's self can be a painful journey. In Shawn Bitz's *The Slim Chance Tour*, the reader sits in the corner witnessing that discovery by musician Slim Chance as well as his biographer, Steven Barber. It's a bumpy ride, but if you like good tears and redemption from a rock and roll Hell on earth lifestyle, you should read this novel."

—Randy Hart, Music Producer, Musical Director for the late, great Roger Miller, and Head Pianist for the Grand Ole Opry

"This is definitely a book I could relate to. I share a lot of common background (and checkered past) with ol' Slim Chance, so reading, (and mentally listening to) him tell his stories was not far from a walk down memory lane. As Mr. Bitz portrays him in the *The Slim Chance Tour*, Slim is a masterful storyteller with an irresistible story and a colorful delivery, and as he meanders through his past, he is likely to carry you along."

—Rick Roberts, Multi-platinum artist and singer/songwriter and Colorado Music Hall of Famer

"Having played music for several decades, I can truly appreciate the believable characters in *The Slim Chance Tour* as well as the wonderful adventures of Slim Chance. We can all relate to Slim's story at some level. It's a great read with many interesting twists and turns. I highly recommend this book."
—Lawren Erickson, Black Hills Musician

"In *The Slim Chance Tour*, Shawn Bitz continues his gift for creating a cast of endearing characters in whimsical circumstances to provide a very entertaining read. Filling a few days with a story that has many laughs, a few tears, and an intense desire to read what happens next is a good enough reason to read this book. But in the end, there's plenty to learn about life in this book as well. I heartily recommend it!"

—Gus Johnson, Black Hills Attorney and Music Enthusiast

"I love a good story told by a non-primary character. Think *Sophie's Choice* and *The Great Gatsby*. Shawn Michael Bitz has mastered this style with *The Slim Chance Tour*. Slim Chance is a fascinating storyteller and Steven Barber's observations are just enough to keep the reader grounded in the present as they travel the aging rockstar's life. Highly recommend."

—Barbara Raffin, Award-winning author of the Saint John Sibling Series

THE SLIM CHANCE TOUR

STORIES IN THE KEY OF G-WHIZ

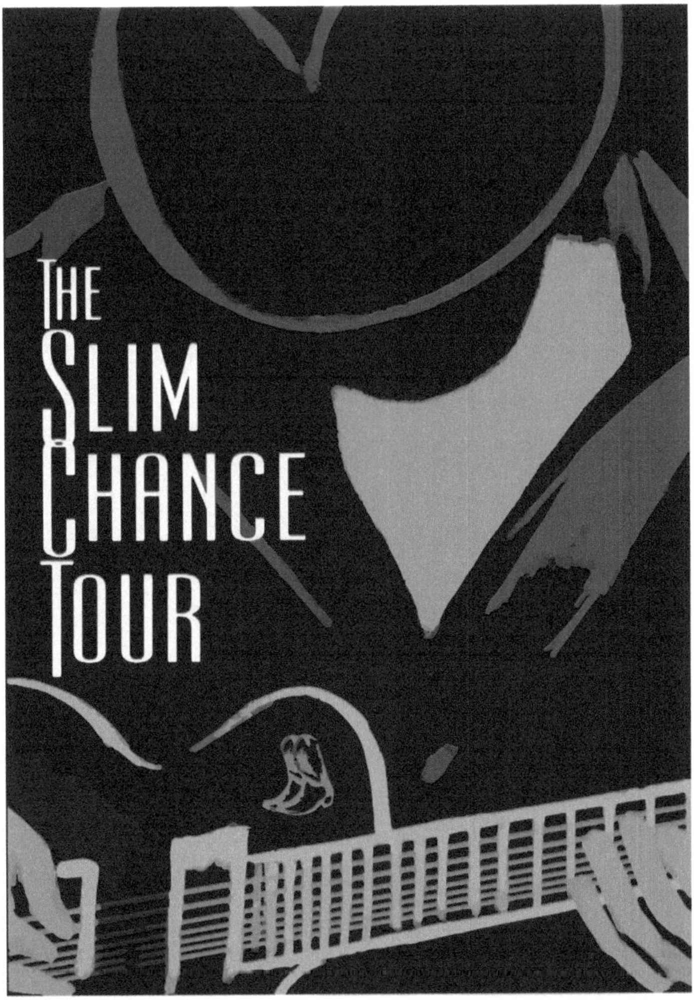

Shawn Michael Bitz

Green Bay, WI 54311

Publishing Editor: Brittiany Koren

Editors: B.A. Koren and A.L. Mundt

Cover Art Designer: Ed Vincent/ENC Graphics

Print Interior Layout Designer: Katy Brunette

Ebook Interior Layout Designer: Maria Connor

Category: Mainstream fiction

Description: *A legendary rock musician is being interviewed for the first time after decades of silence.*

Hard Cover ISBN: 978-1-951375-30-0

Paperback ISBN: 978-1-951375-29-4

Ebook ISBN: 978-1-951375-31-7

LOC Catalogue Data: Applied for.

First Edition published by Written Dreams Publishing in September, 2020.

Green Bay, WI 54311

As always, for my lovely Julie.

"We get old too quickly and wise too late."

—Ben Franklin

Prologue

"Show me what you love, and I'll tell you who *you* are." He said that to me, and I didn't believe him. Didn't believe it could be boiled down to such simplicity.

But that's the magic of the man—of Slim Chance. The kind of magic that invaded my protective walls and evicted me from my hiding place. And he did it without trying. He did this, I guess, merely as a favor to me. A present I, Steven Michael Barber, most certainly never expected to open. He'd laugh to hear me say that.

And what was the love of my life before meeting Slim Chance?

Safety. Predictability. Ever since I can remember. I was the kind of man who sat on the bench and did nothing, perfectly. Avoided change at all turns. Looked good at all costs.

Trust the universe? You've got to be kidding. Trust a God I barely believed in? Preposterous.

No. I would live my life with my head tucked between my knees like a soldier taking fire in a foxhole. Life owed me no favors. It was an unwinnable battle from birth to death, and no matter how much I accomplished, how much applause I received…I would *never* be enough. Life…would never be enough.

Then, it all changed for me. A tired miracle found me and took me away from that foxhole. Away from so much of what I had believed to be true. You see, my eyes had finally been pried open, and I began to see the delicious colors of my life spread out before me. A sense of wellbeing began to surround me like a hug from an angel, if you will.

Steven Barber was reborn. Rebooted. In love with my very own life, and I had so very little to do with any of it. I simply opened up the gift placed at my feet. A gift I am eternally grateful for. A gift I am entirely unable to define. And so, the student became ready, and the teacher most certainly appeared.

I have a story to tell you, and I shall do my very best to not let the words get in the way. As previously mentioned, my name is Steven Michael Barber, and I'm a feature writer for the *Denver Chronicle*. In ten years, I have met some unique characters and had the opportunity to tell a number of amazing stories, but none more engaging than the following.

In July of 2016, I was researching a story in Dayton, Ohio when I spotted a man in a café who captured my attention like a beartrap. Something about him beckoned to me in the back of my mind and I found myself repeatedly glancing at him. He looked like an aging character actor or maybe a movie producer. I quizzed my waitress regarding any details she could provide me, but not only was she not the sharpest knife in the drawer—she wasn't even *in* the drawer.

"Which guy?" she asked loudly, sending a quick text message on her phone after arriving with my order.

I tilted my head towards his table and pointed my eyes in his direction.

"The guy at the table in back." I nodded in his direction, gesturing with a finger to my lips for her to keep her voice down. "The man who ordered pancakes and a cheeseburger?"

"That guy's a rockstar," she said, sucking on fingers that had just handed me my plate of food. "His name is Slim Chance and he's really old."

Slim Chance. *Interesting*. I decided to approach his table under the guise he reminded me of someone I'd worked with years ago.

"Excuse me, um, Sir," I managed. "My name is Steven Barber and I think I may know you."

"You're excused," he said, "and I'm quite certain you do *not* know me. But, since we're starting to get all cozy and such, you mind if I call you Steve?"

"I'd prefer Steven," I answered, edging closer to his table.

"Steve it is," he said, flashing a smile that seemed to warm up the room. "Slim Chance is what my momma named me," he stated and offered me a quite firm handshake.

I was soon seated at his table, immediately transfixed by his whiskey-thick voice and hypnotic pouncing eyes.

He immediately turned the table on me and began firing questions like a Gatling gun, but we both quickly knew he would be the one doing the talking that night.

"Can I buy you a beer?" I asked him.

"Naw, I gotta be somewhere in a couple weeks so I better not," Slim said, winking at me. "And put your money back in your damn pocket. You're in my town now. You know something? They say money can't buy you happiness… but it sure can rent it for a time."

"I'm almost embarrassed to drop in on you like this," I said, "but I'm already glad I did."

"Probably my magnetic personality," Slim said, laughing as he signaled his waitress for more coffee. "As long as you ain't selling something, it's good to have some conversation, Son. Hell, I might even let you get a couple words in from time to time."

We shared the table effortlessly, and once his stories began to flow fluidly I truly did want the evening to never end. Each tale brought me to a new delightful place. He was a masterful storyteller, but it was an unholstered joy he had regarding his life I found so intoxicating.

Hours passed quickly. I would gladly have stayed with him throughout the night if given the chance.

When he suddenly glanced at his watch and began his conversation dismount, I was struck by a surprising sadness and found myself grasping for a reason to keep him there. As he rose from the table and offered his hand, I took it with both of mine and held it for what must've been ten seconds.

"Can I have my hand back, Son?" Slim asked, giving me a sideways glance.

I released it and he slapped me on the shoulder. My emotions came forth overwhelming me, and I wanted to hug him. Thank him profusely for the experience.

As he casually tossed money on the table with our checks, he turned to face me with a look of consternation.

"You have yourself a mighty nice night, Son, and watch out for girlies. They're dangerous creatures."

And that was that. He shuffled off towards the exit and flashed me the peace sign over his left shoulder. In that moment, I was a fanboy who had just met his hero but didn't know it until it was too late. I was already grieving.

That three-hour chance meeting with him deeply impacted me. Haunted me like a menacing dream. His storytelling and offbeat wisdom captured my imagination and I became obsessed with having the opportunity to tell his epic story.

***

After getting up the courage to do so, I contacted Slim Chance a few days later and asked for a real interview.

"Slim," I said, "I work for the *Denver Chronicle*, and they'd like to put an interview in next month's online paper about you."

He told me I was "crazier than a heavy metal tuba solo" if I thought he was going to "tell his life story to some newspaper man."

I tried everything, but he wouldn't budge. I appealed to his ego.

Nothing.

After a few weeks went by, I played the guilt card. Still nothing.

Another few months went by, and I called him again. I begged him like a child at Christmas but didn't gain an inch. He was immovable, and I watched my story idea circle down the drain.

And then, just when I had surrendered the idea, he called me out of the blue to inform me the universe was tugging at him to meet with me and tell some tales. He insisted some would even be true.

And so, after repeated denials, in September of that same year, the man himself finally agreed to sit down with me for a "casual conversation." Not an interview, mind you.

I was treated to the pulsating pleasure of time spent with sixty-seven-year old Dayton, Ohio grape farmer, Slim Chance. Slim, who'd been the lead singer and songwriter for the band Slim Chance and the Codefendants—and later, Slim Chance and the Codependents—invited me into his home and treated me to one amazing adventure and anecdote after another.

I found his spiritual musings to be quite refreshing, and though his wild tales of rock-and-roll debauchery were at times unnerving, there was comfort in their eventual resolve. The best aspect of the experience was how my plans for the "conversation" entirely disintegrated and fell apart.

I had arrived neurotically organized with fabulous questions following a perfect outline. It soon became apparent that Mr. Chance had other plans for me. He had simply decided he'd talk about what he felt like talking about, for as long as he felt like talking about it.

The entire time I thought to myself, if Hunter S. Thompson had studied A Course In Miracles…and was six feet, three inches tall with pulsating blue eyes and a full head of curly silver hair, well, that was Slim Chance.

The following is a word-for-word recorded re-creation of the "conversation" I had with Slim in his cabin along the Great Miami River. None of the names have been changed to protect the innocent. According to Slim, everyone's guilty of something. I hope you enjoy it.

Steven M. Barber,

Denver Chronicle writer

Chapter One

Slim and I agreed to meet at his cabin at midnight to begin the conversation, and thankfully, his directions were flawless.

I think Slim made me wait on purpose when I knocked on the cabin's door with my organized leather portfolio over my shoulder. It was quite windy, with just enough stars to elaborately light the night. The birds were tucked away, and the only evident sound was an eerie howling through the tallest trees.

A curtain moved, the porch light flickered, and the door finally opened. Slim Chance's smile, swallowed by thick, gray whiskers immediately put me at ease. My handshake was met by his vice-like grip, and he pulled me through the doorway into his eager embrace. He smelled of vanilla and cooking oil as he led me to a chair and a waiting steaming cup of coffee.

I looked down at my clothes. Was I dressed too formally? I'd donned dress pants, a dress shirt and jacket, with black leather dress shoes for the special occasion. Slim was in tattered jeans and a t-shirt.

I waited for his voice to pierce the uncomfortable quiet of the room. I sipped my coffee and scanned him, head to toe. My adrenaline pulsed. His eyebrows beckoned for my comment.

"Thanks so much for agreeing to this," I said. "You have a life story well worth sharing, and I'd be honored to be the conduit for such. I have prepared questions for you, though we may not need them. With your permission, I will record everything with this tape machine." I set down the machine on the coffee table.

"I figured as much when you walked in carrying that bag," Slim said. "Steve, the way this is gonna work is, you'll get it as it comes to me. I ain't one for talking about my early days, on account of I can't remember most of 'em. Maybe I don't wanna remember, I dunno. I get flashes, you know, but so much of it's gone, and I ain't gonna get all exercised over trying to get it back."

I nodded. "I understand. Most people I interview are surprised by how much they recall once they begin to discuss their lives in depth."

He gave me a sideways glance. "I ain't most folks, Son, which is why you're here, am I right?"

I grinned this time. "You are indeed."

"I'll give you what I got to give, but so many memories I hold behind my eyes have lost their ability to survive the unforgiving waves and wind of time. They whisper to me in my dreams. So many remain just out of reach, like a shadow I can't catch up to, and life's too short to carry luggage with dirty clothes in it, you know what I mean, Steve. I guess I'm lucky to still be here on the best planet I've been to yet. If I wander too much, well, you'll have to wander with me." He grinned, displaying white, crooked teeth.

"I am able to *wander* with the best of them," I stated.

Slim's eyebrows bounced up and down and his eyes seemed to focus in on my own.

"I have a lot of drawers in my mind I ain't opened in a long time, and some of 'em ain't meant to be opened ever again. I guess everyone has a story worth telling when it comes down to it. I would imagine it's all in the telling. Make yourself comfortable, and we'll see what we see when we see it."

"Yes, everyone has a story worth telling," I said, "but not everyone is able to tell a life story in a compelling manner. You, Slim Chance, are most certainly able."

"Thank you for that, Stevie Boy. Can I call you Stevie Boy?"

"Well," I attempted, "I'd much prefer Steven."

"Stevie Boy it is," he loudly announced, grinning with his chin pressed to his chest. "I know one thing. My life ain't been boring. I just hope I can scare enough of it up to fill that tape machine of yours. Well, go ahead and ask your question and let's get this old buggy started."

"Your childhood," I said. "Where did you grow up?"

"Hell, I'm still waiting to grow up," he laughed. "I was born in the small town of Custer, South Dakota, in the southern Black Hills. Beautiful country, rich with history and good-hearted folks. I grew up in the hallowed shadows of the Crazy Horse and Mount Rushmore monuments. General George Armstrong Custer and the 7th Cavalry Regiment found gold there in 1874, two years before he and all of his detachment were killed by a coalition of Native American tribes in Montana. Anyways, I looked everywhere I could, but I never found any damn gold."

Slim's eyes narrowed as he paged through his mind before continuing. I thought I saw his body tense as he settled into an easy chair with a cup of coffee the size of a funeral urn. He picked off imaginary lint from an armrest, swatting it away with the back of his hand. I could barely contain my excitement.

"I ain't sure what a normal childhood is, Son, but I know I didn't get one. Folks thought I was a peculiar kid on account of I didn't talk and play with the other kids, but I was probably just shell-shocked from my home life. All the fighting and fussing at home had me tiptoeing on eggshells from the get-go.

"I had what the professionals called a nervous disposition. I would later call it a mental malignancy. Corrupted files on my hardrive is what I had, Son. I didn't have friends to speak of. I spent most of my time wanting to be somewhere else, and trying to figure out where that should be. The school had me tested. I came out real smart and all, but my teachers had a hell of a time keeping me interested. A school counselor took me under her wing. She thought I was getting a raw deal at home and was behind enemy lines."

"It was just you and your parents? No siblings?" I asked.

"Yup. Just the three of us. My folks were awfully damn wounded. My momma thought if my old man really loved her, he'd quit drinking. He *thought* if he quit drinking, he wouldn't love her. I think they blamed each other for the holes they had inside. My momma's name was Eve. She was a soft-spoken, generous Christian woman. And pretty. Everyone said so, except for my old man, who constantly berated her with his mouth and his fists. If being mean was a sport, my old man would've gone pro.

"His name was Buck Chance, and he was a southern Florida transplant. He met my momma during a Chance family trip to the Black Hills, and he moved here to be with her after high school. I heard stories about how in love they were with each other, but *I* never saw it. By the time I came along, they were knee-deep in misery. The walls echoed with anger from as early as I can remember. Hell, I never saw my parents kiss. Not once. My old man had some thick bark on him, and you couldn't break through it with a fire ax.

"He was a heavy equipment operator, and it messed his back up real bad. I think part of the reason he drank like he did was on account of the pain, but most of it was because he was always raining inside. His favorite thing to do was get liquored up and pick fights in the bar he drank in, and when he couldn't find one there, he'd find one at home. He had boxing trophies on a shelf in their bedroom. He knew his way around a scuffle.

"I did what I could to be his favorite target to give my momma a rest, and the more he drank, the harder he hit. Until I got big enough to hit back. When I was thirteen, I spent some time in kiddie prison after I knocked him silly with a baseball bat. I warned him to keep his paws off Momma and he laughed at me.

"He wasn't laughing after I brained him about ten times. I hit him with everything I had, and I tried to kill him. I might've, too, if my momma hadn't stopped me. She acted all exercised over the deal when she pulled me off him, but I'll bet you diamonds to donuts my momma had a smile on her face when she washed the blood off that bat."

Slim's guarded smile broke wide open, and I felt myself responding in kind. He nodded to an aluminum baseball bat resting against his fireplace. A monument. Some part of me wanted to pick it up and give it a swing. Or examine it for DNA evidence.

I looked back at him, meeting his eyes. "What was your father's demeanor towards you after that incident?"

"Pure veneration. It's what he would've done, you know? He stopped hitting me so much and started taking me with him to the bar. I'd sit there, sipping soda while my old man got himself wound up. I can't tell you how many fights I saw him in, and he went undefeated.

"One night when I was with him, he beat this younger guy up real bad. It took four guys to pull my old man off, and his hands were completely covered in blood. He walked over to where I was standing and ordered me to look up into his face. When I did, he used two of his fingers to paint lines of blood on my cheeks. Then, he put his face two inches from my horrified expression.

"'You gotta be a warrior in this life, Boy,' he said. 'Are you afraid right now?'

"'Yes,' I managed.

"'Swallow it! Turn it upside down and get mad at me, Boy! Can you do that? Can you get mad enough to turn that fear to hate?'

"He shoved me to the ground, and I stood back up as quick as I could.

He shoved me down again, and I rose even faster.

"'You wanna hit me, don't ya, Boy? You wanna knock me around real good. Those fists you're making right now are for me, and you ain't afraid no more, are you?'

"I wasn't. I wanted to break every bone in his body. He put his hand on top of my head and I pushed it away.

"'That's my boy,' he said. 'That's my good boy.'

"I learned my lesson real good that night."

I nodded with understanding. "Anger is better than fear," I said.

"You got it. He didn't teach me much, but the man did teach me that. I learned to drive while hauling his drunk ass home. One night he passed out in the truck with a beer between his legs, and I snuck it out for a sip. Just as it hit my lips, he snatched it outta my hand like it was gonna bite me. He yelled at me to pull over. I did, and I turned to look at him. He looked smaller than I ever remembered, and the light was gone from his eyes.

"He reached over with both hands, cupped my head and said, 'Booze is the devil's sweat, Boy. I know I got no right to tell you this, but you gotta stay away from it if you wanna keep yourself whole. It'll take everything you have and burn it to the ground. You don't wanna inherit this.' He pointed to his head. 'Please, Boy. Promise me you'll stay away from it.'"

Slim shrugged. "The only promise I ever made to my old man was to never take a drink of alcohol of any kind, and I meant to keep it. Booze was a morbid veil draped over our home, and the last thing I would do was put it anywhere near my mouth.

"My momma tried to stay invisible, and I know she took a lot of pills to help with that. She prayed and sang hymns constantly, and I was damn mad at God for not saving her. In one hand I held a deep desire to know and be close to God. The other hand was a fist, full of rage and resentment towards all things religious or Godly. The dichotomy of that messed me up real bad, Son."

Slim pointed to his heart and shook his head, as if to remove the heavy memory I could see just behind his eyes. He pointed to my coffee cup and shuffled into the kitchen to retrieve the pot. It was then I noticed his casual attire again: tattered jeans, Johnny Cash t-shirt, and bare feet.

He filled our cups, returned the pot, and fell heavily into his chair. We'd just started, and I had a fear he was having second thoughts. As if to read my mind, he stared into my eyes and bounced his eyebrows. It felt like a…hug. Then, to my relief, he continued.

"Momma's spirit shrunk more and more every year she was with him, and I watched her wither like a frozen rose. She and I were close until I was about nine years old. She disappeared around that time, and it hurt me deeply."

"In some ways, one could say you were shipwrecked emotionally," I interjected.

"Yeah, I was. I missed my momma, you know? Up until that time she'd been my champion and only friend. When she wasn't cooking or cleaning, she'd sit at the table and stare into her coffee cup, probably wishing she could climb inside it and hide. She even quit arguing with my old man. He'd bait her for a fight, but she wasn't having it. I could tell she'd given up.

"I wanted to shake 'em both and say, 'What are you doing? Don't you want to be in love and be best friends? Why are you crying so much? Why are you drinking so much? I'm standing right here, can't you see me?'

"I just didn't get why they'd settle for that type of existence. Why they'd want to continue to swim in the cesspool they called a marriage and not work hard to make it good again. Hell, I even wondered if *I* was the problem. Maybe they were happy before I came along, you know? It was the same stuff lots of kids go through.

"Hell was a local call from where I lived back then, Son. There was a lot of pounding on the drama drum in a house always on fire. My best hiding place was listening to records in the basement."

My eyes drifted to several guitars hanging on an otherwise bare wall behind Slim. I couldn't help but notice the cabin's meager, yet tasteful furnishings. He had a home of comfort and necessity. My gaze flicked inadvertently to a dust-covered, ancient turntable and stack of albums.

"What did you listen to?" I asked.

He laughed. "Everything I could get my hands on. Muddy Waters, Robert Johnson, Howlin' Wolf. Little Richard, Jerry Lee Lewis. Johnny Cash, Fats Domino, John Coltrane, and Miles Davis. Sam Cooke, Elvis, Buddy Holly, Hank Williams, Ricky Nelson, and Frank Sinatra. I really liked Ray Charles. There were tons of 'em."

I smiled, visualizing it. "You must've had quite a record collection."

"My old man did," Slim stated. "I'd sneak into the basement and put records on when he was passed out or gone from the house on account of he wouldn't let me near 'em otherwise. I knew the words to every song on every record he had, and I could sing 'em pretty good at a young age.

"We had this full-length mirror, and I moved it to the basement so I could practice my stage moves and such. I strung a tennis racket over my shoulder for a guitar, and I'd practice singing and dancing for hours. I'd picture large crowds in my mind's stadium that went back for miles, all there to see me do my thing. It hooked me pretty early. While most kids were out playing games and sports, I was in the basement singing at a pretend concert, enamored and evolving. I had a dressing room and everything down there.

"One night, my old man came down and caught me carrying on in the mirror after I thought he was out cold for the night. He broke my tennis racket over his knee and kicked over the mirror. Then, he threw every damn record he had in a garbage bag. He pretended to throw 'em all away, but I knew he didn't. He told me no son of his was gonna be a sissy and took the belt to me. I sang at the top of my lungs the entire time he beat me, and I never shed a damn tear. Not one. The harder he hit, the louder I sang. He got tired before I did."

"Sounds like your determination was impressively developed at a young age," I commented, reaching for my cup and taking a sip.

"It made me strive to be a musician that much more. The more he fought me, the stronger the creative current inside me grew, waiting for the day I'd be gone and on my own.

"Everyone around me wanted me to play it safe and pick the path everyone else walked on," Slim explained. "That's what most adults do with kids. They make 'em fit into a box. They led me to a box, but I didn't want any part of it. Nobody was gonna kennel my dream, and I paid no mind to the bait they tried to catch me with. The world hands out love and acceptance for obedience to ideals. It's a quid pro quo I could not cotton to."

"You were young to possess such a powerful vision. Most kids don't have an inkling of what they want to do as adults, other than fantasies," I said, thinking of my own wistful dreams as a teen. I set down the cup.

"The best way I can describe it is music just plain infected me, Son. It was a virus of sparkling passion, and *nothing* could bring the fever down. For most folks, music gives 'em permission to cut loose and step out of their box, you know? For me, music was an angelic path that pointed to the heavens. I felt closer to the idea of God somehow when a record was playing. It was a language He and I spoke together, and it only belonged to us. It was the only time I wasn't angry with Him. When music was playing, it was like He and I were in a truce. How I thought that puzzles me to this very day."

Slim seemed to sink deeper into his chair. He drew in a deep breath, shook his head, and continued.

"I guess what I'm saying is, I had a place that was only mine, and when I was there, I felt I would be okay. Music was the graffiti I decorated my life with. It beautified everything."

I thought that was an interesting perspective, and asked, "Do you continue to believe music is a bridge between spiritual and material worlds?"

"Could be," Slim said. "It originates in a place the left brain can't get to, which is a good thing as it would mess it up. Even children get it. Give 'em a good beat and they'll start moving to it before they learn to walk. It's all very powerful, innate stuff."

"Powerful enough for you to grab hold of it at such an early age," I offered.

I was startled when Slim sprang from his chair. He walked to a darkened window and peered out into the night. He leaned closer to the glass as if he'd spotted something, and then all at once, his voice and posture lifted.

"I remember like it was Tuesday when my third grade teacher Mrs. Kramer asked us all what we wanted to be when we grew up. Some wanted to be teachers or firemen. Others wanted to be pilots, preachers, dentists, doctors, or even the president of the United States. I told her I wanted to be the world's happiest person. Some of the other kids scoffed at me, but I didn't pay 'em no mind. I believed I knew things they didn't.

"I didn't tell the class what I really wanted to be that day on account of I possessed exclusive rights to that information. That dream was mine, and I wasn't gonna share it with anyone who doubted me or my vision. I knew Mrs. Kramer was on my side with all of it. One day I stood in front of her desk and waited until she looked up from a book.

"'Yes, Slim. Can I help you with something?' she asked.

"'I just wanted to tell you that I want to be a musician when I grow up. A real famous one, who gets to travel all over the world and sells a million records.'

"I can still remember Mrs. Kramer's smile and what she said to me that day.

"'When I was a little girl, my mother told we all have a special purpose here on Earth, and it is our job to find it. Now, some people will try to tell you what your special purpose is, but you can't listen to them. Only you know what your special purpose is, and only you can make the decision whether you grow into your special purpose, or away from it.'

"She then told me, 'If you put a group of lobsters in a bucket, the king lobster's nature is to try to climb out, but it will never escape, because the others will always pull it back down.'

"Every day when her class would end, she'd say to all of us, 'Have a nice day, unless you have other plans, and don't let the lobsters get you down.'

"I've held onto those words all my life, Son. Both have become mantras for me when I get to raining on the inside. Which brings me to a part of my story you likely gonna powerfully dismiss."

Slim turned to face me with narrowed eyes and a jaw set with purpose. He turned back to the window, scrubbing off some invisible spot only he could see. Fifteen, maybe twenty seconds passed as he gathered himself.

I scooted to the edge of my chair. "You have all of my attention."

"It happened when I was nine. I was sleeping like a baby when this screeching sound woke me up. I thought I'd dreamed it, but then I heard it again. My entire body went cold, and I sat up in bed like I'd been shocked.

"I squinted into the darkness. Standing at the foot of my bed was a tall figure with no damn face and yellow eyes. The scream that tried to come outta my mouth got stuck in my throat, and I sat there frozen. I couldn't move or make a sound. All I could do was close my eyes and try to wake up from whatever bad dream I was having, you know?

"But it wasn't a dream. When I opened my eyes, this thing had moved beside my bed and I could feel its breath as it leaned in closer to me. Its face got within a couple inches of mine, and it started to hiss. I tried as hard as I could to get my arms to move, but they wouldn't. I was trapped.

"Then, this thing started to laugh. Its breath smelled like ashes and it was hot on my skin. My heart hammered in my chest. All I could think to do was pray.

"I couldn't find the words, though. Not a one. Tears slid down my face and fear flowed through me like a tidal wave. I could barely breathe, and that's when the room started to spin. Words I'd never heard before went around inside my head and kept getting louder and louder.

"I tried to sit up again, but something held me down. Everything inside of me moved faster than it ever had, and every breath I took felt like it would be my last.

"Just as I was about to pass out, a calm suddenly filled my body. I don't know how, but I knew I would be okay. This thing wasn't there to hurt me; it was there to deliver a message."

"Wow! What the hell was that thing…and what was its message for you?" I eagerly asked.

Slim slid smoothly across the room and took a big drink from his coffee cup before easing himself down into his chair. He gazed up at the ceiling, then he combed through his hair with his hands.

I could almost feel the room tighten with the deep breath he took as my neck hair stood and saluted.

"It was a demon, Steven, and it was there to get me to play for the other side. I could hear it talk to me in my head. It wanted me to denounce whatever faith I had in God.

"In my bed, I suddenly felt myself able to move and speak again. So I started to whisper, 'Be still, and know I am God.'

"The figure reared up and hissed louder. I could feel its anger like a grip on my body. The room got colder, but I just kept whispering the prayer. I remember thinking to myself, *God ain't listening,* but something told me to keep going.

"All at once, the figure reared its head back and I heard it scream in my mind. It began to vibrate and come in and outta focus. I half expected its scream to split my skull. Just when I couldn't take another second of it, the screaming stopped. And then it was gone.

"I pulled the covers over my head to warm up. I tried to figure out what had happened, you know? Part of me thought I'd dreamed it all up, but the bigger part of me knew I'd been haunted. I slept on the couch that night, and when I woke up, there was blood all over one side of my face from a nosebleed I'd had in my sleep. I knew then it had all been real; that some part of me would never be the same again.

"I didn't understand it back then, so I just hid it way back in my mind. I've since come to understand I was visited by an evil presence I somehow opened myself up to. I don't know how to explain it better than that. I do know the experience forced me inside even more than before. I became a loner."

I sat back, not knowing what to think of Slim's visitor. Finally, I said, "I would imagine the experience strengthened whatever understanding of God you might have had."

"You would think that, wouldn't you?" he asked. "It didn't. All it did was make me feel more vulnerable and confused. As a kid, I'd been taught everything happens for a reason and nothing happens by mistake. That pretty much told me all the bad things happening around me were God's idea. I blamed God for what happened that night, and the last thing I remember was telling Him to leave me the hell alone."

"Were you ever visited again?"

He nodded. "Several times in my dreams, once again in person. I figured a lot of folks were visited by demons. It wasn't until later I found out that just ain't so. All I knew for sure back then was some things really do go bump in the night. Monsters are real, and I didn't want my soul taking the elevator down, you know?"

I knew what he meant.

"I became older that night and lost a bucketful of innocence. It would be a long time before the scab that grew around my soul would heal. God and I would remain at odds for quite a spell, and my disdain for Him would only grow."

Slim appeared to gather himself and his thoughts as emotions competed for control of his face. A part of me was relieved when he settled on a grin.

"Anyways, we'll get to more of that down the line. For now, let's go back to the lonely kid with no friends and an all-encompassing dream he had resting on his shoulders."

Chapter Two

"So, you really didn't have any friends?" I asked. It was hard for me to believe, considering the power of his personality.

"None to speak of," Slim answered. "I knew some kids at school, but they all played sports after school and I had no interest in it. My old man tried to get me to play football and basketball, but I wouldn't do that, either. I never could understand how chasing a damn ball around makes folks so happy. All of my spare time I practiced being on stage and sang.

"I sang everywhere I got a chance to back then. Some of the kids on the playground didn't cotton to it and did what they could to try to get me to stop. I got to be good at singing and fighting. In a way, they would later go hand in hand.

"And I was a mimic most of my childhood, so I'd fit in enough to be left alone, you know? Man, that's all I wanted back in those days. Just leave me alone and let me find my way. Some kids tried to befriend me, but I wasn't having it. I didn't want distractions. I was a loner by choice. Eventually though, I did start to scare up some interest in girls. I was just too damn afraid to talk to any of 'em. As luck would have it, one decided to sort of sneak up on me."

Slim took a long drink of his coffee, started to recline in his chair, and then sat up straight. As he rubbed the whiskers on his chin, we were both drawn to the sound of a barking dog off in the distance. I thought it was strange he didn't have a dog. Or a roaring fire lit in the fireplace.

"When I was fourteen and just outta kiddie prison, there was this gal who lived three houses from us who had some records and liked me. She was a couple years older than me, and awful shiny. One day, she invited me to her house to listen to music. I was damn impressed with her collection—and everything about her. She had a classy chassis.

"She introduced me to the Beatles, and they really lit me up inside. I'd never heard anything that moved me so much. She was a big fan and told me they would become the biggest band ever. Anyways, she put on a Beatles record, and the next thing I know, I'm getting a strip tease and she's naked in no time.

"I formulated a plan to marry her on the spot."

"I should think so," I said.

Slim went on, as if he hadn't heard my comment.

"Her daddy was a cop, and I was terrified he would bust through her bedroom door and shoot me for raping his daughter. I almost left right then and there, but I'd never seen real boobs before and decided I'd take a bullet if I had to.

"That started a nefarious regime I truly looked forward to every week. We met at her house every Tuesday after school when her folks were both at work. My job was to sit on the bed and watch her strip and dance for me, and I mastered the task. I was told not to touch her, even when she rubbed up against me. She picked the songs, and she had damn fine taste. I guess she just wanted an audience, and by God, I gave her one, every Tuesday.

"Sometimes she'd light a cigarette and sip something out of a glass when she danced. She'd get this glassy look in her eyes and touch herself, you know. She'd whisper sexy stuff in my ear and drag her hair across my face slowly, like a knife blade. Just when I couldn't take it anymore and I'd have to touch her, she'd gyrate outta my reach. It was like trying to dance with smoke.

"Patty was a naughty girl. My kind of naughty, I would find out.

"One Tuesday, she switched things up a bit. I showed up at the usual time with my tongue already hanging out of my mouth, and she met me at the door with a bottle of booze and two glasses in her hands. I looked into those bright green eyes and decided on the spot booze probably couldn't hurt a smart guy like me. I had no idea I was about to let Pandora out of the box, but it wouldn't have changed my mind had I known. I was powerless to refuse her anything, Son, and damn happy about it all.

"We enjoyed a couple of adult beverages and I coughed and hacked my way through my first cigarette. Does it get any better for a naïve, fortuitous fourteen-year-old boy? It most certainly did.

"She led me to her bedroom and put a record on. I assumed my position on the bed and she spun me around and put a lip lock on me. I still think about it from time to time. She looked me right smack in the peepers and told me to take off my clothes. It took me three seconds. To make a long story short, I lost my virginity. She did all the driving.

"I thanked her profusely and she laughed. She walked me to the door, kissed me again, and said, 'We're moving, Slim. Daddy got a new job in Sioux Falls. I'm going to miss you.'

"And just like that, it was all over. They packed up the house and were outta town in no time flat. I was damn sad to see her go, and my heart rained a long while. I guess I'd never let myself care like that about anyone before. Not even my folks.

"That experience did something permanent to me. I can think of only a handful of times I approached a woman first after that. I liked 'em aggressive and confident, which is what I pretended to be, you know? That's what turned my crank. A woman who knew what she wanted and went after it. Patty was the beginning of all of it for me.

"I always wondered whatever happened to Patty and her great record collection. For a long time, I'd hear a Beatles song and fall into a Pavlovian puddle. I'd get aroused and just laugh, you know? It felt good to go back there. Back to my first time, and a place where I was safe from the echoes. She surely poured gasoline on my coals, Son, and to this day there's just something special about Tuesdays for me."

"I suddenly am quite fond of Tuesdays myself," I stated, smiling in spite of myself. "So, when did you first start to play music?"

"You're being kinda nosey, ain't ya?" Slim asked with a straight face.

"Um, I guess I am, yes," I answered, momentarily caught off guard.

"I'm just pullin' on your chain, Son. I quit schooling in the tenth grade, and when things got too sticky at home, I left South Dakota to go live with my momma's daddy in California. I never looked back, and I never spoke to my old man again. I kept in touch with my momma some, but she got real sick and died from pneumonia. I think she gave up after I left and was ready to go. She was forty years old.

"My grandfather and I flew back for her funeral, but I refused to go in the house. My old man tried to talk to me, but I wasn't having it. I never shed a single tear for my momma. My grandfather insisted she was in a better place, but I didn't know if that was true. I guess I felt happy she was finally out of the rain and didn't have to hide inside herself anymore. We stayed just as long as we felt was proper, and then hightailed it back to California."

"I would imagine your grandfather was a crucial influence in your life," I said.

Slim's eyes twinkled, and a smile almost framed his face. He began to nod his head repeatedly as he rose to fill our cups and retrieve something from his refrigerator. He tossed me a piece of the best jerky I'd ever tasted, and then began to pace the living room like an attorney working a courtroom.

"My grandfather saved me, Son, and I loved and worshipped him. He took me in and gave me a safe place, you know? When I moved in with him, I started to breathe deep for the first time in my life. He rescued me from the stranglehold that had me all but completely down. The agreement he struck with my old man was I'd spend a year in LA, and then come back to finish school. My grandfather and I laughed it up about that one. He knew I was too far gone to ever return to them. Or school.

"I told him, 'You know I ain't going back, right? Back home or to school.'

"'I figured,' he said.

"'I know what I want, Gramps. I'm gonna play in a band as soon as I can.'

"'I figured that, too.'

"'Do you have any advice for me, other than to practice hard?'

"'Bass and drums, Son. Make sure those bases are covered, and you can build anything you want. They don't have to play fancy. They just have to be tight and together. And don't let a woman join up with you. Not unless you want a firestorm on your hands. And stay off the dope.'

"'I wanna be a great singer, and a real fast lead guitar player,' I said.

"'Fast fingers are a dime a dozen, Son. It's more important to know how to bend a string just right. That's where the magic is. All guitars have their own voice, and all you have to do is find it and let it talk. It's not about being flashy and fast. It's about being there for the song. Giving the song what it needs when it needs it. If you can do that, you'll become a great guitar player.'

"He'd had his own band called The Regulators in the late 40s and early 50s, and he played lead guitar and sang most of the songs. They got real successful and toured the country almost endlessly. He said the only thing that kept 'em from fame and fortune was the booze. Anyway, he gave me my first acoustic guitar and showed me a bunch of what he knew to get me started."

Slim pointed to a wall directly beside me, where two concert posters for

The Regulators hung posthumously framed in gold. Below them sat a photo of a handsome, muscular man dressed in jeans and a t-shirt, wearing a guitar, a silver cross, and a pervasive smile. A shrine to a beloved mentor.

"I slept with that damn guitar. It was righteous redemption in my hands, and I played it until the blood from my fingertips ran down the fretboard. When the pain got to be too much, I'd just ice my fingers and go at it again. I even let the blood stain the wood. It was my signature on my dream.

"My grandfather told me music would take me wherever I wanted to go if I put in the work and kept my nose clean. Well, I put in the work, but my nose would get quite dirty in the coming years. I don't know if my grandfather ever knew about my drug and alcohol use. It would've bent up his heart real good.

"His faith was everything to him. He tried to point me down the same road, but I'd driven too damn far down another. He always told me if I ever wanted to learn more about God and the Bible, he'd be available. He knew I had a powerful anger inside about all of it, and he wanted to help me heal. I pretended to stand in the worship line and most folks left me alone."

Slim tossed me another piece of jerky, reached in the bag, and threw me another. He tore off a large bite and had it chewed and swallowed in three seconds. He pointed at me with the remaining piece, and I began to work on mine.

I fixed my gaze on his strong jaws, working against the dried flesh, waiting for the words to start up again. His pacing continued, and my eyes followed him.

"Anyways, I made a pal named Rico who lived in our neighborhood. He was a damn fine guitar picker and singer. Folks teased him about his teeth that couldn't decide which direction to grow in, and his inordinately large ears. I thought he looked eccentrically cool.

"The two of us spent every day together learning what we could from books and records, sneaking booze and cigarettes from Rico's old man.

"Rico introduced me to the electric guitar and the fine art of smoking weed. The first time I smoked, I caught a buzz that changed the trajectory of my life and the way I looked and felt about everything. My life changed colors, Son. I finally felt bigger than the fear I carried with me everywhere I went. I suddenly became the confident cat I'd always reached for. I decided then and there high was the way to be for me. To feel that good all the time would be a goal of mine for many years to come.

"Rico told me not to smoke it all day, every day. He warned me about frying my circuits and such, but I never paid any mind. As far as I was concerned, I'd found the secret to breaking happy records. I was reborn.

"We'd planned to start a band together when we got good enough, and then Rico's daddy died from cancer and his momma moved 'em back to her hometown of San Francisco. Rico was like a brother, you know. He was my dreaming partner. Some say hearts don't break, but mine got dented when he left my world. It surely did.

"He was the first best friend I ever had, and I rained inside for quite a spell after he left. Hell, it just made me practice guitar more, as I didn't have anything else to do."

"South Dakota to California must have been quite a change for you," I said.

Slim's eyes widened, and a warm smile came over his face as he shook his head back and forth. Poured more coffee. A glance at the fireplace. Would he start a fire? Was it cold? I couldn't tell. I was so comfortable in his presence.

"Los Angeles in the late 60s and early 70s was like being on a celestial carnival ride," he answered. "Something about the palm trees and the sun fed me back then, and the darker my skin got, the stronger I felt. I lived on my grandfather's patio and slept there most nights. To this day, I sleep with the windows open so I can hear the night's whispers and moans.

"Six months after Rico left, I met some guys and formed a band called Plastic Ocean. Three lead guitars and a drummer. We thought we were innovators. Three busy guitar players playing over the top of each other while a cat played nonstop drum solos. We obviously didn't know beans about dynamics and such, and we sounded like a whole mess of a mess. We were horrible, and we fought all the time over what kind of songs we should play. Our band broke up before we ever played a gig." He laughed at that, before he became serious again.

"Then I met Harry Beaumont. I called him Hammer on account of he hit his drums so hard. Hammer was older than me, and already a virtuoso drinker and smoker. He became the lead singer for a new group, and we called the band Hammer and the Nails. We were a three-piece outfit with another buddy named Tommy Tolo on bass. We called him Tunes. We played surfer music and stuff like that. Hammer taught me about dynamics and how to bring a song's emotions up and down. I wrote some songs, but Hammer thought they were 'crude and pedestrian.' I didn't care. I knew I was on my way.

"We practiced every night in Hammer's basement until his old man caught his momma with another man, and burned the damn house down with Hammer's drums in it. That band was over before it started, too."

He stared off in the distance a moment, then made eye contact. "I got an interesting side note about Hammer. He and I stayed in touch after our musical collaboration took a dive. When the Vietnam War was in full force and the draft lottery was knocking on Hammer's door, he had to do some quick thinking. There'd be no going to Canada. He didn't want to be a fugitive and such.

"So, Hammer started eating. Everything he could get his hands on. By the time his army physical came around, he weighed 350 pounds and had high enough blood pressure for two of us. He flunked the physical, and his problem was solved."

He slapped his knees with both hands and sent a piece of jerky flying across the living room. Slim nodded knowingly.

"Holy batcopters! Hammer ate himself out of the Vietnam War," I said.

"He did. It took him a couple years, but he lost every damn pound he'd gained. Pure genius. I never worried about the draft and such nonsense. I was a full-blown dope prodigy by then, and nobody was gonna let me get anywhere close to a machine gun.

"Anyways, a few months after Hammer And The Nails folded up the tent, I met a guy who changed everything for me. Mortimer Slade was his name, and ain't that a doozy? He was the coolest cat I'd ever met, and my same age, but you wouldn't know it by looking at him. Even then, he was tall and tenacious, and I followed him around like a hungry puppy.

"Some folks have charisma. Morti would walk in and hit a room like a lightning bolt. He played keyboards and guitar, chain-smoked menthol cigarettes, and introduced me to malt liquor and chocolate mescaline. He also talked me into being the lead singer on account of he couldn't hit a note with a bazooka."

"Morti the mentor, so to speak," I said.

"It was his idea to call our band Slim Chance and the Codefendants when it was just the two of us. It was also his idea to focus on writing songs. All we needed was other musicians. So we went to a battle of the bands, and when the band that won was loading their gear into a station wagon, Morti walked up and introduced us.

"'Congratulations, boys,' he said to the four of them. 'I want you to meet your new keyboard player and lead singer. I'm Mortimer, this is Slim, and we're all going to be rich and famous.'

"They all looked at him like he had a snake in his mouth.

"Well, for most folks that would've been the end of it, but Morti had a way with getting his way, you know? We all went for pizza, and found out we all liked the same music and such. Morti suggested a jam session, and they went for it. They liked our songs, and they loved our drugs. They fired their singer and hired us. Puck the drummer, Rev the bass player, and Flash the lead guitar player became our new best friends, and these cats were as cool as we were. We were a band."

Slim filled our coffee cups and returned to his chair. I settled back in my chair, hands behind my head. I knew, with a precise certainty, I was exactly where I was supposed to be at that very moment. A kid on Christmas morning. An athlete at the free throw line. A reporter in the presence of a master storyteller. A master storyteller who had truly hit his stride. Slim continued.

"So, the five of us moved into a one-bedroom apartment in the San Fernando Valley, and we slept on the floor in sleeping bags. We lived on macaroni and apples, on account of we had a tree right there, you know? We not only didn't have a pot to piss in, we didn't have anywhere to put one. I loved every delicious second of it."

"Ah, the wonders of youthful simplicity."

"Indeed," Slim nodded. "We couldn't get a gig at gunpoint the first few months, and the boredom got to us. Our booze and dope use really exploded. Pot, hash, mescaline, and then speed we'd grind up and snort. Once in awhile we'd take some Quaaludes and have a drooling contest.

"A couple of the guys got heavy into LSD, but I pretty much abstained from it since it'd put me out of commission for several hours. I had things to do. I had songs to write. Gigs to book. The other guys didn't mind laughing until they vomited, or having their silverware curl around their fingers and such.

"Morti was the only one who didn't fall face-first into drugs. He controlled 'em. Dope had its way with me from the get-go. The other guys did drugs to get high. I did drugs to feel normal, you know? I truly believed I couldn't enjoy anything unless my mood was altered.

"And I loved speed. That hammer would hit the nail in my heart and I'd have to reach way down to get that next breath, hoping I hadn't snorted too much. There were times my heart would race, stop, race, and for a second, I'd think

I was a goner. Funny thing was, I'd beg God to not let me die, just so I could do it again. It was the only time I'd ever talk to Him.

"It's hard for folks to understand why a fella would put poison like that in his body. For me, it was hard to pass up feeling that euphoric and confident. I was indisputably invincible. No matter what the cost, I was willing to pay it to feel like that, you know? Unless you've been so high you swear you could reach up and pluck the moon from the sky, you just wouldn't understand."

"Please do not be offended, Slim, but I cannot imagine assaulting myself like that. I'm hesitant to take cold medicine."

"You'd make a horrible drug addict, Son. You don't seem to have the chops."

I grinned. "Curses, foiled again."

"I remember one night we got ahold of this powder from a dealer we all called Squeak, on account of this noise he made through his nose when he talked. He told us it was the best speed in the city, but none of us wanted to try it, since it was a different color than we'd ever seen. There were stories about how Squeak would spike his drugs with whatever was handy. Anyways, I got tired of staring at it, and did a few lines.

"Next thing I knew, I woke up face down on the kitchen floor in a pool of blood after I'd nearly bit my damn tongue off. It turned out I'd snorted PCP cut with strychnine, and Squeak had quite a laugh watching me have what must've been a seizure.

"Well, Squeak wasn't laughing when our drummer Puck broke his nose with a pistol butt. Then Puck jammed that pistol in Squeak's mouth and politely asked for our money back. I went through Squeak's shoulder bag and found a treasure trove of dope and cash. Cocaine, hash, mescaline, white crosses, pot, LSD. He had everything, and several thousand bucks to boot.

"Man, I thought we'd hit the lottery, but Morti was no fool and talked sense into the situation. He knew if we took this cat's stash and cash that somebody would come looking for us. And they wouldn't send boy scouts. That was just simple math. Ain't nothing free in the drug world, Son.

"We negotiated a gratuitous deal and took the white crosses, and Squeak left with a broken nose, a couple black eyes, and his bag. Funny thing was, his squeak had gone away."

"Can I assume you and Squeak severed business ties following this?"

"You can, but you'd be wrong. When you found a dealer you could sort of trust, you stuck with him. Squeak had the best dope and the best connections, and he continued to be our guy. After that night, we laid down some rules governing dope-dealing deportment, and we had no further problems with Squeak or the dope he peddled to us.

"In the beginning, it became more about the drugs than the music. We thought that's where the inspiration for the music and our creativity came from. And it was what I lived for. The next great buzz. That and the hope we'd get to play our music someday."

"How did you guys survive financially while the band was developing?"

"Tupperware parties and a lemonade stand. Naw, I'm just funning with you. We tried to sell dope, but I ended up doing most of it. As a musician, I wasn't gonna sell out, you know? I wasn't sure what to do, but I knew I wasn't gonna get a job."

Slim rose from his chair and shuffled over to the thermostat to adjust it. Did he turn it up or down? I was so caffeinated, I had no idea if I was hot, cold, or comfortable. The furnace turned on. I guess we were cold.

"Our drummer—we called him Puck on account of he put so much tobacco in his lip it looked like he had a hockey puck in his mouth—was the only one of us who had a job to speak of. A paper route in this uppity neighborhood near Beverly Hills. He got to know the comings and goings of those folks. Puck had this batshit crazy girlfriend at the time named Lucy, who always thought we should rob one of the houses. She was a beautiful lady, but her elevator didn't exactly go to the top floor.

"Lucy had these mercurial moods that changed quicker than a hiccup, and poor Puck had to weather all of 'em. She also decided she'd be our tambourine player and backup singer. Even though she had no rhythm and a voice that sounded like a tortured rabbit, she was overtly talented—at dancing nude."

"A lucrative occupation I have heard."

"She made big money as a stripper at an elite gentleman's club. Called herself Bambi. Puck even put a pole up in our basement so she could practice. She'd walk around the house nude, and we never complained, on account of she had curves like a country road. I remember we'd all sit in the living room and pretend to watch television, staring at her out of the corner of our eyes. Puck would get all exercised and haul her off to their bedroom. She loved every damn second of it.

"One day, Puck cornered me in the kitchen with this wild look in his eyes, chewing on the inside of his cheek like a rabid chipmunk, and said, 'You all have got to stop staring at Lucy, man. It's freaking her out, and I'm going to start kicking some ass!'

"'Tell her to put some damn clothes on,' I answered. 'What the hell are we supposed to look at with a naked woman walking around? Come on. We're your damn brothers, for crying out loud, and nobody is kicking anybody's ass.'

"'She's just staying in character, Slim. It helps with her dancing at work.'

"'Oh for the love of Pete, Puck. Pull your head outta your ass and get some air to that messed up mind of yours. She's doing it to get attention and to stir the soup. If Bambi wants to stay in character, tell her to do it in the basement, and to put a robe on when she's out around us. She thinks we're all in a movie about her life.'

"'You really think she's doing it to get attention?' he asked.

"'She's a stripper, Puck. Do the damn math. Women have to be half-cuckoo to do that, man. Wake up. She's got you swimming up Crazy Creek, and this ain't good for the band. Nobody is trying to get with her behind your back. She's pouring poison into your head. She ain't good for you.'

"'But her tits are perfect. And her butt and legs and face are, too. Where am I going to find another woman like her?'

"'Are you serious? We're gonna see five just like her at the show tonight, and they're gonna be lined up to meet you. And maybe one of 'em won't have Multiple Personality Disorder. She's cheese in a mousetrap for you, my brother. Open your eyes, Puck. Your stinking thinking's got you chasing a tail, and there ain't no dog. Your tick ain't got no tock.'

"Just then Lucy walked in, holding ample breasts in both hands and says,

'I've got great news, guys. I've saved up enough money to get fake boobs. I can't wait. Oh, Baby, you are going to love, love, love them. Rick says I'll double my tips, and then I'll have enough money to do my nose and cheekbones. I might get butt implants, but I'm not sure. How's my ass look? What about my calves? Maybe calf implants, too. I'm so excited!'

"Rick—the P in front of his name was silent—was the manager at the club she danced at, and he was a slimy weasel who tried to get with all the girls. I always knew I was on level ground when Rick would drool out of both sides of his mouth. Rick the Prick talked all of 'his girls' into getting breast implants and facelifts. He ran a damn Barbie Doll farm, and it nauseated me. I detested his very existence.

"Not being able to help myself, I said, 'You know, your butt and calves look pretty damn good. I'd maybe have some elbow and ankle work done. That's where the real money is. Two often overlooked areas on a beautiful woman. Ain't that right, Puck?'

"I looked at Puck, whose eyes had fogged over with his Lucy virus, and she looked like I'd given her a calculus equation to solve. Her eyes just about crossed. I shook my head and walked out of the room while she examined her elbows. It was gonna be a long summer for all of us."

"Did she dress more appropriately around the house after you spoke to Puck?" I asked.

"Hell, no," Slim answered with an exaggerated frown. "When Puck was off doing things, she'd flaunt herself around like a flower on fire, waiting to see our reaction. We tried to ignore her, but you can just about guess how well that went. The more we ignored her, the more she'd up the ante. Sit there with her damn legs spread out, or bend down to pick something up, slowly. We were like basset hounds at a barbecue. It went way past appalling, Son.

"I do have to give Lucy credit for floating most of the bills until we got up and running. Without her help, we wouldn't have been able to keep the apartment, and don't think the hypocrisy was lost on me. We just had to hold on until we started getting some better gigs, you know?

"Lucy had crazy in her from hell to breakfast, but she sure tried hard at anything she did. She practiced riding the pole in the basement about five hours a day, and she could bend and gyrate that impressive chassis of hers like you wouldn't believe. We were all sickened and immensely turned on by her.

"Her voice was flat as a piece of paper, and Puck tried to work with her on both her singing and playing. When she tried to join the band, she played and sang her little heart out, and when a couple of us gave her the thumbs down, she couldn't believe it.

"Puck and I about came to blows on that one when we told her Lucy wasn't gonna be part of the band. He threw a tantrum. She threw a tantrum. Hell, she threw two tantrums. She locked herself in the bathroom with a butcher knife, and commenced to carve on herself like a damn pumpkin. We had to call the cops and the oxygen squad on that deal.

"She did about two weeks in a spin dry, and came out crazier than she went in. She refused to take the prescription drugs they gave her because they made her feel drowsy and out of it. Well now. When she said that, she was playing a song I could dance to. I thought it would be a damn shame to let barbiturates go to waste, so I took 'em. Not as prescribed."

Slim winked at me and bounced his eyebrows. He slowly closed his eyes and tilted his head back. Stretching neck muscles, or celebrating a memory? Likely the latter. A question formed in my mind. I allowed it to float away.

"Anyways, Lucy got the bright idea we should rob a dentist's house, and we did just that. Twice. We found out they were on vacation, and it took us two nights to get all the loot. A neighbor scared us off the second night, and we were long gone before any cops showed up. We were smart enough to take the license plates off the van we drove both nights. We even wore gloves, masks, and black clothes. I insisted on it. I watched a lot of crime shows on television, and I wasn't gonna make it easy for the detective squad.

"By the time we got it all sold, I think we made around five thousand bucks. That kept us afloat until we finally got an audition for an agent who signed us and put us on the road non-stop for quite a spell. Once that happened, we all had plenty of dough to make do and then some. We rented a small house with a basement, and that was where we rehearsed.

"As luck would have it, Lucy met a zillionaire at the strip club she fell ass over teakettle in love with, and we didn't have to put up with her damn drama no more. Puck was sad to see her go, but we all agreed he was in a much better lane without her. Hell, we all were, and it was nice to have our house back. Nice to have the band back."

"The Yoko Ono Syndrome. Widely acknowledged to be deadly for some groups."

"Malignant, Son. A metastatic growth you can't slow down. I can think of five or six women who almost tanked the band in a period of just under two years. Every time I turned around, one of us would start seeing some shiny gal with a screw loose, and the next thing I knew, we were all fighting. They were always beautiful, and usually leaking all over the place. Morti said they were necrotic tissue that needed to be removed so the wound could heal. It was a bad record we just kept playing.

"Anyways, it's said crime doesn't pay. Well, I guess it did for us, but I was a big believer in karma, so I was done stealing after that. I remember the guilt ate at me something fierce, but the others weren't bothered by it none. I never knew for sure, on account of I didn't want to, but I figured they broke into other places. Things would just show up in our band house, you know? I never wanted to know, so I never asked.

"I used to say I was a burglar who took early retirement. We were just kids chasing a dream around with way more dumb luck than sense. And I place myself on the lucky side of the big fence that I chased my dream. Most folks never even get a whiff of their own. I call that an epic soul miscarriage.

"It most certainly is. Did you all get along well on the road?"

"Son, we were so damned tickled to get paid doing what we loved to do. I was eighteen and living a dream, and the good news was there was nobody around to tell me what I could or couldn't do. The bad news was, there was nobody around to tell me what I could or couldn't do, you know? We all learned it together. We didn't have one damn clue about the business of music and what we were trying to do. We just played our butts off and had the time of our lives. It was real good.

"The toughest part was getting enough sleep. The five or six of us travelled in a van and trailer, and sometimes we'd have to load up after a gig and drive all night to get to the next gig. Again, that's where the speed came in handy in those days.

"I remember going three or four nights without sleep quite a bit. About the third day is when you start seeing things that ain't there, and electric shocks go through your brain like tiny firecrackers. We used to have contests to see who could stay up the longest, and nobody could beat me.

"It made playing gigs interesting, I'll tell ya that. It's hard enough to keep track of everything happening on stage when you have all your senses, you know? There were nights we'd play a gig and I wouldn't remember a damn thing about it. I went through the motions on automatic pilot a lot. Muscle memory. We'd finish a show and drive eight, ten hours, and none of us were in any shape to open a can of soup, let alone operate a vehicle. I don't know how we made it."

"I bet you get plenty of rest these days."

"Not as much as you'd think. To this day, I gotta force myself to go to bed. I've never been a morning person. I always loved the soundtrack and rhythm of the evening. When the sun goes down, I go to a better place inside. I've always been real good friends with the night.

"In the old days, I couldn't sleep without some type of medicine. It was usually opiates and vodka, but I wasn't picky about it. I'd knock myself out cold, and if I got real lucky I'd sleep three hours. My mind would only stay still for that long, you know? The damn thing had to get me up so it could tell me what I needed to be worried about.

"I was one hell of a pharmacist, too. If I got tired, I'd take some speed or snort some cocaine. If I got too wired, I'd take a Quaalude and a couple shots of brandy. Maybe smoke some pot. If I got to feeling down, I'd find an opiate. I knew what to take, how much to take, when to take it, and when it was okay to take it again.

"Well, for the most part, anyway. One drug I always had trouble regulating was heroin. A few of us weren't exactly casual users, you know? As if there was such a thing. I don't let myself get all exercised over what I pissed away, but it was a damn fortune."

"I'm just curious. Could you estimate how much money you spent on drugs and alcohol?"

Slim was serious for a moment. "I added it up once in a treatment center to be over two million bucks."

My eyebrows nearly jumped off of my face and I began to wonder what I could do with two million dollars. Slim's voice coaxed me back.

"That's the best my drug-addled brain could remember," he continued. "My cocaine habit cost me four hundred dollars a day, and I only drank booze if it was very expensive. Heroin was the big dog for me, and I dropped a lot of coin on it. I didn't get as beat up as a lot of guys did, and thank God I was working as much as I was. Some highs are elusive, you know, but heroin always did the trick for me."

This brought to mind my favorite John Prine lyric and I shared it. 'There's a hole in Daddy's arm where all the money goes. Jesus Christ died for nothing, I suppose.' Slim nodded and pointed his finger at me.

"Some folks write songs that are much bigger than they are. They go places they ain't supposed to be able to get to, but they do. Seems like John Prine could go there whenever he wanted to. And guys like Taupin, Dylan, Lennon, and Waters. They traveled on a different train entirely. They'd kick out these visceral lyrics that would make my head spin. I guess it made me work harder, though. There was that.

"Anyways, I never took an overdose of anything, but I knew a lot of folks who did. Back in those days, we all carried Narcan with us for the 'just in cases.' We figured that would save us if we went too far, but sometimes folks died anyway. That would scare me for a day or two, but then I'd run plum out of give a shit. I thought I was bulletproof back then. Hell, I still do in some ways. Except when I gotta bend over to cut my toenails and I remember how old I really am. The older I get, the farther my mind and my body get from each other."

"I'm not sure I follow. How are they farther from each other?" I said.

"My mind still thinks and acts like I'm thirty, but my body feels like it's seventy. I can't believe the old guy snuck up on me like he did. See that wood stove in the corner? My mind believes I can walk over and lift it off the floor, but my body has to be careful just lifting the wood it burns. Time is a tricky old girl, but all in all she's been damn good to me."

Slim sprung from his chair and did a dance on the way to the kitchen with his coffee urn. I could hear him making more coffee and humming a John Prine song. I purposely did not look at my watch. He returned to the living room, rubbing his hands together while the coffee machine coughed and brewed.

Watching him, filling the silence I said, "Some say time heals all wounds, but others say time is no friend of man."

"And some say getting old is a bitch," Slim said. "I say getting old is an honor, and it beats the dickens out of the alternative. I got old accidentally, Son. I didn't expect to be here. You wouldn't believe how many folks I've known who didn't make fifty. Dope and booze took most of 'em. Or cigarettes. Some couldn't carry the pain any longer, and they just set it all down. There was a time back in the day when it seemed like every damn time I turned around, I was carrying another casket, blitzed out of my mind on the same stuff that killed 'em.

"I think of all the times I played Russian roulette with myself, you know? All the dope I did, and the hundreds of thousands of miles we drove drunk outta our minds. I'm damned lucky and blessed to be here with you today, Son. So much could've gone really, really wrong.

"Anyways, we're on the right side of the dirt, we're healthy, and we got coffee and grocieries. That's what I call a damn good start to any morning."

Chapter Three

"Who were the other members of the band?" I asked.

"Well, there was Ringo, Paul, George, John, and me." Slim counted on his fingers to add emphasis.

I laughed. "I am certainly no student of music history, but I am quite certain you are pulling my leg."

"I'm pulling both your legs now, ain't I? Open that picture book in front of you. Page six, I believe."

I opened a leather-bound scrapbook and turned to the sixth page, which had a band photograph. In it were five young men who wore their hair long, their clothes tight, and their eager dreams on their sleeves. I smiled and showed it to him. He beckoned me over with the book. I obliged and stood beside him. His index finger landed on the member to the far left.

"Puck was on drums, Morti on keys, I was front and center, Rev was on bass, and our lead guitarist was a cool cat named Joshua Marquis from North Dakota. We all called him Flash.

"That cat could play faster than anybody I ever saw, but he rarely did. He was real tasty, you know? He knew that when not to play was as important as when to play. Problem was, he'd always be so drunk by the end of the night, I'd have to muddle through his parts, and he'd just stand there grinning like he'd just crapped his pants—which, by the way, he did on occasion. It didn't stop the show, but it sure slowed it down.

"He'd slap me around some if he knew I told you this, but he used to wear diapers during our gigs."

"Diapers? Oh, my." I inserted.

"Yep. Adult diapers. Thank God I never had to change one. I used to beg him not to drink too much before gigs. He'd laugh and point at my medicines.

"I wanted to tell him, 'But I don't crap my pants on stage,' but he was my brother and I didn't want to hurt him.

"Anyways, that was the gauge he used when it came to booze and such. As long as he avoided fecal fracases, everything was copacetic.

"It was best to catch him early in the night when he was still sober. I asked him once how he learned to play so fast, and he told me when he first started on the guitar, he'd snort a whole bunch of speed and play chords and scales over and over as fast as he could. He did it six hours a day for over a year, and came away with lightning in his fingers. He was an extra something, Son.

"I got another side story on Flash. He was having a bad time with his asthma on the road, and I kept telling him he had to quit smoking cigarettes. He tried everything and still couldn't kick 'em. So, he goes to this hypnotist, and whammo, he's off the smokes.

"The problem was, he was also helplessly compelled to whistle and howl at blonde-haired women. Every single one he saw. It drove them, him, and the rest of us crazy, and got him in trouble more than once. He told me he was going back to the hypnotist to have the hex removed.

"I failed to concur.

"'I've got to do something, Slim,' he said. 'I can't help myself, and one of these days it's going to get me killed. Or worse.'

"'You can't go back to that same hypnotist,' I told him. 'She obviously put this hex on you so you'd have to come back and pay her more money to remove it. It would never end. Next time, you'd be afraid to touch your own pecker, or wanna touch mine. You gotta find a new hexer.'

"Which he did, and of course he fell hard for her. She liked him a lot, too, and she'd meet us on the road from time to time. Flash told me he had the best sex with her he'd ever had on account of she'd hypnotize him before hand. She'd snap her fingers and he'd turn into a sexual velociraptor."

"You don't per chance have her number, do you?" I asked.

"Ha. The whole time he dated her, Flash stayed away from other women, which impressed the hell out of us. He stayed off the cancer sticks, too."

"Too bad she didn't hex him to stop pooping his pants," I added.

"Don't think I didn't meditate on that some," Slim said, pronouncing every word alowly. "If I'd mentioned that, he'd have grabbed me by the neck and popped my head like a pimple. That one was off limits for all of us. Whenever Flash was around her, he stayed off the dope and booze. He quit wearing diapers and started writing more material for the band. We even let him drive once in a while, and that had never happened before.

"She was always offering to hypnotize me for this or that, but I never took her up on it. She told me she was real exercised over my drinking and drugging and that she could help me stop both. I thanked her kindly and told her I'd keep her in mind if I ever felt so inclined. It would've taken a doozy of a hexing session to get me to stop taking my medicines.

"She was real good for Flash. I think they were together for almost two years, and it really knocked him for a loop when she left him. I never found out about why any of that went down like it did. He'd never talk about it, and I never asked. I always just figured she wanted to get hitched and have some kiddos. Flash would never have gone for that. Hell, we were all consummate bachelors, committed to as little as possible besides the music and the band.

"The most dedicated bachelor of all of us was Dennis Hutto. AKA Puck."

Slim's finger tapped repeatedly on a shirtless, well-muscled, dark-haired young man wearing bellbottom jeans and a mischievous grin.

"Puck was a born again and again Baptist redneck from Mississippi who usually wore a confederate flag t-shirt, pants tight enough to choke a straw, and so much cologne you knew he was coming from a block away. I'd always ask him to stand downwind of me, you know? He had a drawl that would make you howl, and the drunker he got, the more he drawled on. He acted and sounded like he was touched in the head some, but he never fooled me. He was the guy who always knew what was what in all situations. The quintessential redneck eagle scout.

"If equipment needed fixing, Puck took care of it. If the van broke down, Puck took care of that, too. If one of us had a mouth that wrote a check our body couldn't cash, Puck would bail him out and make sure no harm came to him. He never got flustered, never lost his temper, and he was always as sober as he needed to be. He could be counted on in any situation.

"He was the only cat I've ever met who truly had no fear of anything. If someone dared him to do something, he'd be on his way to do it before the other guy got the whole sentence out. I saw him do things that would've killed most folks, and he never gave any of it a second thought."

"Such as?" I asked Slim, curious.

"I saw him cut a hole in the ice at a lake and jump in naked. I saw him leap over a car that was speeding at him, and watched him almost blow himself up with dynamite, holding it while the fuse burned down to nothing. His favorite thing to do when the band was off was to jump outta airplanes, waiting to pull the cord at the last second.

"Once he showed me how to hypnotize an alligator, and then he went and put his damn head in its mouth. He'd put LSD in his eyelids, and he almost died one time from a 190 proof alcohol enema. He once dated twin sisters at the same time, in disguise. He was a certifiable lunatic, Son.

"He was a hell of a drinker, but only did drugs on special occasions. Now that I think about it, we had lots of special occasions. And he always had at least two guns on him. Whenever we got into a tight situation, my first move was to locate Puck and stand close to him. It was like having a Navy Seal in the band, you know? He was truly a man's man. The kind of guy who did his own dentistry, you know. Impervious to pain and impervious to fear. Of anything.

"The thing I appreciated most about Puck was he had fists of concrete, but the heart of a saint. He could lift a car engine with his back and bare hands, and would cry during a diaper commercial on television. I called him a delightful paradox. I also called him Brother Puck, and meant it.

"He had a dandy sense of humor on him, too.

"One morning we got visited by a couple Jehovah's Witnesses at our bandhouse. Puck watched 'em walk up the sidewalk and disappeared into his bedroom. I was about to answer the doorbell when he shoved me aside, holding a machete in his hand and naked as a newborn except for a pair of cowboy boots."

"Welcoming committee," I offered.

"He welcomed 'em alright. He swung that door open, wild-eyed and such, and you should've seen the look on their faces when he invited them in for breakfast."

"I have a picture in my head," I said.

"He told them he had a girl tied up in the basement, and asked them if they knew how to get blood stains out of shag carpet. They stood there paralyzed with their mouths hung open, and by the time they'd backpeddled and hightailed it away from the house, I'd about wet myself from laughing. I half expected the police to pay us a visit, but they never did."

"You did not have a girl tied up in the basement, right?" I asked, laughing.

"Not that day," Slim anwered, giggling like a schoolboy.

"I remember one night, this tortured, stunning younger gal tried to pick a fight after we'd finished up a gig. She stormed into our dressing room and glared at a very intoxicated Puck.

"'Don't just stand there, Sweetheart,' Puck said. 'Go somewhere else.'

"'You asshole,' she yelled. 'You can't just ignore me like I'm one of your stupid bar bimbos!'

"'I got good news and bad news for you, Darling,' Puck said. 'The good news is you are not one of my stupid bar bimbos. Your classification would fall under the motel bimbo heading. The bad news is…yes, I can ignore you…and I will continue to do so indefinitely.'

"If she wasn't crazy before he said that, she went past it after. Way past it. She threw chairs and kicked over the catering table before the bouncer intervened and corralled her.

"Puck shook his head and made the sign of the cross with his forearms.

"'The power of Christ compels you. The power of Christ compels you,' he kept saying to her as she was carried out the door.

"When she'd been removed from the venue, I asked him, 'What the hell is wrong with her?'

"'Daddy complex with a couple eating disorders,' he answered. 'We spent about a week together one night, and I can't shake her off, man.'

"'Did you sleep with her?' I asked.

"'Didn't sleep a wink,' he answered.

"He always delivered his punch lines with a straight face, and never broke character. And what a character he was. He was also a great drummer, and he could keep perfect time in a hurricane. Once he set a tempo, you couldn't budge him. He was the best kind of drummer to play with. Sometimes you gotta drag a drummer with you, and that'll make a guy exhausted by the time the gig is over. Puck was effortless to play with."

"And Rev?"

Slim turned to the next page of the book, and there stood a young seminary student with short blond hair and an almost pained expression. Slim's finger lingered over the student's face as his eyes misted. My hand wanted to go to his shoulder, but I kept it holstered.

"Ah, yes. The Reverend Bretavious McClanahan, bass player extraordinaire. He was the son of two Irish Catholic parents from Denver who insisted he become a priest. He said his family didn't give him a choice in the matter. He was gonna be a pulpit pounder, and that was that. He told me he'd tried to wear the priest collar, but it didn't fit him too good.

"Rev loved the ladies, and they loved him back. He'd have had one hell of an argument with that celibacy part, I'll tell you that. I never understood why priests can't get married. Why they gotta stay single and broke. Seems like cruel and unusual punishment to me."

"I wonder if they'll ever figure out this priest celibacy concept has not exactly panned out?"

"I dunno. They've had 1000 years to figure out priest celibacy makes about as much sense as putting earrings on an eggplant. If I ran the show, I'd allow all priests to get married. And what the hell's wrong with a woman being a priest? Or would that be a priestess? Anyways, I'd let 'em do whatever they wanted to do. I guess I'd make a horrible Pope.

"Rev always read the Bible on the road, and pretty soon he'd start to jaw about it to the rest of us. Puck would hang right with him on account of his background, and the two of them would flop around and pretend to speak in tongues. I probably would've got more out of the lessons and such if I hadn't always been cross-eyed drunk. Rev was always trying to steer me towards sobriety, but my wheels were rusted and facing one direction.

"The best thing about Rev was he never judged. Anybody. And he wasn't above raising some hell on occasion, either. He just always had an off switch the rest of us didn't have, you know? He'd have two beers and that would be it. He'd take one pill and stop. He'd take one hit off of a pot pipe and call it good. I never understood how he could do that. I thought he knew the secret, but I'd ask him for it and he'd just laugh.

"I remember once we were on the road somewhere and he and I bunked together in a hotel room. He came back from a run and found me face down in a puke bucket. He picked my head up by a handful of hair and I came to and looked up at him.

"'How's that working out for you?' he asked. 'You giving that booze a second viewing?'

"'I'm okay. Just help me stand,' I managed.

"'You've got to slow down on the drugs and alcohol, my friend. I love you and I don't want to see you die. How much did you drink?'

"'Twice as much as you think I did.' I laughed.

"'Will you pray with me? Ask God to deliver you from this madness?'

"'I ain't asking for something I want no part of, Rev, and God ain't gonna listen to me anyway. You got your way of dealing with things, and I got my way. I'll be okay, man. I just wish you'd tell me your damn secret to dealing with this mess.'

"'There's no secret to it, Slim. I like to dip my toes in drugs and alcohol. You like to swim in the deep end.'

"Two hours later I was on stage, rocking like nobody's business. Amyl nitrate was a wonderful resuscitator and could drag me out of a serious drunk enough to get my legs under me. And speed. At that time, speed was the root word in my drug vocabulary. I lived on the stuff.

"The reason I brought up that conversation is I knew Rev was right and that I was already in trouble, but I always kept the truth outta my reach. He was a great friend and brutal confidant to me. He never pulled punches, but he also never preached at me. He was a true man of God, and he would've made a heck of a preacher teacher.

"Rev was older than the rest of us, and before joining the band, he'd entered a Catholic seminary. Things had gone well for him until he did an exorcism without permission from the Vatican, or however that works. Some kid's mother had begged Rev for help, so he and another seminary student tied the kid down and did their exorcising thing, you know? The noise bothered the neighbors, and the cops got called and kicked the lady's door in. There was Rev with this tied-up kid, and he and the other student were arrested on the spot.

"The Catholic Church's legal squad got the charges dismissed, but Rev had to leave the seminary. I asked him about the exorcism, and he told me he'd never go near anything like that again. His face turned white when he talked about it, and I could see in his eyes the experience continued to haunt him.

"'We went into a situation that was totally over our heads,' Rev had told me. 'It was like tossing a thimble full of water on a campfire.'

"'Do you think the kid was really possessed?' I asked him.

"'There was something deeply wrong with him, Slim. I don't know if he was possessed or not, but his eyes were blood red and he had strength he shouldn't have had. Thank God the police showed up when they did, because I was freaked out of my mind. Do you believe in the devil, Slim?'

"'I know he's real, and I believe I don't wanna talk about this no more, Rev. Some things are better kept in the drawer.'

"Rev must've seen something in my eyes, and he wouldn't let it go."

"'Did something happen to you?'

"'Nope. I just don't like giving evil any airtime, okay? Let it go.'

"'Okay, but if you ever want to talk, I'm always here and you know that.'

"'You'll be the first person I flag down. And, Rev? Thanks for always being a good pal. For never judging me or putting pressure on me to see things your way.'

"'Oh, Slim. I know you, and I know that you will come back to God when you are ready. He loves you and so do I.'

"He told me getting kicked out of the seminary was the best thing that could've happened, and that he wasn't cut out for the priesthood. He sure was cut out for playing rock and roll, I'll tell you that. He was a damn fine musician and singer, and he wrote some really good songs, too. I was lucky and blessed to have him on my team.

"The other thing that sticks out in my mind about Rev was he never liked the attention being in an up and coming band brought to him. He was very humble about all that. Folks would ask us to sign autographs or take pictures with 'em, and Rev would always just suddenly disappear. When folks would tell him how great he was, he'd turn all red and slip inside himself. I always liked that about him. He wasn't playing music to get something. He was always playing to give.

"The last time I talked to him, he had himself a wife and two kids, and was the musical director at a Presbyterian church. Can you believe it? My buddy, Rev, the recovering Catholic."

Slim turned back to the band photograph and held the book closer to his narrowed eyes, robbed by time. Color filled his face as he petted the form of the final Codefendant. Imperceptible whispered words barely escaped his lips and a memory dripped from his eyes.

"And that must be Morti, right? Where did he fit into the scheme of things?"

"Mortimer Slade was the band's conscience, and parent. Whenever an important band decision needed to be made, Morti made it. He was really the only adult in the bunch. He'd cut loose on occasion, but mostly he kept himself in check. He'd go a week without a drink or a drug and think nothing of it. Then, he'd just go on a bender with the rest of us and keep up just fine.

"Morti always hammered away at everyone to write songs, and he was the band's music director. He always believed the band would be signed to a record deal, and thought we'd better have a whole mess of songs ready to go when it happened. He was a slave driver when it came to rehearsing and such.

"That was a difference between him and me. I knew we were a damn good band, and that was enough for me. He knew we could be an exceptional band, and he fought us tooth and nail to get there. He always said good bands were a dime a dozen. He wasn't interested in just giving folks a show, you know? He wanted to give them an unforgettable experience.

"Morti loved learning. When we weren't on the road, he sat in on business and law classes at Santa Monica Community College, posing as a student. He figured, why not get a free education, you know? While the rest of us zombies were drunk by the pool, Morti worked on marketing plans and attended classes. He also devoted two hours a day to writing new music, and nothing got in the way of it. I just never had that kind of discipline. Hell, I never had any discipline to speak of.

"Another thing about Morti was his explosive charisma. I was the front man, but the band's true magnetism emanated from Morti. Whenever we needed it, Morti would spring a charisma leak and take over a crowd. Puck called him Morti the Magnetic. He had enough star quality for all of us.

"And he was a hell of a practical joker. We always tried to one-up each other in that department, and I could never hang with him. One thing he used to do that I got a kick out of was walk into his bank wearing a ski mask. He'd just casually stroll up to the teller and wait for her face to drop like an anchor, politely do his banking, and stroll out. He'd have security guards spilling their damn coffee on themselves. If anyone asked him why he was wearing it, he'd tell 'em he had leprosy and go to shake their hand. He even had guns pulled on him, but he kept doing it. It was a hell of a hoot."

I grinned. "That may be one of the coolest pranks in the history of prankdom."

"Is prankdom a word?"

"I'm quite certain it is not, though it seemed to flow out so effortlessly."

"Morti ran around with a half-shaved mustache for about a month once, too. You should've seen the looks he would get from folks. Then, he'd act insulted by their attention and tell them it was a birth defect and he was ashamed of it. They'd apologize all over themselves. Tell him it looked just fine, you know? Damn. How was I supposed to compete with that? I can't even think of the pranks I pulled, as they paled in comparison to his. He was one in a million.

"He was also a movie freak, and down the road after he left the band, he bought himself a movie theatre in Tucson, Arizona. He said he loved to work the projectors, and really enjoyed talking movies with folks. One of these days, I'd sure like to run into him again to catch up."

"You mentioned there were six of you in the van. Who was the fifth Codefendant?"

Slim wiped emotions from his eyes and chuckled to himself as he pointed to a picture of a portly, ponytailed young man holding a pistol and a bottle of Jack Daniels. His wide grin seemed to be the largest part of his body, and his t-shirt sported the words *Peace Sucks*. My eyes were drawn to his movie star good looks. Paul Newman. Steve McQueen.

"In the early days, we had a cat who came with us named Leroy Zeeb—who we all called Rufus—who ran the soundboard and helped carry equipment. He could figure out any electronic device in no time, and he had a damn good ear when it came to mixing the band's sound. I never had to worry about how we sounded out front when Rufus was on the mixing board.

"That was a gigantic weight off of my mind, I'm telling you. You can be the best band on the planet, but if the soundman doesn't find a good mix, the crowd thinks you're horrible. They're worth every penny, and Rufus was as good as we ever had.

"He met a ton of pretty girls on account of he looked real shiny and knew twenty-dollar words. He'd always pick the prettiest woman in the room and make bets about whether he could bed her. He won more than he lost. Rufus looked good and he was as strong as an ox, but the brain in his head was like a marble in a box car when it came to common sense."

"You lost on me that last one," I stated.

"Rufus loved to chase older, married women. Neither a popular or particularly safe sport to engage in."

"Ah. I'm guessing their husbands displayed little affection for him."

"He was constantly getting kicked around by some pissed-off hubby, and he had guns pulled on him on a real regular basis. It's not that he couldn't take care of himself sober, but he was usually so drunk when he was women hunting he was unable to defend himself.

"Puck and I saved his bacon a number of times, but we got tired of putting ourselves on the line for his bad habit, you know? I'd talk to him about it until my tongue would go numb, but he wouldn't listen a lick. He was morbidly stupid when it came to women, and nobody could wave him off the married ones.

"He got himself beat up so bad after a gig one night in Madison, Wisconsin, it took him six months to learn the language again. We had to leave him behind in the hospital, but he did catch up to us eventually. We were awful glad to have him and his finely-tuned ears back. He swore off chasing women for good repeatedly, but it wouldn't last. He had an addiction to dangerous liaisons. His habit was carcinogenic, Son. Deadly deeds."

Slim closed the scrapbook and rose to refill our coffee cups in the kitchen. Another piece of jerky flew at me, and I snatched it out of the air like a fly ball He remained in the kitchen for only a few minutes, but the uncomfortable silence seemed to stain the cabin. Slim returned to the room with two plates of meat, cheese, and crackers. I was suddenly famished. He bounced his eyebrows and returned to his chair.

"Rufus was my hallucinating partner when I felt so inclined. We meshed well during dope trips, and I never had a bad one with him. Our favorite thing to do was drop acid at the beach and start a big fire. We'd peak together and that damn ocean would come alive, Son. It would speak to us, and you ain't heard nothing until you hear the ocean say your name over and over, you know? We'd go into these laughing fits that would make us both sick. I think laughter like that adds years to a fella's life. Well, minus the vomiting part.

"Once when we were playing shows in Arizona, Rufus and I took motorcycles across the Painted Desert and took a bunch of peyote buttons. It was 110 degrees, and we made a fire and danced around it in the rain, but it wasn't raining, you know? He had a vision where his grandfather appeared to tell him he had to change his ways. He cried all night and most of the next morning. I got to spend time with my mother in a field of lush grass and butterflies.

"She appeared to me in this white gown, with flowers in her hair and a gold necklace. She held me tight, and everything inside me collapsed into her. She smelled like lemons, and her breath on my skin brought tears to my eyes. She told me she was proud of me, and that she was sorry for leaving me like she did. I was so sad when my vision switched to something else. I looked for her everywhere that night. I craved her like the breath you take when you're coming up from under the water.

"It wasn't until the next afternoon we were able to function enough to ride the bikes back into the city. Rufus and I shared something sacred during those couple days. We took peyote and acid together many times after that, but never matched that experience. I can still see that part of the desert in my mind. Sometimes I go there in my dreams to this day.

"Last time I saw Rufus, he'd learned some lessons and had settled down with a gal we all knew from the old days when she was just finishing up law school. We called her Suzie Q, and she was one smart gal. She gave up her law practice and started stripping, since she made more money naked. By the time Rufus ran into her again twenty years later, she'd long since given up the pole. I don't know if it's true, but I heard she taught herself computers and invented some damn combat game. The next thing you know, ole Suzie Q's a millionaire, and tag, Rufus is rich.

"Anyways, we were all a damn good team, and for a long time, we got along just fine. We were brothers, but we felt like soldiers. Fighting the good fight, shoulder to shoulder, come what may. When you're on the road and spend that much time together, you get so you can finish sentences for each other, and know what the other guy's thinking.

"We got along the best in the earliest days when we didn't have any money, you know? We all just shared what we had and did it gladly. We laughed a lot, but it was some tough going.

"The more successful we got, the easier it was for us. Simple math. Bigger gigs meant bigger money. More money meant better hotels, rooms, and food. Better transportation. Better dope and booze. We had money to hire roadies to haul and set up equipment. And get us girls and drugs. We thought we were something special when we started getting fancy dressing rooms and catering tables. Hell, when we first started, we were lucky if we even had a stage to stand on.

"We earned everything that came to us, I'll tell you that. We worked our butts off, and we were as tight as a gnat's ass as a band. We could literally read each other's minds on stage. It was a hoot to play with those gents.

"You want some more groceries?"

"Excuse me? Groceries?"

"Meat and cheese and such. I can fetch you more."

"No, thank you, this is plenty and delicious."

"I'll cook us up something proper down the road a piece. I don't wanna eat too much—it'll make me sleepy. You got a question?"

"Yes. Did you perform mostly in California?"

"We played music in the key of everywhere. We covered the country like a sweaty blanket, and by the time we'd been out for two years, I'll bet you diamonds to donuts we'd been everywhere but Alaska and Hawaii. We'd crawl back to California once in awhile to sleep it all off, and then back at it we'd go.

"It got to be I didn't feel comfortable unless I was on the road, though I wasn't a fan of travel. I was a fan of arrival. I loved living in motel rooms, and the promise of another adventure just down the road kept us all eager and full of energy. The more we played, the better we got at everything we were doing.

"When we started out, we didn't really play well together, but we looked good and sold more of an image than we did the music. That changed, and we became a damn good band. I think we surprised ourselves by how good we became."

A wide grin spread across Slim's face as he rose to retrieve my empty plate. From the kitchen, his voice rose above the noise of the water now running in the sink.

"We put over a half million miles on the first band van before it curled up and died for good. We were driving in a blizzard on the Raton Pass in Colorado and blew the motor. By the time we got it towed into Raton, New Mexico, we'd all about froze to death. Maybe it was karma, but it always seemed to go like that for us. We'd get ahead or get a break or two, and then something would bite us in the ass.

"Anyways, we had gigs to get to, and we needed a big van. The old guy who towed us into town knew a guy who knew a guy who had a brand new one just sitting in his driveway, but he wanted a bit more for it than we had on us at the time. We hadn't got the hang of saving and budgeting yet. That would come later.

"As luck would have it, it was a Thursday night when we broke down. The following Saturday was the annual policeman's auxiliary ball, and the band booked to play the gig couldn't get there on account of the snow. We were sitting in a motel room fretting over what to do when there was a knock on the door, which sent us all scurrying like cockroaches to hide all the dope and such."

Slim suddenly appeared in front of me, and I realized I'd closed my eyes listening to his hypnotic voice. He touched the top of my head and handed me a plate of sliced apples. Again, his eyebrows bounced across his face as he returned to his chair.

"When I opened the door and saw a tall policeman in a cowboy hat standing there, my ticker started jitterbugging something fierce. But when he politely introduced himself as the town's sheriff and explained he needed a band for the following night's festivities, my butt muscles started to unpucker."

"He needed a band, and you needed money for a van," I proudly stated. "Makes sense."

"Well, ain't you a damn detective. Yep. We all struck a deal, and Slim Chance and the Codefendants played the Colfax County Policeman's Auxiliary Ball that Saturday night. They even rented tuxedos for us. And, they paid us twice what the other band was gonna get, on account of Morti's negotiating. We had plenty of dough for the van, and enough left over to get us down the road to more gigs.

"I don't have to tell you we were on our best behavior that night. It was truly the only show the band ever played sober, and I remember how tickled we all were by how well we played. Go figure.

"Well now, we played the gig and they liked us just fine. In fact, the mayor presented us with a gold key to the city, and we got our picture taken with him and the entire police force. If they'd have known how much dope we had hidden in our equipment, I don't think they'd have been so accommodating. The weather cleared that Sunday afternoon, and off we went in our shiny new Dodge van, which turned out to be one of the best damn band vehicles we ever owned.

"One thing about being a road band was you always had mechanical problems with the vehicles, and electrical problems with the equipment. There was a stretch there where bad luck seemed to be glued to our fannies, and for a time I just expected things to go the wrong way for us.

"I should say that on the other side of tumult and tragedy for the band over the years, there also seemed to be a saving grace, like a guardian angel. I can't begin to tell you how many times we were screwed, glued, and tattooed to trouble, when something would come outta nowhere to save the damn day. It got to the point we started tracking it. Something good would happen, and we'd look at each other and wait for the hammer to drop. Or, we'd get hit with another disaster and wait on the corner for the next blessing.

"Back and forth like that it went.

"I remember my grandfather used to say, 'I don't know if it's a good thing or a bad thing that this has happened. I just know that this has happened. You've got to let things breathe, Slim. Let them unfold the way they are supposed to without trying to control them. Control is just an illusion, anyway. Learn to let go, and don't pick it back up like a let go yo. Put it in the God box.'

"'What's the God box?' I asked him.

"'When you find yourself worried about something, write it down on a piece of paper and then put it somewhere where you won't look at it. Ask God to handle it, and let it go. Whenever you start to worry about it, you just tell yourself it's none of your business anymore. It's in the God box.'

"He also used to beg me not to become what he called a fence rider."

"A fence rider?"

"Someone who makes a decision to not make a decision about faith. My grandfather believed the biggest tragedy a man could experience was to not to have a personal relationship with God. He called that 'empty living,' and he believed more folks than not fell into the category. He knew I was awful twisted around when it came to God and such, and it bothered him deeply. But he knew I was a believer, and I guess he figured that was a good enough start. He used to tell me he knew I'd get it all sorted out. He just wished for sooner than later, you know?

"He used to say, 'We all start out sitting on the big fence, Son. Some folks never jump down off of it, and spend their lives in fear. Others jump down on the dark side, and spend their lives hurting others chasing empty sins.

Folks like us, we jump down on the other side. It's the toughest side to stand on, but it's worth every ounce of whatever gets tossed at us. It's the passionate side. Where love and peace live. God gave you a good heart. Follow it and your head will come along whether it wants to or not. Feed your faith, Son; it's hungry.'

"I can still see him in his chair, cheek stuck out a mile with chewing tobacco, rocking back and forth with twinkling eyes. I'd sit on the floor in front of him, patiently waiting for another pearl of wisdom to come tumbling outta that mouth. Every morning he'd tell me he loved me and make me hug him.

"The last thing he would always say to me before he went to bed was, 'Just in case I pass and get to go see Grandma, always know how proud I am of you, Son.'"

"Grandma?"

"She passed real early on, and I never got to know her. He'd dance with her picture and talk to it all the time. He never remarried and seemed peaceful about that. He was always happy, you know? Always smiling. I loved everything about him and craved his affections. He was as close to a father as I'd ever had, and I never got to thank him enough for giving me what he had inside, you know?"

Moisture formed at the corners of Slim's eyes, and he let them fill and drain tear trails down his tanned, whiskered face. He slowly rose from his chair and his eyes pointed directly at mine. My eyes began to blink repeatedly.

"I'm still mad at myself that he passed when we were on the road. He went real sudden like, and if I'd known he was as sick as he was, I never would've left him. Even though I know he'd have wanted me to be out playing shows like I was, I still beat myself up pretty bad about it all, you know? His omnipresent love and support sustained me, and I sure wish I could've been there for him at the end. I'm damn glad I have so many memories of him, and I replay 'em all the time. I never laughed with anybody the way I did with my grandfather. He was the best man I ever knew, and I hope he knew how much I loved him."

"Your eyes have a twinkle when you talk about him. I'm sure he took notice of that as well, and knew how important he was to you."

"Thanks for that, Son. Anyways, I know he would've been proud of the way things turned out for the band. Through all the ups and downs we had over the years, I think the universe treated us pretty damn fair. We had way more ups than downs, I'll tell you that. Lady Luck smiled on us more times than I could count, and she seemed to always be close by when we really needed her. When I look back on it all, we may have had her on speed dial.

"I will tell you this. If my band did have a guardian angel back in those days, if she wasn't a drinker before she signed on with us, she sure was afterwards."

Chapter Four

"I adore the band's road stories. I'll bet you have hundreds," I grinned at Slim.

"Not hundreds, but I've got enough to keep us busy tonight. A lot of 'em got lost over the years. The dope. The booze. Time. They took 'em. I used to have a mind like a whip. Now it's more like a zipper that keeps getting stuck. It still works, but you gotta fiddle with it some. Sorta like another part of my body. I got a couple stories in mind that are worth telling, but a lot of 'em don't seem worth digging into.

"There was the time we got hit by a tornado at an outdoor show in North Dakota and lost all our gear and instruments. The time the stage collapsed underneath us in Iowa and I found out a few months later I had a damn broken back and didn't know it. Both good stories, but they ain't speaking to me.

"Then, there was the night we all got drunk and got into a bowling ball fight. That one cost us about four grand in damages and bail money to get out. And, the time two of us got genital crabs from the same gal. Twice. The time our hotel caught on fire in Kansas City and Puck did a TV interview in his underwear and got the reporter's phone number. Another time, two of us passed out on stage during the same show. There was the night when…um…."

The color drained from Slim's face and he suddenly had no idea what to do with his hands.

"The night when…what? What happened?" I asked, almost demanded.

"Some of these ain't for public consumption, Son."

"That's going to drive me batty," I whined. "What if I turn off the recorder and we keep it off the record?"

"Nope. I mean it, Stevie Boy. Leave it alone."

Slim's face turned bright red and the look in his eyes backed my insides into a corner I had no way of escaping. I nodded apologetically and let it drop then and there.

"I do remember a couple other events you might get a kick out of, though."

"First, Slim, please tell me how two of you contracted genital crabs from the same woman, *twice*."

Slim guffawed out loud. "There goes me and my big damn mouth. Look, me and Rufus had a threesome with this gal and we both got the worse case of genital crabs in the history of the state of Minnesota. We were playing a three-night stint at a club in Minneapolis, and we both got to itching real bad the next day.

"Crabs ain't hard to diagnose, and we got the stuff to treat 'em at a pharmacy and doused ourselves, our clothes, and our motel rooms. She showed up for our next gig that night and apologized all over herself for giving us the critters. She swore she'd taken the cure and was okay to go again that night. We chewed her out for infecting us, and then chewed ourselves out for telling the rest of the band, who teased us like heartless playground bullies.

"Well, she did her best to seduce the both of us, and neither one of us took her up on it. We knew better than to risk getting 'em again. We were smart guys. Budding rock stars. We had integrity to live up to, you know? The last thing we were gonna do was besmirch our good names again for some bug-infested gal!"

"And your resolve wore off," I proudly noted.

"That next night, we both stepped knee-deep into stupid, Son. Both of us signed up for a repeat performance, and we got 'em again from her. I can't begin to tell you how much teasing we received after the second infestation. Morti started calling us Itch and Scratch, and Deja Screw. Thanks for asking about it. Can I tell my other damn stories now?"

"Please, be my guest," I insisted.

Slim rubbed his hands together, and somewhere in the back of his eyes, a flickering light began to show through. I peeked at the recorder. It was still running.

"Well, this first story is a doozy and then some. The time we played an, um, interesting show in Santa Cruz when we were just starting out. I think it might have been our second or third major gig. Our booking agent put us in this real hot club called The Catalyst to see how we'd do. We knew if we did well there, we'd be on our way. If you wanted to tour where we wanted to tour, all roads led through The Catalyst, and we were tickled to be there for our shot.

"We'd made it through the first set, and we were really cooking with gas that night. The folks were digging the dickens outta us, and the club owner told us we were as good a band as he'd seen in years. It was one of those magical nights when everything was working and no matter what we did on stage, the crowd dug it.

"I remember we were in the dressing room on break, snorting huge lines of coke and guzzling wine like vampires until we had to go back on. In those days, we'd get as drunk and wired as possible to promote maximum creativity, you know? That night we were about as creative as we'd ever been, and I remember thinking I might have pushed it a bit too far when I came to, staring up at a ceiling fan and Rev's concerned face.

"'Cripes, Slim. You went down so fast I couldn't catch you.'

"'Maybe you should leave him down there,' Flash said. 'Maybe he needs to learn a little lesson. Like not blowing an important audition gig for us.'

"'Help me up,' I managed, which Rev and Puck did. 'Man. What the hell's in that bottle on the table over there?"

"'Everclear and punch,' Puck answered. 'With a hint of MDMA, morphine, and various pills I found and ground up.'

"'What the hell you drinking that for on a show night?' I gasped.

"'I'm not. I was saving it for after the gig," Puck said. 'You're the one drinking it on a show night, you idiot. Rev? Reach in my bag in that side pocket and get me that white bottle. I gotta wake up our fearless leader before we return to battle.'

"Rev retrieved the bottle, which turned out to be amyl nitrate, or what folks called poppers, and Puck gave me a couple whiffs. I was awake, alert, and once I got my eyes uncrossed, ready to hit the stage. It took me a couple more hits off the poppers bottle, but I managed to finish the second set in marginal shape. The crowd by that time was standing room only, and the energy of the joint was dripping off the walls. The whole place was electric and alive. The kind of crowd you live to play for.

"We were just about to return to the dressing room when a gunshot rang out and folks started to lose their damn minds all around me. Then, two more gunshots echoed off the walls. I froze in place and saw a body on the floor and a whole mess of blood spilling outta it. Folks were screaming and running for the exits, and I suddenly found Puck's face in front of mine, but I couldn't hear the words coming outta his mouth. He had a gun in his hand and was waving it towards the back of the stage. For a second, my polluted mind thought maybe he'd done the shooting, you know, and I didn't know what the hell to do, so I did nothing.

"The next thing I know, I'm being whisked backstage by Flash, Puck, Morti, and Rev, and we ran into our dressing room, then slammed and locked the door. To make a long story short enough to stomach, a guy was murdered by two gunmen that night, and we hid in our dressing room until we heard the police and oxygen squad sirens."

"Did they catch the shooters?" I asked.

"Yup. Caught 'em that night," Slim answered. "One surrendered, and the other got shot and killed by a policewoman. We heard it was all over a gal who was having an affair with the guy who got killed. It was a hell of a way to finish such a dynamite show. I can still see the blood-spattered walls. Black and shimmering against the neon lights.

"We hightailed it outta town after we got paid and interviewed by the police, but none of us saw anything. Like I said, we'd just gotten started as a band, and it brought us closer together in a real hurry. It was a while down the road until we all relaxed about it. Because of how well we did at that club, we took off like a rocket. The murder somewhat soiled the experience. That's all I have to say about that, I guess."

"Wow. That's one heck of a way to baptize the band, Slim. Let me catch my breath, and then I'll be ready for another story. Ok, I'm ready," I immediately said.

"I've got another gunplay ditty for you," Slim began. "We were playing a three-night gig at a Playboy Club in Chicago during a rough snowstorm. In those days, the Bunnies served drinks in the bar, and bands and comics performed in the Club Rooms. We were playing away on Saturday night, and the power went off. The crowd was real light on account of the weather, and pretty soon the place started getting cold. We took that as a sign we needed to start drinking, real hard, and we abided said vision.

"All the tables had candles, so there was some light in the place, and of course, plenty of hard booze. Well, the six of us got into a drinking contest with some of the Bunnies, and pretty soon Flash talked us all into a rousing game of strip poker."

"I am just spitballing here, but stripping down naked with beautiful women under candle light had to have been an improvement on most nights."

"It was an upgrade. Hell, the gals were only three hands away from being nude as it was. To make a long story short, everybody got naked, Morti, Rev, and Flash disappeared with a couple Bunnies, and Rufus, Puck, and I settled in for some substantial drinking."

"What, no Bunnies for you?" I loudly inquired, spreading my hands out wide.

"It's not like we weren't into them. They just weren't into us. It bummed the three of us all the way out. We'd been looking at those magazines for decades, and here we were with eight fantasy gals and we couldn't close the deal. Morti, Rev, and Flash teased us about that for as long as we'd take it—about two days' worth. I still can't believe we got shut down like that. It was an ego crushing of epic proportion.

"Anyways, we got dressed and started up a poker game with a few of the locals, who turned out to be professionals. Drinkers, that is. We were hall of famers ourselves, and the next thing I knew, we had a drinking contest. Tequila, if I recall correctly, which always turned me into a putrid pile of malarkey.

"I could hold my own with just about any alcohol, but tequila did things to my senses I couldn't handle or control.Rufus drank it all the time and it just made him horny.When Puck drank tequila he was totally unpredictable.And, of course he was always armed.

"By the time the fat lady sung on that one, I went unconscious, Rufus went after two married women and almost got his butt kicked—by the two women— and Puck decided he'd pull out his pistols and do some target practice with some empty bottles. I was out cold the entire time, and the story varies from here depending on who tells it.

"According to Rufus, who was a bit banged up and exceedingly intoxicated, an off-duty police officer snuck up on Puck and disarmed him with a pistol of his own.

"According to Puck, the inebriated off-duty police officer challenged him to a shooting contest, and the two of them unloaded on some bottles set up on a table in front of a concrete wall.

"According to the seven sober police officers who stormed the joint after the power and phones were restored, both Puck and the off-duty officer were under arrest for illegally discharging their weapons, and other various charges I am unable to recall.

"When I came to, Puck was already on his way to jail, and Rufus was curled up like a bear cub, sleeping it all off. Morti, Rev, and Flash had themselves one hell of a night with some of the most beautiful women we'd ever seen.

"Puck spent sixty days in the county jail before they let him off with a fine and time served, and we had to hire a fill-in drummer for the next two months. His name was Tony Adams, he was bald as a cue ball, and he had enough dragon tattoos to cover a small horse. We called him Ink. He was a bit older than the rest of us, and wiser as well. He didn't drink or do dope of any kind.

He got a hell of a kick out of watching us assault our senses, though. He said it was a good reminder of why he didn't do the same.

"One of the things I remember about Ink is he was constantly doing pushups and sit-ups. We'd all be on the bus, chain smoking, guzzling booze, and snorting dope…and there he'd be on the carpet, working out. He asked me to join him one day.

"'You want to get some exercise, Slim?'

"'You know CPR?' I asked.

"'No, but I could make something up.'

"He was a damn fine drummer, but couldn't remember how to start a song to save his butt. I'd call off a song and he'd give me this deer in the headlights look, and I'd have to start it with guitar. So much for the seamless flow we were accustomed to with Puck.

"Puck met us in Baton Rouge, and man, it was good to have him back. He showed up fifteen minutes before the gig, and we had to bust butt to set up his drums. I remember being in a panic, thinking he wasn't gonna make it We'd already let Ink go, and Puck was supposed to have joined us the night before. I almost garnished his entire pay for scaring me half to death, but we were so glad to have him back, I let it go. Two months off and he still never missed a lick. He even remembered the song list.

"He was prohibited from carrying a weapon of any kind for five years of probation. I think he made it two weeks."

Slim retrieved the coffee pot, but I'd already had enough coffee to blow my heart out of my chest. He shrugged, filled his urn, returned the pot, and settled back in. Wind picked up outside of the cabin, and I reflexively closed my collar.

"A towering tale. Please, Sir, may I have some more?"

"No pudding for you, Smarty Pants. One night, when the band was off, Rev and I entered a wet t-shirt contest in a bar in Topeka. They thought we were kidding until we stripped down to our skivvies and shirts and stood in line with the females. We were told it was against the rules to have men enter, but the crowd was about to burst at the seams from the prospect. Rev was a damn fine talker, so I turned the oration over to him.

"He stood on a table and yelled, 'We have all the physical attributes necessary to compete in this sacred contest, and we most certainly shall! We will not be shackled by discriminatory prejudice! We spent all this money on breast implants, and by God, we're going to show them.'

"To say the judges were a little confused would be to say the KKK is a *little* judgmental.

"Anyways, the owner of the bar pulled me aside. His grip on my arm was a bit too tight for Puck's liking, and Puck roughly removed it. The owner puffed himself up as much as he could, but the look in Puck's eyes let all of his air out.

"He turned back to me and said, 'Look now. I don't know what you two are up to, but I'll give you free drinks tonight if you back off right now.'

"'And deprive the audience of these?' I shouted, flashing him my bare chest.

"The crowd by now was hysterical, and Flash somehow grabbed the host's microphone and asked the crowd, 'Do you want to see some man boobs?'

"Boy, did they!

"You couldn't miss the fear on the gal's faces. They were in it to win it, and didn't appreciate the focus veering elsewhere. To make a long story easier to handle, they couldn't keep us outta the damn thing, and Rev won it in a landslide."

"Of course he did," I remarked. "I would imagine the female entrants were furious."

"The girls were crushed, tears were shed, and we were threatened by their boyfriends. Puck and Rufus were in the mood for a tussle, but we were outnumbered and severely intoxicated. We read the writing on the wall and departed out the back exit to a rousing audience ovation.

"The boyfriends caught up to us in the parking lot, but they reconsidered their stances after Puck pulled a pistol and waved it around his polluted head like a lariat.

"Rufus started yelling, 'We haven't shot any rednecks for almost a week now, Puck. We still doing ten points for a torso hit and twenty points for a headshot?'

"'And one hundred points for a circumcision. Fifty for a vasectomy.'

"Those boys backtracked in a hurry, and we were off like a prom dress. Rev got a trophy and a hundred bucks, which pissed me all the way off. My nipples were perkier than his. I was convinced the judges had been bought and paid for by Puck on behalf of Rev. We laughed all the way back to the motel that night and then some.

"Rev and I were always doing crazy stuff back then. Always trying to one-up the other guy, you know? I cringe when I look back on some of the things I did. I was entirely, naively oblivious to consequences, as there rarely were any. Wandering around LA like a maniac, it's a wonder I didn't get in more trouble than I did.

"My favorite activity in those days was to get as drunk and high as I could possibly get and see if I could function. I liked to test myself and see what I could get away with. I was a wild animal, Son, surrounded by folks who didn't call me on it. Not that it would've mattered, I guess. In my mind, I was doing what I was meant to do. Living like a rock star.

"I remember one time Rev and I got all dolled up to go pretend shopping on Rodeo Drive in Beverly Hills. I'd decided it was appropriate to drop some acid and smoke some opium beforehand, so I did. I also drank an entire bottle of rum. By the time we got to this fancy men's clothing store that sold two-hundred-dollar pairs of underwear, my hallucinations had reached epic proportions, and I was as drunk as a really drunk skunk. I was not suitable for public consumption by any stretch of the imagination.

"The last thing I remember was the clerk who was helping us try on clothes turned into a dancing cigarette, and I found that to be quite humorous. So humorous, in fact, I laughed until I threw up in the two-thousand-dollar shoe section. Rev said the clerk had a panic attack and dropped to the floor in a fetal position, whimpering like a wounded puppy.

"Another female clerk rushed to his aid, but couldn't handle the sight or smell of my regurgitations and started dry heaving. The poor gal beelined for the restroom, and must've alerted the manager, who arrived on the scene with a look on his face he'd probably never tried on before.

"Rev said the manager started to cry and walk around in circles, yelling, 'This is Beverly Hills! You absolutely cannot do this in Beverly Hills!'

"Anyways, he called 9-1-1 for the fallen clerk, and ordered us to evacuate immediately. Rev thought that was probably a good idea, on account of I was chasing butterflies around the store in nothing but my two-dollar underwear. By the time he got me and my clothes gathered up enough for an exit, the oxygen squad had arrived and were attending to the collapsed clerk.

"That's when the manager began to scream at the two of us at the top of his lungs. Rev told me I tried to dance with the poor guy, and he took a real awkward swing at me that got me laughing all the more. A morbidly obese security guard was finally rousted, and he and I played a little game of chase around the store. Rev told me I did a real fine job of evading Deputy Dawg, who broke down mid-chase, hyperventilating and such.

"Somehow, Rev lured me over to him, and he bear-hugged and carried me outta the store, where two police cars came to a screeching halt. Rev told me I was still in a dancing mood, and tried to jitterbug with him on the sidewalk. Those cops took one look at us and the next thing we knew, we were secured in the back of a squad car while the officers investigated the scene of the crime.

"I 'came to' about five hours later in a holding cell, scratching my head and wondering why I was locked up, why my cellmates' faces kept changing colors, and why I could see inside my own brain. To make a long story short, my band mates bailed me out, and we hit the road the following morning for a three-month tour of the Midwest. I missed my court appearance and would later have a bench warrant for my arrest slapped on me, but that's another story. It was just par for the course in those days."

"I take it you learned your lesson and quit shopping for two-hundred-dollar underwear while intoxicated and hallucinating?" I stated.

"You would think so, wouldn't ya?" Slim winked at me. "I learned a lot of lessons back in those days; I just never committed 'em to memory. What's that saying? In youth we learn, in age we understand. Thank God most of what I did was harmless.

"We all had loads of fun in southern California, and spent a lot of time on the ocean, where we swore we'd build a mansion one day. We hung out in Malibu a lot, rubbing shoulders with the fabulously famous few. We felt we were doing research and development, you know? To figure out how they got there, and how we could as well.

"We also spent a lot of time at Venice Beach, learning goofy stuff from all the crazies. Best people watching place I've ever been to. Where else are you gonna see a beautiful woman roller skating in a string bikini with a python wrapped around her damn neck…at midnight? We called it the Psycho Circus back then, but we didn't mean anything by it. It was just a place where our pieces fit into any puzzle around. Everybody was free to be free, and nobody raised a brow at nothing—and I mean *nothing*.

"The saddest part about all of it was I had to be high to enjoy anything, and I was always so high, I rarely remembered much of what I did. It's a damn good way to miss most of your life. I look back on my life, and there are so many empty spaces. Folks told me I had one hell of a time, and for the most part I have to take their word on it. California just took me over, Son."

"How long was the band based out of Los Angeles?" I asked.

"Oh, we were in California for just over ten years, I think, but didn't spend much time in LA. We could make more money and had a better following away from home, which always puzzled us. We were basically ignored by our hometown, but we were heroes a couple hundred miles away."

Slim shook his head back and forth, and after all that time, frustration still hung over him like an angry cloud. He fidgeted in his chair, and finally got comfortable. I stood and stretched my back and neck. Nodded for him to continue.

"LA clubs like The Roxy, The Troubadour, The Rainbow, and The Whiskey all booked us, but we usually received lukewarm responses. We'd play clubs like The Filmore in San Francisco, or CBGB's in New York, and the joints would come apart. The line of folks waiting to get in would be two blocks long. We'd play Las Vegas, anywhere, and sign autographs for an hour after the gig. I never could figure it out, you know? We'd do the same show with the same songs and energy, and LA crowds would turn and walk the other way.

"We didn't let it bother us, though. We were doing great everywhere else, and the money was real good. We finally got smart and hired a moneyman to help us with some investments. Before that, we pretty much just pissed away everything we'd get on dope and dames.

"We even started saving money in a band fund. We got so good at saving, we bought a tour bus and a five-bedroom band house with a pool in Studio City. We were hardly ever there, but it was a great place to be when we'd get back. We'd have parties for days on end, and it had a great rehearsal space in the basement.

"Another good reason to be away from home was we'd all usually have a gal or two we were seeing, and for some damn reason we seemed to pick crazy ones. I know crazy is a word that gets tossed around a lot, but a few of the gals we went with were nuttier than a saddled chipmunk. They were all show ponies, and show ponies are hard keeping. The prettier they were, the harder they fell, and they were LA gals. Something about that city is poison for the pretty ones.

"I dated this one gal named Alice Hernandez, who was a sexual savant. She had enough pretty to get whatever she wanted from whoever she wanted to get it from, and had a towering intellect to go with it. When she was in a gentle mood, she was one of the most fun gals I've ever met. When the demons woke up, she'd get meaner than a cornered coon with hemorrhoids. We broke up and got back together twenty times. The old ho heave. I was what you call…what's the word? Oh…an idiot.

"Alice was a swimsuit model who worked all over the planet and made more money than she could spend. She had a place on the ocean in Malibu, and I'd live there with her until she'd turn into a werewolf again. She was also a wannabe tambourine player and singer and, God bless her, she had about as much musical talent as a rattlesnake. Which is what she'd turn into when I wouldn't let her get on stage to play with us.

"Reminds me of one of my favorite musician jokes, and you'll have to pardon the blasphemy:

"This young, brilliantly talented musician dies tragically before his time, and goes to heaven. There's St. Peter waiting for him at the gate.

"St. Peter says, 'I've got good news and bad news for you. Which do you want to hear first?'

"The musician says, 'It's been a rough day. Give me the good news.'

"'God created a recording studio, and everyone who played music from Mozart to Jimi Hendrix are all waiting there to work with you.'

"'Right on,' said the musician. 'What's the bad news?'

"'Jesus has this chick that sings.'"

"Fabulous joke. I have to remember that so I can tell it to a friend of mine," I said.

"Just tell him that I made it up, Son," Slim insisted. One eyebrow stretched high, he laughed and slapped his thighs.

"You got it," I stated.

"Some nights," Slim continued, "Alice would just stand in front of me beneath the stage and scream obscenities at me at the top of her lungs until I'd have security remove her. She stabbed me in the leg once with a stiletto, and one show she threw a heavy leather purse on stage and knocked my microphone right back into me. If I hadn't had my mouth open, it would've hit me in the face. That one knocked out a front tooth and I got to swallow blood the rest of the night."

"I'll bet she felt bad about doing that," I offered.

"She felt just horrible about it. So horrible in fact, she snuck up on me behind the venue as we were leaving and tried to take my damn head off with a lead pipe she'd found. Like I said, show ponies are damn hard keeping, Son, and sometimes hard to get rid of.

"Another night, Alice took it upon herself to cut the power in the house when we were rehearsing, and stood in front of the fuse box with one of Puck's pistols. Rev tried to talk her outta the gun and she pointed it between his eyes. So, I aimed my flashlight at her eyes, and when she closed 'em, I shoved her down and grabbed the gun. I didn't intend to hurt her, but her damn head hit a doorjamb pretty hard and she went out like a light.

"Well, after she came to, she called the cops and reported me for assault, which I was charged with. The officers didn't believe any of us on account of we were 'long haired hippy dippy dope fiends' and such. I was cuffed and hauled away before I could get two more words out, and I spent a night in jail before she fell back in love with me and had the charges dropped.

"It wasn't too long after that happened she drove my Mercedes, on purpose, into the front window of a grocery store. I'd arrived home late for dinner, and she'd decided to make another one of her famous points. I loved that car."

Slim ran both hands through his hair as his eyes slammed shut, and he shot up and out of his chair. He shuffled towards the fireplace, thought better of it, and continued to pace.

"I can't begin to tell you the hell I went through trying to untie myself from that woman. I tried to reason with her, but that was like trying to train a grizzly bear to sit and shake hands. We'd break up and she'd follow me everywhere I went and make a scene, you know? There was a brief time where I half expected her to take me out."

"Take you out? You were afraid she might *kill* you?" I gasped.

"I was. Hell, she as much as told me she would. For about three months, I had eyes in the back of my head, watching and waiting for her to make some damn fool move. And we were on the road, for crying out loud. I even started carrying one of Puck's guns in my boot. She had me all exercised, and I just couldn't shake her off me. I did everything I could think of to anger her so she'd finally hate me enough to leave. Nothing worked, Son. I finally had to pay her off."

"You bribed her to break up with you?"

"Five thousand dollars, a big bag of weed, a jar of cashew nuts, and an acoustic guitar."

"Quite a combination to make her go away. That is simply amazing to me. Did she ever come back, you know, to haunt?"

"I always expected her to, but I heard she'd met a door-to-door encyclopedia and vacuum salesman who swept her off her feet."

"You just made that up," I stated.

Slim laughed. "Caught me again. I don't know what happened to her, but I was damn glad to have her gone. I called her my beautiful tragedy, and I really learned my lesson. I must've waited at least a week before I started up with another one. Her name was Tina, and she was a cocktail waitress at a club we hung out at.

"Tina was six feet two with eyes of blue, and had played volleyball at UCLA. I affectionately called her High Pockets, and man she was a beauty. So damned pretty I had to pace myself when I looked at her, you know? I fell hard for her, but she didn't cotton to my drug and alcohol use. I tried to explain to her I was in total control of both, but she didn't buy it for a second. So I hid my dope use from her, and you can deduce about how well that went.

"She got me into health food, exercise, and tantric sex that always about gave me a damn heart attack. And, I did slow down on my dope and booze binges some. We'd get up in the morning and take a jog around the neighborhood, and she'd put all kinds of fruit and veggies in a blender and we'd suck that down. We lived on fish and rice in the evenings.

"And that tantric sex stuff freaked me out. The goal was to prolong the experience. Sometimes I would hide from her at bedtime, hoping she'd drift off so I wouldn't have to go through it. I know that sounds kooky, but the sexual gymnastics thing wasn't for me. I just wasn't up for that kind of work, you know? I liked quick, hungry sex, and television and cigarettes in bed afterwards. But everything was about exercise with her. I could never get her to just sit still.

"I gotta admit, I felt and looked better than I had in years, but pretty soon the chemicals slowly talked their way back in and took over. I knew she wouldn't put up with it for long. She flushed my stash down the toilet one night after an argument, so I burned her running shoes. Her shoes cost about fifty bucks. My stash cost about three grand. I guess she won that round.

"Like I said, I tried to hide my drug use from her, but she could sniff it out in a jiffy. I always wore sunglasses since she'd check my pupils with a damn flashlight. One time, I took way too much mescaline and ended up with horrible stomach cramps. I told her something I ate didn't agree with me, and I might have pulled it off if I hadn't talked to the wrong head of the three heads I was seeing. I even tried to kiss it and came up empty. She stormed out the door and I didn't see her for a week or so.

"She couldn't stand me being high, and I couldn't stand being sober. She thought if I cared enough for her, I'd stop using. Just like my momma did with my old man. I didn't want to put my size ten foot in my size twelve mouth, so I stayed silent, which was probably worse. I couldn't get her to understand it wasn't about choice at that point, you know? I was powerless over dope and booze, and not unhappy about any of it.

"We dated on and off for a year or so when I'd come back from the road, but she got tired of me being gone all the time—in more ways than one. She was a real nice gal and would've been one heck of a catch. Hell, she'd only had the one personality. That was new ground for me, I'll tell ya. Truth be told, she was the first lady I ever loved, Son. She was a rainbow when I was black and white, and her colors ran off my page. I carried that hurt with me into several relationships. I guess it was the cost of doing business. The drug and alcohol business."

Slim stopped pacing, put his hands on his hips, and reached up to strum the strings of a guitar hanging on the wall. As he shuffled back to his chair, the vibrating strings rang out like a siren.

"I can see that was painful for you to talk about her. Your first love and it didn't work out. Maybe you should…"

Slim clapped his hands together loudly, shook his head and pointed a shaking finger at me. I got the message, nodded, and during an uncomfortable silence I checked the battery on the tape machine while Slim fell into his chair.

"That's enough about gals already. Where the hell was I before all that bullshit?"

"You were talking about how you had to play shows away from Los Angeles," I answered.

"Indeed I was. We played a lot of outdoor festivals in those days, and they were the best gigs on account of the big stages, crowds, and sound systems. We also did a lot of gigs in Las Vegas in the lounges, back when the lounges were a hotbed. Vegas was run by the mob, and it was a cleaner, safer town then. They kept all crime to a dull roar. Hookers had their areas they worked, and they stayed there. Show tickets were affordable, and a decent tip to the maître d would get you just about anything you needed or wanted.

"When the corporations took it over, they sucked the character outta everything. The place got bigger and more lavish, but Vegas lost some of its magic in my book.

"You know, the last time I was in Las Vegas was around 1997. I'd gone there to catch some sun and hook up with an old musician pal I hadn't seen in decades. I went with a hundred-dollar bill and the Ten Commandments, and my goal was to not break either."

"How did that pan out for you?" I wondered.

"I did no gambling, and managed to stay on the celibate side of the line. A buddy I was with didn't fare so well, and he lost about ten grand on the tables. I called him Lip—he liked to do coke and you couldn't shut him up. He got to feeling sorry for himself, so he bought himself a couple hookers and a large pile of cocaine, which I stayed away from as well. He took one of those pecker pills and said he had sex all night whether he'd wanted to or not.

"I remember Lip saying, 'My penis wouldn't go down, Slim. Damn Viagra. I should've taken Niagara. I gave those girls the rest of the coke and sent them on their way. They about killed me.'

"Lip's old man owned a bunch of car dealerships, and Lip had more money than sense. I'd met him back in LA in the 70s when he was a folk singer, and he opened for us some. He was a damn fine singer/songwriter in those days, but like I said, you couldn't get him to shut up. He'd get all wired on speed and talk for ten minutes between songs and lose all his momentum.

"It got so the soundman would turn off Lip's mic in between songs. After a while, the clubs told us we had to find another opener. Lip didn't pay it no mind. He just laughed it all off and would play on the street or anywhere that would have him. He didn't need money.

"Anyways, I really miss the Las Vegas of the 70s and early 80s.. It had a soul, you know? It had a beating heart. We used to hang out at the Sands after our shows, as we knew a guy who'd get us in to see Sinatra and his cronies. Elvis was in town a lot at the Hilton, and we got to meet him. Hell, he even came to one of our shows one night, and we all about lost our damn minds. Vegas was a mystical playground in those days, and I'm glad we got to be a part of the wonderful nature of it all before it changed."

Slim retrieved his coffee cup and again began to pace the room. I saw a light of recognition switch on in his mind, and he spun around to face me. He sat back down, suddenly revitalized.

"I remember the strangest gig we ever played around that time. We were approached after a show in Reno by this bull of a man with a neck the size of a basketball, flanked by two armed goons who looked like they knew how to cook pasta. He'd been sent out by his boss to hear us play on account of he'd heard good things, and they'd strutted into our dressing room like they owned the place.

"Anyway, Mr. Bull Neck informed us we would be playing a birthday party for his boss at his estate in Vegas, and when we quizzed him for details, he said, 'Don't worry about it.'

"I couldn't figure out how sound came out of his mouth, as his lips never moved when he talked. He told us the date, but we were already booked to play a festival. When I told him this, his right eyebrow went up, and he pulled out a wad of bills that would've choked a rhino.

"'How much?' he asked.

"'How much what?'

"'How much you getting for the gig?'

"'Ten thousand and expenses,' Puck announced quickly. It was a lie. The contract was for eight grand and expenses.

"Mr. Bull Neck didn't even blink, and peeled off eleven thousand dollars in hundreds and shoved them in my shirt pocket.

"'The man wants you there the day before.'

"He handed me a gold envelope and turned to walk away. As he was leaving the dressing room, he turned and said, 'Dress nice,' and disappeared through the door. The goons stared us down, nodded, and followed Mr. Bull Neck out. There wasn't any sound in the room as we all chewed on and digested what just happened.

"We showed up at this monolithic mansion three weeks later in our weathered band vehicle and trailer, and parked next to a Rolls Royce limousine after passing through a security gate. We were frisked and whisked through the mansion, out to the back pool and garden area by a cat with a shoulder-holstered pistol. He didn't speak a word, and only had one eyebrow. I think he may have grunted in Italian a couple times.

"The invitation in the gold envelope said a sound and light system, a sound and stage crew, and a stage would be provided, and you should've seen that set up. We all thought we'd died and went to God's cabin. The sound and light system would've filled and lit up Yankee Stadium, and you could've put three bands on the stage.

"Three more armed goons showed up with Mr. Bull Neck, who asked, 'This gonna work?'

"We all nodded like puppies watching a yo-yo."

"This surreal event was a mobster's birthday party," I proudly stated.

"Badda bing, badda boom. We all got shown to our rooms, and then we joined the birthday boy and his trophy wife for an evening meal and some skeet shooting out back. The Man, as we called him, never spoke a word to us, and wore dark sunglasses the entire time. His wife wore this painted on smile, and it was obvious she was blasted. She had to be thirty years his junior, and had these fake boobs that arrived seconds before she did, you know?"

"I believe I do. Boobs happen to be a hobby of mine," I remarked, faking a blush.

"I called her Silicone Sally, and she was nice and all, but you could tell she was cut from a different cloth then the rest of us. When she talked to you, her eyes were always somewhere else."

"Please, tell me Rufus behaved himself around Silicone Sally," I said, crossing my fingers.

"He did. The goons walking around with automatic weapons might've had something to do with that. I think she might've been sweet on Morti, since she sat in his lap at one point. I'll never forget the look on his face as his head swiveled around looking for who was gonna shoot him. She brushed the hair out of his eyes and flowed all over him like syrup. Poor Morti about passed out.

After the skeet shooting, we watched a movie in this home theatre you wouldn't believe, and servants kept bringing us popcorn, candy, and soda. Then, we all went bowling in a damn bowling alley he had in a building hooked to the house. The whole time, we were drinking champagne, and I was semi-blasted when the evening's main event kicked off."

"What would that have been?" I asked.

"It was a stripper extravaganza by the pool, with a full bar. Puck and Rufus were so happy, they both kissed me on the cheek, and Rev pretended he didn't approve, but couldn't hide the grin that snuck up on his face. Flash and Morti missed the show on account of they'd inhaled too much champagne and went to bed.

"The man sat in a special chair and got lap dances for about an hour before he staggered off to bed, escorted by bodyguards. And just like that, the stripper party was over. The girls gathered up the hundred-dollar bills that had been tossed at 'em like confetti, and were whisked away like nothing had happened. Before we knew it, we were the only ones sitting by the pool, until Mr. Bull Neck showed up and basically ordered us plebians to our rooms.

"'Nighty night, boys,' he said without moving his mouth.

"I remember my bed was about an acre long and had the most comfortable pillows known to man. The walls were covered with impressionist art, and there was Italian marble on the counters and floors. There were great columns and arches everywhere. It was a marvel, Son. A veritable palace.

"My manservant asked if I wanted the fireplace on. Well, of course I did. He pushed a button on the wall, and I had a fire to sleep to. Another button closed the drapes, and there were buttons for the bed, too.

"I also had a big screen television with about two hundred channels. Back in those days, that was something. I stayed up most of the night just switching back and forth with a big grin on my face.

"And you should've seen the breakfast spread. It was served to us all in another dining room with ten televisions on the wall, a fountain with goldfish in it, and servants running around like mice. The food was outstanding, and I wasn't even mad when I got woken up for it. We had prime rib, eggs, and hash browns. I remember it like it was Tuesday."

"Sounds fabulous. You hungry?" I asked, pointing my eyes towards his kitchen.

"Getting there. The birthday party was filled to the gills with bodyguards, rough looking goombahs, and their show pony wives or girlfriends—who didn't hold back when they got their boob implants. They ordered extra large. Everybody chain-smoked and guzzled booze, and we sat at our table like nervous teens at a Sadie Hawkins dance. We didn't even do any dope before we played, in case we got shot. Or worse.

"The damn party was like a Disney film. There were ice sculptures, fire breathers, jugglers, dancers, and a cake the size of a dresser. It truly was something, Son, and the place was better guarded than Fort Knox.

"Mr. Bull Neck approached our table and said, 'You're up,' and walked away.

"I'd never been nervous to play before, but I was that night. We all were. I'll tell you one thing, that group was the best sound team we'd ever worked with, and we never even had a sound check. They told us they'd worked some of the biggest tours in the world, and I believed 'em. The stage crew moved around like ballet dancers, and they were top shelf too.

"Thank God the crowd applauded after the first song, and we all loosened up and let her fly. And just when we thought we were rocking the joint, Bull Neck walked up and gave us the hook.

"'That's enough,' he said. 'Pack up your stuff and wait for me out front.'

"We packed up and loaded the trailer, then stood out front of the mansion and nervously waited for Bull Neck, who arrived about twenty minutes later. We hoped we weren't in trouble.

"'The Man says thanks,' he said without moving his lips, and he handed me another gold envelope. 'You ever get into trouble you can't handle, call that number.' Then he just shuffled away.

"We never did find out who the man was, or if he even liked us that night. The envelope had ten thousand bucks in it, and a business card with a phone number we never called. It was a hell of a gig."

"It certainly was. It would be quite interesting to know who was at the other end of that phone number," I wondered.

"Yeah, it would. None of us had the guts to ask or introduce ourselves to the Man or any of his people. I just always figured he was some family's fairy godfather, and left it at that. What I couldn't figure out was…why us? He had enough money to hire anybody he wanted, and he picked us. It still puzzles me to this day."

"It was probably down to you or The Rolling Stones, and they likely demanded too much money," I said.

"I'm starting to like you more and more all the time, Son."

"Do you like me enough to share the mysterious story you won't tell me?" I hesistantly asked.

His eyes told me all I needed to know, but I pushed him further regardless.

"Slim, if you have something you need to talk about then…"

"If I got something to talk to you about I'll damn well talk about it God dammit! I said no and I mean no, get it? You gotta learn when to back off, Stevie Boy. Now is the God damn time for it!"

I swallowed hard and was pushed back in my chair by his sudden eruption.

"Maybe this ain't such a good idea. Digging up all this shit might be bad for me."

I nervously watched Slim's face change to a deeper color of red. I so wanted to rewind the situation. Everything I tried to say fought to stay deep inside of my throat. His eyes locked onto mine and they backed me down quickly. I lowered my head, shook it, and stared at my wringing hands. The sound of him suddenly rising from his chair startled me.

"I gotta think on this some," he said as he quite slowly shuffled towards and disappeared into the bathroom and closed the door.

"Nice fucking work," I whispered to myself.

Had I blown it? I stood up from my chair. Sat back down again. What could I do to fix it? To fix him? My stomach seized up and I thought I might get sick. All I could think to do was to lean back and take in long, deep breaths and wait for him to return to the room.

And a long wait it was. My heart skipped a few beats when the bathroom door cracked open and he emerged. His hair was wet and slicked back on his head. I searched his face for any hints of hope he'd rebounded and would continue. Slim eased slowly down into his chair as I leaned forward in mine.

"We're gonna keep going with this, but that damn drawer stays closed, got it?"

I eagerly nodded. A scolded child who suddenly knows he's not about to be spanked.

"It ain't easy to dig around in my dirt for some of this stuff, Son. I ain't a damn machine and I got powerful feelings about a lot of it. Feelings I ain't shook hands with in a very long time. I know you got questions you feel you gotta ask, but I need to you to keep in mind that my life ain't exactly been a comedy. We'll get to what we're supposed to get to here. The rest of it stays where it belongs. Now, where were we?"

"I'm sorry, Slim. I truly am."

"Just help me remember where I was."

"You were talking about how you had a more welcoming fan base outside of Los Angeles," I answered, breathing a deep sigh of relief he was going to continue.

The room was loudly silent. At least a minute crawled by before he finally continued.

"LA was a tricky lady. You had to find a niche or a gimmick, and we didn't have either one. Hell, nobody could pigeonhole our music, you know? We played a little of this, a little of that. Most bands would just play to what was selling at the time. Some band would get hot, and you'd have ten just like it overnight. But we were proud to be who we were. Besides, why chase what was popular today when it would be gone in a month or so? We just figured at some point, we'd be playing what was hot and popular, so why veer?

"All we would've had to do was listen to rock radio and copy what we were hearing, and we could've owned LA. We just weren't interested in research and development. We changed things up so often, our sound changed from one night to the next, and that's how we wanted it. It kept things fresh for us.

"Our manager at the time actually wanted us to talk with British accents on account of how well those bands did in America. I thought he was crazier than a narcoleptic air traffic controller. I remember Puck and Rev thought it was a good idea, and the three of us got all exercised over it. Then it seemed like we were fighting all the time, and I couldn't get enough water on the flames. We were like brothers for so long. Best friends who always had each other's back, you know? Then it all changed.

"I remember stretches of time we'd be on the road and nobody would say a word to each other. Not one word. We'd play the gig, and everybody'd go back to their rooms and not see each other until the next morning when we'd leave for another place. We'd drive ten hours to the next city in total silence. It was painful, Son. A veritable nightmare."

"So many bands experience that dynamic," I offered. "They work together so well in the beginning, and then somewhere, for some reason, they find themselves in a dysfunctional family."

"In the beginning, our dysfunction is what functioned so well, if that makes any sense. It's what fueled us. The weirder things got, the better we played. We all made room for each other's luggage. Our common goal overrode everything. I think every band is haunted, you know? Touched by the ghosts of all its members. It's a weird balance of the coin. One side represents all the good qualities, and the other side represents the dark side. Well, our coin flipped to the bad side and we couldn't get it turned back over.

When we started, we were able to place principles before personalities, you know? The common goal we shared overrode everything. You could've hit us with a locomotive train and we'd have stood back up like it was nothing. The drugs. The women. The money, the road, and the fights gave us our creative edge. I know I always wrote better when I was gripping that damn guitar like I wanted to hurt it. And, when I was sad. I always wrote better when I was raining.

"Then towards the end, nobody would even look at each other. We'd all just built up these walls, and nobody was gonna tear his down first. I played with a lot of guys over the years, but that particular group was awful special to me. We learned the music business together, side-by-side. It was without question the best incarnation of the band that ever was, and it dented my heart to know we weren't close anymore.

"Maybe they just got tired of it all, and they wanted to have normal lives. Maybe they got tired of chasing a moving target. It's a hard life, Son, and you gotta want to fight to keep it. Especially when things start to get really good, you know? Most folks can deal outta adversity. It's the prosperity that often brings on the cards that are harder to play. It was for us.

"Sometimes I think everyone wanted to be the lead guy, and for better or worse, I was that guy. But I wasn't afraid of their talent. Hell, I welcomed it. I needed help, you know? They just never grabbed the brass ring when the merry-go-round came around to it. They sat back and waited for it to drop in their damn hands."

"You would have been agreeable to sharing the limelight?" I asked Slim.

"Hell, I'd have loved it. I didn't care who got to ride the biggest horse, just so we all rode in together.

"It sounds to me as if the band was like a lover for you, Slim."

Slim suddenly looked tired as he returned to his chair. He reached for his coffee, thought better of it, and allowed himself to collapse in the chair's embrace.

"I didn't know it at the time, but my emotional well-being rested on the shoulders of what we all shared together.

"For me, the band was a well-tailored suit. It was the only thing I wanted to wear long-term. For them, the band was like a really fancy coat that didn't fit anymore. It hurt me deeply, Son, and no matter what I did, I couldn't put it back together. When that band began to fall apart, something inside of me unwound, and I didn't know how to get it wound back up. It was the beginning of some emotional problems I kept buried for as long as I could, but down the road there wasn't enough dirt.

"I called a band meeting when I couldn't take the tension anymore. We all got together in our living room, and everyone stared at the floor. I asked 'em if there was any hope of saving what was left of us. Nobody said a damn word, Son. They all just stared at me, and I knew we were done. I remember being numb inside for a moment, and that surprised me. And then it all turned to a crushing sadness that choked off my breath. I watched them walk out of the room, and I started to rain inside like I had never rained before.

"I just sat there and cried like a damn baby. I didn't leave that room for several hours, and when I did, I knew something big inside me had shifted. It was almost like losingthe cornerstone of my inner being. All those years, I thought I was so strong on the inside, and I came to find out my strength was tied to my family. My brothers. Our creation. Our band. My band. I truly felt like I was standing on smoke that day, and it would be several months before smiles would make their way back to my face."

"I would imagine you felt somewhat abandoned. Possibly betrayed," I added.

Slim shrugged. "In a way, I felt betrayed. I'd given them so much, you know? I just felt like they went and took it all for granted. Today I know it wasn't that simple, and we all had our part in it. At the time, I wished it had been a better divorce. Hell, what am I saying? I wish we could've worked the damn thing out and kept going. Today, I see it all for what it was. It was a wonderful ride with some tragically talented cats. They were truly some of the best years and times of my life, and I'm forever grateful for 'em. Sometimes you just can't keep the water out of the boat, you know? No matter how fast you scoop.

"It was a real heavy time for me, and I wasn't gonna let it slow me down. There were tons of fabulous musicians lined up to play with me after word got around we were splitting up, and I had my pick of the best of 'em. I think all the guys in the band thought I'd be dead in the water without 'em, but I knew I'd bounce back on my feet.

"Two things that kept me going back then were hope and delusion, Son. I simply refused to grieve, you know? I was focused on the next chapter and keeping the buggy rolling.

"Anyways, we broke up, sold the band house, and split the proceeds. I immediately retooled, and we changed the name to Slim Chance and the Codependents in 1974."

Chapter Five

"Why did you change the band's name?" I asked.

"Lance, our bass player at the time, was dating a marriage counselor who specialized in codependency. She suggested it, and we went for it. She also suggested I get in touch with my inner child, and that I quit drinking and doing dope. She might as well have suggested I swallow a bucket of earthworms.

"Before I dive into the new band I wanna touch on a couple things. Nancy was a piece of work. She was this semi-famous therapist who wrote books on relationships, and she was crazy about Lance. Lance always had another gal on the side. Nancy found out about it and went batshit crazy over the deal. The poor lady misplaced her damn mind.

"Here was this relationship expert, driven over the falls with jealousy and stalking Lance like a nymphomaniac ninja. She'd show up everywhere we were playing, and Lance would hide in the dressing room. He got a restraining order on her and she got arrested twice I knew of. She ended up losing her therapy practice over the deal. She was an avalanche of desperation, and I felt sorry for her. She was a nice lady and really tried to help folks. She couldn't help herself, I guess."

"Physician, heal thyself."

"Yeah. She spent all this time correcting others, and she had the same faults. She couldn't see it. She insisted it was all about true love. They say love is blind, and it got her in both eyes.

"I got an interesting story about Lance. We called him Lancelot on account of the size of his…um, sword, if you know what I mean. He looked like a damn tripod."

For emphasis, Slim hung his arm down between his legs and waved it around like an elephant's trunk. We were both thrilled by the giggle that slipped out of my mouth.

"Anyways, right when the new band was hitting on all cylinders again, Lancelot got the damn fool idea he was gonna be a porn star. So, he quit the band and headed for Los Angeles to be in dirty movies. I was so angry when he told me I about cut the damn thing off. We had a doozy of an argument. I called it 'The Battle of the Bulge.' We did manage to patch things up before he departed, I guess, and folks gotta do what folks gotta do, you know?

"Lance passed the first audition, which was basically taking his pecker outta of his pants and setting it on the table. He told me the producer removed his sunglasses to see if what he was seeing was real.

"The next audition went a bit different for him when he found out he didn't have the mojo to perform in front of a camera. That damn snake of his crawled under a rock, and there wasn't nothing that would coax it back out. Poor guy's porn career was over before it started, which may have saved his life. Who knows?

"He limped back to us with his tail and his pecker between his legs, begging for his spot back, but we'd already given it up to a sweetheart of a player named Gary Rose. We called him Suds because he always had a beer in his hands. Hell, he'd take one in with him to shower.

"Suds could sing like a bird, and was the best bass player I ever played with. The problem was, we found out Suds' real name was Lawren Erickson, and he was wanted in the state of Nebraska for two counts of aggravated assault for beating his ex-girlfriend and her boyfriend half to death. He'd fled south, changed his name, and became our bass player in a matter of a month. We found out about his little problem when US Marshalls stormed our band house and we all found ourselves with automatic weapons pointed at our peepers.

"Not a comfortable scene, Son.

"Good news, bad news on that one. Good news was, they ignored the pound of pot on the coffee table. And, if they'd have searched the house, they would've found illegal guns and enough speed to put us all away for a long bit. And, Lance was ready to jump back in on bass, and already knew the show and the songs. Bad news was, Suds needed a really good lawyer."

"I should say so. Where were you based at that time?" I asked.

"Boy, that reminds me of a guy I ain't thought of in a spell. We were based in New Orleans, and I got to be pals with a cat who worked at a funeral home in The Quarter. We called him Mountain, on account of he was almost seven feet tall and weighed about four hundred pounds. He played football at LSU, and would've gone pro if he hadn't blown out his knee. He'd sneak us into the funeral home before gigs so we could get bombed on embalming fluid.

"By the way, don't ever get bombed on embalming fluid."

I laughed. "I shall do my very best to abstain."

"We thought we were rock stars and that we should act accordingly, which gives you an idea of how far our depth perception was off. I mean, we were famous in certain circles, but a damn sight away from rock stardom. We hung out with real rock stars all the time back then, and those cats were royalty, you know? Some of 'em had sweet recording and publishing deals, and had more money than they could hide. Others were hooked to a pole and worked like dogs to pay back their labels. We weren't signed, but we always made more money than we needed. We were upper-middle class rockers.

"Anyways, Mountain traveled with us to help with equipment and watch out for us, which he stayed busy doing. He saved my bacon after a gig one night when I got lippy with three bikers bullying a transvestite who was a pal of mine. She was minding her business at the bar when they surrounded her and pushed her off of a barstool. I quickly intervened, and pushed away a biker who was about to kick her. They turned on me like wild dogs, and I knew I was in deeper than any rope outta trouble would reach.

"I remember thinking I was gonna hit the first one within reach and then boogey towards the exit. But then they started to circle me with knives, and I knew I was a goner.

"The next thing I remember is seeing Mountain come from the corner of my eye, and before even I knew what had happened, we had three unconscious bikers on our hands. The bar owner told us to split, which we promptly did, and on the way outta the joint I kissed Mountain on his bearded cheek, which turned his face as red as an apple. My gentle giant protector had saved my butt yet again.

"He was always defending underdogs, and I always admired him for that. Mountain's favorite move was to slam his gigantic fist on top of a bully's head to knock him out. We'd all hoop and holler like the dickens, and he'd just stand there with this goofy smile on his face you could barely see beneath his beard. Man, I truly loved him.

"He was a dog lover, and famous around our circle for breaking up a dog fighting operation. Literally. Mountain found out this group of guys had dog fights on land outside of New Orleans, and he showed up with a bulldozer and two armed buddies."

Slim held an imaginary rifle in his hands and pointed it at me. His eyebrows danced as he aimed just above my head. The memory seemed to wake him up, and he pushed his coffee away from him on the table.

"By the time the fat lady sung on that one, he'd leveled the place—and most of the vehicles in the parking area. The armed buddies kept the idiots at bay while Mountain made his slow escape, and then they disappeared into the night. I would've given just about anything to see that. The cops didn't spend a lot of time solving that caper, I'll tell ya that much.

"Women loved Mountain, but I never saw him with one. I do know he loved his momma, and he called her every day until she passed. The rumor around was that Mountain was gay, but he and I never discussed it. I always felt like it wasn't my business unless he wanted it to be, you know? I just loved the guy, and my life became a better place to be when Mountain entered it.

"Last I heard, he'd gotten his mortician's license and bought a whole mess of funeral homes in the Deep South, and every single one of 'em had a fleet of hot pink hearses. How can you beat that? You can't, Son. You just can't."

"How long was the band based in New Orleans?" I asked Slim.

"A couple years or so. We played all the clubs in and around New Orleans for about a month before we ran into this promoter named Rollie Whitehead."

Slim reached over for the scrapbook and flipped through pages, humming to himself. He settled on a page and beckoned me over to his chair. There was a young Slim, arm-in-arm with a well-dressed gentleman with a fancy cane and a lion's mane resting on his head. Just behind them, a limousine with an opened door.

"Rollie was a psychological case study waiting to happen. He was a gun-carrying, sociopathic, white supremacist vegetarian who secretly dated a black transvestite behind his fifth wife's back. His fourth wife ran away with his third wife and a hell of a lot of alimony money. He also had six kids with four strippers. His current wife couldn't keep a smile on her face for nothing.

He gave her everything she wanted, but all she wanted was him, you know?

"And, he slept in a padded coffin."

"No!" I exclaimed.

"I swear to God he did," Slim insisted. "His entire office was decorated with vampire memorabilia, and he drank red wine by the gallon. He was a freaky cat, man. Pale as a ghost, and you'd only see him at night. I always wondered how he did so much business when his day would start when most folks were winding down. That was Rollie.

"He had this red Cadillac limousine he went everywhere in, and his driver was this Japanese cat who nobody messed with. We'd spend hours just driving around the city in the back of that buggy, yacking and laughing about how we were gonna spend all the money when our time came. Rollie always got us to believe in ourselves and to aim higher than we ever had. He was my music business mentor, and though he was a sick puppy, he treated me real good.

"We got a lot of good work from Rollie, and he kept us busy up and down the east coast and into Florida. He set us up in a real fancy tour bus, and boy, that was the only way for a touring band to travel. Those early days in vans about did me in, Son.

"We had a driver who we called Bug—his eyes stuck out because of all the speed he took in order to stay awake driving. Bug was a damn good driver, and could back the bus and trailer into a coffee can if he had to. He was a Patsy Cline fanatic and played her on the sound system whenever we'd let him.

"He had this really bad red toupee that we called a toupee de ville, and it would constantly slide down over his forehead without him knowing it. Before joining our team, Bug had been a dental hygienist, but he got canned after he couldn't stay away from the Nitrous Oxide. You'd never see Bug without a cigarette hanging outta his mouth, but while we were on the road, he'd run at least five miles every day when he could fit it in."

"An anomaly, to say the least I would think," I remarked.

"He was that. Bug was with the band just over a year until he inherited a whole bunch of dough when his daddy died. He bought himself a mini-mansion on Lake Pontchartrain, and took up golf. He even ordered a Russian bride, and when showed up young and eager to please, he was damn tickled over it. And man, was she shiny. They looked like a father and daughter squad when you saw 'em together, but he never paid it no mind.

"We played some great shows with some big name bands. One thing I'll say about Rollie is, you always got your money up front. And, you always got what the contract stated. That wasn't always the case with promoters.

"The problem was, we were opening for other bands and not getting the money some of the guys thought we should, which caused a stir. They never knew how good they had it, you know? We played major gigs with great exposure, and we had a connected promoter who believed in us and saw us headlining someday.

"I used to tell 'em all, 'If you think you can do better, then grab your stuff and get down the road.'

"That would usually keep the peace for a week or so, until the bitching and the egos started up again. It was like raising kids. Adult children. It made me want to form an acoustic duo."

"Who were the members of the band at this juncture?" I wondered.

"You'd need a scorecard to follow that one, Son. There were so many in and out. I remember a drummer we all called BP on account of he lived on coffee, cigarettes, and potato chips."

"BP? Blood pressure?" I asked.

"You got it. He got a girl pregnant and left the band to work in her father's drycleaning business. He was damn sad to give up the music, but he had mouths to feed and a father-in-law who literally put a gun to BP's head and asked him what his intentions were with his daughter.

"So, we hired a cat we called Boo for how he always scared children. With his obesity, sweat stains, long beard, and wild, stringy hair, Boo looked like a strung out caveman. But he was a cool character who always had a quick joke and a toothpick between his teeth. He was a really good drummer, but his thing was heroin, and he chose it over the band. Chose it over everything. The morning after a show in Indianapolis, two of us found him dead in a hotel bathtub, and it shook us all up pretty bad. He was white as a piece of paper, with a needle stuck in his arm. Sometimes I still have dreams about it.

"The saddest part of it all was, he didn't have any family, and we didn't know where to bury him. We figured Indianapolis was as good a place as any, so we interred him there. The band paid for a real nice sendoff for him, but we were the only ones who even knew or cared he was gone. When Boo died like that, I got real careful about what and how much I was putting in my arm. I sort of figured he died so I wouldn't have to. I know that sounds cold. It just was what it was. We picked up a fill-in drummer and never missed a gig over the deal. The show must go on, you know?"

"That would be a traumatic event for anyone, Slim. I'm sorry that happened to you and I cannot believe it did not prove to be a wakeup call. Maybe it's not my place to say it, but it seems that would have been the perfect time to find sobriety."

"You're right. It ain't your place to comment on things you know nothing about. I probably spilled more booze than you'll ever drink in your damn lifetime, Boy. You ain't got nail holes in your hands and feet, do you?"

I was stunned. Paralyzed. The anger building behind his eyes had me cornered inside myself and I was unable to speak.

"Answer me. Do you got nail holes in your hands and feet, Steven?"

"No," I whispered.

"Then you ain't got the right to judge anything about me or anyone else."

Slim stared vacantly at me for what seemed like a minute. Several emotions seemed to fight for control of his face. I found myself in a struggle over what to say next that would be appropriate. His silence stirred up fears inside of me. Fears I'd spent much of my adult life outrunning. My mind drifted aimlessly, and I fought to bring it back to the task at hand. Just as I was about to speak, he snapped back to the room, smiled, and slapped his knee.

"It was a dangerous game we were all playing, and sometimes folks lost it all. I was so numb back then, and quite insulated by hubris. I couldn't afford to get all exercised over it. Folks were depending on me, and I had to produce. It was a tough deal, Son.

"Speaking of a tough deal, are you ok? You look a little worn around the edges. You need to take a break?"

"To be honest, Slim, and I apologize for the bad timing of this, but I am experiencing some anxiety and I may need to go to my car and get some medication to calm myself down. I have a history of panic attacks and one may be around the corner if I'm not mistaken."

"Well hell, Son. Do what you gotta do for yourself and we'll work through it. You say you got anxiety medication in your car?"

"I do, Slim. I literally have not had to take any for several months and I don't know why this is suddenly happening now."

"I used to take anxiety pills like candy just so I could leave my damn house. I ain't had to take one in years, but I still get myself worked up over things something fierce if I ain't careful."

"My therapist tells me I get anxiety because I don't feel and express my anger," I said.

"You mad at me, Son? For jumping on you back there?"

"I honestly don't know, Slim. I never seem to be able get angry at anything or anyone. You did scare me. I will tell you that much."

Slim rubbed the whiskers on his chin, closed his eyes and drew in a large breath. His eyes sprang open and the color of his face darkened.

"The first head doctor I ever saw told me dealing with anger is the key to everything, and that most folks stuff it down. She told me it's the cause of most diseases of the mind and body. I dunno. My jury's still out on that one, but she might've been onto something there. Anyway, you feeling any better?"

"What I need to do is to get the hell away from my own thoughts and focus on what you are saying," I insisted. "Please, continue. I'll get through this."

"Okie dokie, but you keep me posted, Son. You know, we all need a little emotional CPR once in awhile so don't go being hard on yourself over this. It took me a long damn while to figure out I needed help from time to time, and good for you for speaking up to me about it.

"Anyway. Onto some other members—two guitar players I remember who were with us for a while were Jeb and Whitey. Nice guys, and real heavy drinkers. Jeb was Louisiana Creole, born and raised in New Orleans, and he could dance and cook like the dickens. He played this beat-up Gibson that was held together with duct tape and glue, and that damn guitar had the best tone I'd ever heard.

"The thing I remember most about Jeb was he was in love with his high school sweetheart, and he'd never been with another girl in his life. They married at sixteen, and had been together fifteen years when he first started with the band. They had three little ones, all girls, and Jeb loved 'em real hard. They were a nice family, and an inspiration to all of us.

"Women threw themselves at Jeb constantly when we were on the road, and he never gave 'em a second glance. Not ever. I admired him so much for that. In the circles we traveled in and the business we belonged to, that was inconceivable behavior, Son. He loved his wife, his little girls, his music, and, God bless him, his whiskey. He didn't have room in his life for nothing or nobody else.

"Whitey was addicted to sun tanning and bourbon, not in that order. The thing I remember most about Whitey was he had this trained Seeing-Eye dog he bought off of a blind man's widow for a bottle of scotch and a a big bag of dope that travelled with us, and when we weren't playing, Whitey would put on these dark glasses and walk around pretending to be blind. He'd hold a cup out, and folks would toss him bills and change. That was the money he used for booze and food, and he just bankrolled his gig money. We all got quite a kick outta that.

"We were playing a show, I forget where, on Halloween night, and Whitey was a bit drunker than usual, which would've killed most folks. We were playing away when Whitey started commenting on Halloween costumes he didn't approve of, you know, pointing and chastising them on the microphone.

"By the time we finished playing our set, Whitey was chomping at the bit for combat of any kind, and I had to separate him from Count Dracula and Captain America before he got his ass whooped. I thought I'd calmed both him and the crowd enough, so I headed for the dressing room. About fifteen minutes later, a bouncer carried a bloodied and battered Whitey in and set him down on one of the couches.

"'What the hell happened to him?' I asked Bouncer Bill.

"'I don't know,' he answered. 'I found him out by the dumpsters like this, and he's pretty much out cold. I think somebody already called for the cops and an ambulance. I thought you'd better deal with it.'

"'Gee, my pleasure,' I managed, checking Whitey for signs of life. He was breathing through what looked to be a broken nose, and possibly a dislocated jaw. He was starting to come to, and I helped him sit up.

"'Bourbon,' he whispered. 'And a cigarette.'

"'You've had enough bourbon, Whitey. What the hell happened? Who did this to you?'

"'A big, pink rabbit,' was all he kept mumbling.

"Whitey slowly focused his crossed eyes on me.

"At this time, two police officers and the oxygen squad came into the dressing room. The EMTs checked him over and determined his nose was the only thing broken. They started to load him on a gurney, and he shut that operation down in a hurry by taking clumsy swings at anyone within reach. A large police officer subdued him, got right in his face, and told him to calm the hell down, which he immediately did.

"'Who beat you up?' the officer asked him.

"'I already told everybody,' Whitey slurred. 'A big, pink rabbit!'

"'You mean like the Easter Bunny?' I asked. 'You got your ass kicked by the damn Easter Bunny, Whitey?'

"Whitey nodded and fell back down on the couch.

"'Did you see what he or she looked like, um, under the costume?' the second officer asked. By now, all of us were holding back belly laughs as best as we could, but they weren't staying put.

"'It wasn't no damn woman! No woman hits that hard, and no, I didn't see what *he* looked like. He looked like a big damn pink rabbit that blindsided me when I went out for a cigarette and kept kicking me when I was down. I'm glad you all find this so damned funny. Are you going to stand here laughing at me, or are you going to go catch that son of a bitch?'

"The officers took down Whitey's information and set out to locate and arrest the Easter Bunny.

"As the officers were leaving, one of them leaned into the other and said, 'We need to be vewy vewy quiet when we're hunting wabbits.'

"We all busted up like a bunch of teenaged girls, and poor Whitey never lived down getting a beating by the Easter Bunny. What a hoot."

"I do not believe it's much of a stretch to assume it was a woman who struck Whitey down that night. A pink Easter Bunny costume sounds female to me," I offered.

"Yeah, we all figured that, too, but let it lay, you know? Poor Whitey got teased about it enough as it was. To this day, I think about that night and I get a belly laugh. Whitey's mouth quit writing checks his fists couldn't cash, though, I'll tell you that. It humbled that boy right up.

"How you feeling, Son? You got a smile on your face, so that's certainly a damn improvement from awhile ago."

"I feel better, thanks, Slim. It's going away. I always think it's all behind me for good, and then sometimes, it shows up like a bad penny. Thanks for your patience and understanding. Please, continue."

Slim began to say something, stopped himself, and leaned back in his chair. He nodded to himself and then to me. His eyes were warm, and I could feel his concern from across the room. The safety of the room-his presense-wrapped around me like a heated blanket, and I knew I somehow knew I would be ok for the rest of this journey.

"Now I ain't making judgments here, but Whitey was trisexual. He made love with men, women, and his guitars when he played 'em. He was a hell of a looker and drew folks towards him like he was made of gold. I never cared either way about his sexuality—or anybody's, for that matter. Some folks took issue with it though and it pained him deeply.

"One night he approached me and said, 'Does it bother you that I lay with men and women, Slim? I mean, do you think I'm a sick man for it?'

"'The only thing that bothers me is you get laid five times more than any of us do, Whitey. Seriously, of course it doesn't bother me.'

"'What about God? Do you think He's mad at me?'

"'I think God's got more important things to think about than your damn sex life. Only thing I'll say to you is you make sure you protect yourself, and treat whoever you're with as good as you know how to. God probably cares about that more than anything.'

"'You're a nice man, Slim Chance. Thanks for always voting for all of us, and for giving me the chance to play music at this level. Thanks for picking me.'

"'No thanks needed, my friend. You earned it, and you keep earning it night after night. It's a pleasure sharing the stage with you. Now, listen—and I'm serious about this. Don't listen to those amateur humans who give you guff about your love life. Nobody has any right to judge you, Whitey. I like to believe God looks in people's hearts, and yours is a damn fine ticker.'

"He left the band after a long bit, and started a chain of pizza joints around Boston. He did real well from all I heard, and supposedly he even beat melanoma. I always warned him against that damn tanning affliction, but he'd just laugh me off and pour more baby oil on to scald himself like a damn rotisserie chicken. He even rigged up sun lamps on our tour bus when we traveled. Damn, he'd get dark.

"Jeb is a real sad story, and I hate to think about it even now. He was as good a guitar player as I ever had, and he had a voice that only comes along when God's in a really good mood, you know? He was our guy, and I thought he'd be with us for the long haul. He and I thought alike on just about everything, and we got real tight.

"And then he got drunk and flipped his Corvette about ten times on the freeway doing 120 miles an hour. He ended up in a wheelchair, paralyzed from the waist down. But I think another part of him shut down that day, too.

"We all supported him as best as we could. We even had a special chair rigged for him with guitar pedals he could operate with levers and such. Some folks thought we were playing the sympathy card by keeping him on. It pisses me all the way off to this day to think of some of the things folks said about him.

"Anyways, he got to feeling too damn sorry for himself, and the booze really took him down quick. He just couldn't keep up on stage anymore. We had to cut him loose, and it bent my damn heart up something fierce.

"The last show he played with us, he hugged me after the show and wouldn't let go. I had to take his arms off of me, and he was crying hard. Man. I can still see that panicked look in his eyes like it was Tuesday. He was about to lose the last sanity handhold he had.

"I set him up real good financially when he left, and his wife and kiddos surrounded him with as much love as they could muster. We lost track of Jeb along the way. Last I heard, he was still drowning in whiskey. It's a very sad story, Son."

"It is," I agreed. "Did you ever have any sober members?"

"I had a keyboard player for a while named Barnibus Dunkelburger. We called him Paws, since he only had four fingers on his chording hand. He was a dandy of a player, and could really rip it. Paws abstained from booze and dope, as he thought they would wreck his life. Damn coward.

"But he liked the ladies, and he liked 'em young. Not illegal young, but way younger than he was. We called him a sexual surgeon for operating the way he did. They just couldn't say no to him, you know? He made 'em all dress up in a cheerleader outfit he always had with him. Then, he'd take these Polaroids and show 'em around, all proud of himself. I never cottoned to any of that behavior. I told him to keep his damn pictures to himself. Anyways, he stayed with the band through thick and thin, until thin got to happening a bit more than thick.

"I can see all of their faces, the other guys we played with over the years, but some of the names are gone. One gentleman I worked with lost a long battle with depression and committed suicide, and outta respect to him and his family, I ain't gonna talk much about him. His pain beat him down until he murdered it with a bullet. God rest his soul.

"He once told me, 'My whole life, I felt like an animal who just missed getting on Noah's ark…and it's starting to rain.'

"I know what that feels like. I never told him that, and I wish I had.

"Another fella that comes to mind is a cat named Larry Johnson, and he was a keyboard and guitar master. We called him Rope. He had chord-like muscles, and was stronger than two of us put together. He came down with lupus, and it got him real bad. So bad he couldn't play anymore, and he gave up live gigs. I hear from Rope every year on Independence Day."

"Your band had more than its fair share of tragedy with its members, Slim."

"I always thought they were loaned to me, you know? I got to have them for as long as I was supposed to. I wasn't in control. Their lives and their well-being should've been what counted. Somewhere along the way I forgot that."

"Anyways, after Lance quit the band again, we picked up this splendid bass player named Jimmy Thomas who we called Thumper. He lost a leg to diabetes and drinking. He always played in shorts so you could see his prosthetic device. That always bothered me for some reason. He wore it like a badge, like, 'Look at me, I lost my leg.'

"Thumper always had a sawed-off, double-barreled shotgun attached to his bass rig, just in case we got stage rushed by the Russians. He only pulled it once in a club in Tampa, Florida, when two bikers took issue with the fact we wouldn't play any Elvis songs. I did my best to schmooze 'em and such, but they wouldn't back down, and started throwing full beer cans at us. I made an announcement for a bouncer, but the place was so full and loud, we couldn't get their attention.

"We were halfway into a song, and Thumper grabbed his shotgun, jumped down off the stage, and proceeded to jam the gun into the bigger biker's forehead. That raised his eyebrows a bit. The other biker had his hand behind him, and I half expected him to pull a pistol. Just when I thought we were gonna have us a shootout, two bouncers finally showed up to remove the bikers. Thumper casually strolled back to the stage with the shotgun over his shoulder and launched into a bass solo like he'd never played before.

"After the gig, I asked him, 'Would you have shot him?'

"'Naw, the last thing that idiot needed was another hole in his head,' he replied. 'I was really hoping he was going to say something so I could break my teeth-knocking-out record. Right now, it's at three, but I was feeling a five.'

"Thumper bought himself a hardware store after he left the band for good. The last time I spoke with him, he'd found Jesus in a parking lot behind a Chinese restaurant, with a bottle of whiskey in one hand and a pistol in the other. His replacement was a cat named Pork, and I got a story about him for later."

Slim paged through the scrapbook, and then for some reason, shut it and placed it on the table beside him. He picked up an old toothpick and slipped it between his lips. I wasn't certain, but he appeared to inhale from it.

"I also had this real good guitar player for a while, who I wrote some songs with back in the day. His name was Eddie Shama. Because of his gambling, we called him Lucky. The thing was, he wasn't a good gambler. Truth be told, he was borderline bad. I recall times we'd have to get his gear outta pawn shops just so he could play the gig. But all he ever talked about were his rare wins. His losses always slipped his mind.

"He also liked barbiturates and highbrow scotch. One night, he overdosed after a gig and the Narcan we gave him didn't quite do the trick. The oxygen squad came and brought him back. He was back on stage the next night like nothing had happened. I was gonna tell him to slow down on the dope, but I was doing more than he was, you know? He would've just laughed at me.

But as it turned out, he did slow down some for a bit after the Reaper stood over him like he did.

"He and I wrote a lot of good songs together, and he was a really nice cat. Very generous—he would've given the shirt off his back to anybody. And for a gambler, he never cared a hoot about money. It was the chase that hooked him. It was all about playing as long as he could, come hell or high water. When he was gambling, his pupils dilated, Son. That ain't a normal reaction to a damn game of blackjack, you know? He called it the Throne Zone. When he felt like he was a king.

"I'm happy to report he got clean after he left the band, and stopped gambling as well. The last time I talked to Lucky, he was dating a real nice gal, and they were gonna have a baby. That was years ago, and I have no idea where he's at now.

"One thing about the musicians I played with is they were all extremely proficient. Because of my reputation and the gigs I always had lined up, I was able to hire the best players around. But musicians come with baggage. All humans do. Those musicians I hired over the years all seemed to have more than their fair share, you know, and most of 'em were goofier than a mustache on a melon. Just when I'd start to get settled into the groove of a group, whammo! Artistic folks ain't exactly wired the same way as most people. We have different priorities.

"To be honest, I always kinda missed that first unit I played with. The Codefendants. I took it all for granted when I was in the middle of the ride. To have that kind of consistency and brotherhood was unmatched for me in the years that followed. I just never got the same chance to really bond with the guys I played with after that first band busted up. I mean, there were a lot of really good things about painting with new blood, too, but man, it could get really old fast when the colors started to run.

"Anyways, it was the Wild West, Son. I never knew what the hell was gonna happen next."

"It sounds to me as if it would have been nerve-wracking, Slim."

"It was, and then some," he nodded. "It's a damn good thing I wasn't in touch with my feelings. My medicines kept my volume down, and that kept my hopes and delusions up. Don't get me wrong—there was a lot of smooth road, too. But we had more than our fair share of…what we called, *excitement*. Anytime you put five or six guys together in a creative situation, you're gonna get all you can carry.

"Two things I insisted on with my musicians were a tight bass and drums combination, and dependability. Whenever I put a band together, I always started there."

"Your grandfather taught you that?" I proudly added.

"That he did, Son. That he did. And I didn't care if you shot heroin into your damn eyeballs after the gig, but you better show up on time and do your job the next day. I was never afraid to fire a man if he needed firing, and I let a lot of 'em go over the years. Mostly due to dope and booze. We all thought we knew our limits—a funny thought now. Hell, we had our heads so far up our butts, we were staring at our ribs.

"Sometimes there were cats who'd sit in for part of our tour when their bands were taking down-time. The all stars of other groups would join us for shows, and Rollie would bill us a supergroup. Sometimes it worked like a charm, putting that many egos on stage at the same time—other times it was like putting a puzzle together in the wind.

"I remember this one cat that joined us for a couple shows. His name was James Lee White, but folks called him Hondo. He was a damn fine guitar player, and the lead singer in another band. One night, we were rocking a joint, and he shoved me outta the way and started singing on my microphone. Making up words to one of my songs.

"I shoved him outta the way and took back my place. The crowd was digging it, and thought it was part of the show…until James Lee took a swing at me, and we ended up going ass over teakettle off the damn stage.

"That happened to be a night when Mountain was with us, and he lifted James Lee off the ground by the throat and had a little chat with him backstage. We took a break and went back to the dressing room, and there was James Lee, sitting on a couch like he'd just been spanked by the principal.

"He behaved like a true gentleman for the rest of the shows he played with us, and we got to be pals. We both loved dope, booze, women, and music, so we had a lot to converse on. Rollie paired us up because we both were celebrities around those parts. To be a good sport, I decided to let James Lee sing a few tunes, and he did a real fine job with 'em.

"Rollie liked to keep things interesting and new for all of his bands, and it gave the music different spices and tastes. Some of the personnel combinations he cooked up didn't make any sense to us, but there was a method to his madness. He knew stirring the musician pot would create magical musical dishes and keep us all up on our toes. Lethargy wasn't an option.

"We just did what he told us to, and the gigs kept flowing in. Most of us were always so high we couldn't operate an electric toothbrush, let alone promote our band. Rollie was a damn fine teacher when it came to promotions and the business side of music. He believed he could make anyone a star, and that kind of thinking infected all of us in his stable."

"Slim Chance and the Codependents was basically you and an amalgam of a rotating group of musicians?" I asked.

"Yep," Slim nodded. "It kept me on my toes, but it also kept the music and the shows fresh and exciting, you know? The musician rotation made it necessary for me to really pay attention and to, as best as I was able to, moderate my dope and booze use before and during the shows. I was happy to be working and rubbing shoulders with these up-and-comers, you know? I thought maybe some of their sauce would rub off on me. Rollie had big plans for us that were always just right around the corner. Everything was *always* right around the corner with him.

"Nobody else in the band trusted Rollie, but I thought he always treated us just fine. It seemed like everyone around the Quarter liked him, and if they knew that you were working with him, you got special treatment. Like VIP rooms, free drinks, and such. He always dressed in this red, crushed velvet leisure suit with butterfly collars and a gold watch the size of a hubcap. He was always smiling. Always had a good story about this famous person or that.

"Until they found him dead in his office with a needle in his arm, that is. I never believed it for a second, as I never saw Rollie do any dope of any kind. He was a wine drinker, and that was that."

The story seemed to stop Slim's heart in his chest. His eyes closed as he regained his inner balance, and again, part of me wanted to put my hands on his shoulders. Shoulders that seemed to carry more than any man's should.

"The rumor around the Quarter was Rollie had gambling debts that went way over his head. I spent a lot of time with him, and I never got a whiff he was a gambler. If he got himself in trouble, it was something that had to do with where he was putting his pecker. I even heard his wife paid to have him killed when she couldn't put up with his behavior any longer. But it was all nothing more than dubious musings.

"Rollie once told me, 'The only people I've ever made really happy in my life are divorce lawyers. The rest of you all just put up with me.'

"All I know is I about fainted when I heard he was gone. I'd just been with him the night before. I couldn't catch my breath, and all the times we'd shared together started running like a damned highlight reel just behind my eyes. I couldn't make it stop, and I had to lie down. To talk about it, to this day, tightens my belly. He was a messed up cat and everything, but he was real good to me, and I called him a friend.

"We were supposed to meet him that same afternoon they found him, to sign papers for a national tour with Dr. John and The Meters. Another break we'd been waiting for. I guess we never did get around that damn corner."

"I am so sorry for the loss of your friend and mentor." I wanted to comfort Slim, but wasn't sure how.

"Yeah, that one knocked the wind outta things. It wasn't long before we all started fussing and fighting with each other. The band broke up the first time at a bar in the Quarter right after a gig, over a bag of pills and a gal we were all sweet on. That one went to fisticuffs, and I got my damn nose broke. Which, by the way, helped my singing voice reach higher registers after my sniffer healed up.

"We patched that one up the following day over a pile of cocaine, a bottle of scotch, and some cartoons. It was like that for a couple months. We'd go along pretty well for a week or so, and the tent would come down again. Rollie had always been the peacekeeper for the band, and with him gone, it was only a matter of time before we blew up for good.

"It happened on stage during a gig. We finished a song, and my bass player turned to say something to my drummer, who threw his sticks and walked off stage. The rest of 'em looked to me for guidance, and all I could do was shrug and follow him. That was it. The end of another band era."

"Did you have the energy to soldier on at this point?" I wondered.

"By that time, I was dirt tired, and I just didn't have it in me to patch things up again, you know? I felt like I'd worked so damn hard to build a great musical engine, just to have it crumble in my hands again. Once again, I was awful hurt and pissed off at everything and everybody. Some friends of mine tried to coax me out of it, but I wanted to ride the pain pony a bit longer. I didn't know what else to do, so I loaded up and headed home to South Dakota.

"I wanted to change things up, so I went to college for five minutes at the

University of South Dakota, but I couldn't get used to having to attend classes. Hell, they wanted me to get up in the damn morning, Son. Before noon and such. I remember when I registered for classes, I asked the gal who was helping me if they had special classes for rock stars that didn't get started too damn early.

"'Are you a rock star?' she asked, peering over her glasses at me.

"'Damn near,' I answered.

"'Would I have heard of you?'

"'Damn near.'

"'Try me. What's your name?'

"'Slim Chance. My friends call me Slim…Chance.'

"'I have heard of you, Mr. Chance. I believe my husband has one of your records. Well, well. We have a famous musician on campus, likely looking for special treatment he will not receive under any circumstances.'

"'I like you,' I told her. 'All the good ones are always married.'

"'Are you flirting with me, Mr. Slim Chance?'

"'Do you have goosebumps on your arms?' I asked.

"'Do I have what?' she answered.

"'Goosebumps. On your arms.'

"'No, I do not.'

"'Then I haven't flirted with you yet.'

"She helped me register for five classes that started as late in the morning as possible, and I thanked her profusely for her efforts. I even signed a couple autographs for a few fans of the band. I thought maybe I could make this college thing work.

"I didn't exactly see eye-to-eye with following proper procedures, you know?I lived in a dorm room with a cat from Nebraska named Christopher Cathey, who I called Hitch on account of he liked to hitchhike everywhere he went. This would not be as interesting had he not been born without thumbs. Hitch had a lot to learn about dope, booze, and women, and I took him under my wing.

"For example, I taught him the importance of crib notes, and I taught him how to meet, befriend, and date the shy girl who worked in the department that printed up the tests for the instructors. All the tests, Son."

"That would have come in handy for a couple of dilettantes," I stated.

"Damn *determined* dilettantes to you. We didn't cotton to the rules others abided. Hitch sorta lost his way when it came to grades that semester, since his hangovers got in the way of class attendance. I never had hangovers—and that was because I never really stopped drinking. The poor lad tried to keep up with me, but I already had a PhD in chemical abuse, as well as a master's degree in debauchery.

"When I first met Hitch, his idea to start the morning was Raison Bran and orange juice after thirty minutes of calisthenics. I thought it was normal to wake up, smoke a joint, have six shots of tequila, snort a line of speed or coke, mix a very large to-go drink of rum and coke, and then walk to class smoking a cigarette. Most folks would call that a massive party. I called it a Monday morning.

"Hitch was all for making the change to the dark side, but I had to halter break him and show him how to ease into purposeful oblivion, you know? He was an eager student and studied real hard. The problem was, poor Hitch didn't go to class because he was unable to function. I *didn't* go to class because it all bored the hell outta me.

"One teacher gave me an F for unexcused absences, and I took issue with it. I got 100% scores on all three tests that semester, and I asked him what the hell was wrong with that? He told me I missed too many lectures. I told him missing the lectures didn't seem to be holding me back none. He told me I was lazy and had a bad attitude.

"I told him he was an insecure idiot with common sense deficiencies who had no business teaching history until he started learning from it…and that he could kiss my lazy, bad attitude ass."

"Ouch," I said.

"You ever see a face turn into a thunderstorm? We didn't exactly bond that day."

Slim's grin lit up the room as he winked at me and rose to shuffle to the kitchen. I hoped he would bring back hamburgers and fries. I settled for more fruit and jerky.

"I left his office and walked back to our dorm room to pack up my belongings. Hitch was devastated when I told him my college days were over, and he wanted to leave with me.

"'What the hell am I supposed to do with you gone?' Hitch exclaimed.

"'You do what you were supposed to do in the first place,' I answered. 'Go to college. Get a degree and a good job. Marry some sweetheart and get pregnant. Have a good damn life without my complications.'

"'What you call complications, I call the best thing that's ever happened to me. I don't want to have a boring life, Slim. I want to really live.'

"'You don't wanna go down my road. It takes everything I have inside of myself to keep the buggy from flippin' over. You ain't cut out for this kinda life. I live in a hedonistic hurricane. You're suited for sunshine, Kid.'"

"I'm guessing you wanted to save him from the consequences of your lifestyle and life choices."

"I did. He actually cried when I walked outta the room. I felt bad for him, but I knew the best thing for him was to stay as far away from me as possible. He couldn't hold it together like some of us could. Drug and alcohol abuse ain't for the faint of heart, you know, and I cared about him a lot. He was a real smart kid. I figured he'd be okay once he got back on the beam after I was gone.

"So, I drove myself the hell outta town. My plan for going to college in the first place had been to become a defense attorney for misunderstood and underappreciated dope fiends such as myself. I was gonna help pass legislation to legalize all drugs, and become the voice and figurehead for a national movement calling for government funding of artistic endeavors."

"You were going to make a push for a Nobel Peace Prize."

"At the very least. I always thought criminal law would be a hoot, you know? As long as I had other folks to do the damn research. I wanted to be a trial lawyer, and that was that. I wanted to dress up in thousand-dollar suits and strut around courtrooms like a peacock, expounding and pontificating and such. I would fight for dope fiends who were drowning in the pools of injustice. I'd unlock the prison doors and release the throngs of mishandled drug offenders. Maybe I'd run for governor or the Senate. Smoke dope during press conferences and piss off some pundits. I had it all planned out.

"Well, I ended up in Alaska working a fishing boat with a bad leak and a chain-smoking, alcoholic captain from Russia who knew three words of English and had breath like a mug full of mule puke. His wife was our dyslexic navigator, and she carried around a wooden paddle to swat her husband with repeatedly. That woman could hit a bucket with tobacco spit from twenty feet."

"Sounds like they were a lovely couple," I noted.

"Yeah, they were a real Hallmark couple. Their favorite sport was to get drunk and into a knockdown, dragout so they could have loud makeup sex on the deck. You won't believe me when I tell you this, but spreading fish blood and guts all over each other turned 'em on."

"That doesn't do it for you?" I asked. "Just the other day, I covered myself in fish blood and entrails. My favorite body spread is a ground-up tilapia with just a sprig of perch."

Slim belly-laughed, and it made me so proud to have given him that. I felt so close to him. I hoped the sun would refuse to rise and the night would never end. Part of me wanted to sit right beside him. Part of me wanted to be *him*.

"I'm a trout man, myself. They did this about three times a week, and always when I was trying to get some sleep. The good news was, they spoke in Russian the entire time, and I never had to know what they were saying to each other in the throes of passion.

"One night, the three of us got stupid drunk, and they tried to teach me some Russian board game I couldn't get. He got so frustrated with me, he grabbed me by the throat, and for a second, I thought he was gonna choke me out. Well, his quick-thinking wife jammed her tongue down his throat to create a distraction, and I beelined for my cabin. He later knocked on my door to apologize, and I didn't understand a word of it. She was standing behind him with that damn paddle, cocked and ready.

"My plan was to work a year and save up enough money to buy land in Montana to build a studio. I made it nine days, and when the blisters on my hands got blisters, I retired and drove to Seattle, where I formed and managed an all-girl band called Toxic Shock. I can't begin to tell you how bad I screwed that one up, but man, I was glad to be back on land, Son."

"Toxic Shock. Sounds quite interesting, Mr. Chance."

"Toxic Shock was a five-piece, down and dirty rock group, and those gals could really play. And, they wore lingerie on stage, which didn't hurt their show attendance any. There were other female groups in town, but the musicianship was poor, and they were gimmick groups more than anything. Toxic Shock was a great band that could really get down in the trenches and rock, you know? This band was a money-maker outta the gate, and we were playing five or six sold-out shows a week for great money until the inevitable happened."

"You slept with one of the girls," I too quickly inserted.

"I stepped right off the common sense ledge, Son. I had me a sordid affair with a gal named Lexy, who was a pretty fair singer and guitar player. We got to smoking hash and blowing the smoke into each other's mouths and such.

Well, we got too close, and you can figure the rest. At first the other girls were okay with it, and Lexy and I got along pretty well—until she caught me with Joan, the bass player."

"You slept with two of the girls." I shook my head like it had flies surrounding it.

"Three. I had a fling with Katie, the drummer. Katie had the dirtiest mind of any human being I've ever encountered, and an oral fixation that came in awful handy. I don't like talking about sexual stuff, but she had a talent that needs to be told about here. Katie could hum John Phillip Souza tunes perfectly while she performed oral sex. Like I said, I ain't comfortable discussing such things, but damn, ain't that a hoot?"

"That's a hoot and a half. Maybe two hoots," I managed.

"I probably would've taken a shot at Cindy the keyboard player, but she was a lesbian, and Ruthie the sax player would've just plain kicked my ass. I didn't have a lick of sense in me in those days, but I can't be too hard on myself over the deal. Those girls were awful shiny, and we all had hormones stuck on open throttle. Anyways, they fired me and patched whatever needed patching up between 'em, and kept playing.

"I kept in contact with Cindy through letters and such. She'd always send me a birthday card with a red lipstick kiss inside. Those gals actually signed a deal with Virgin Records later down the road. I think they were called Kitty Kat by that time. I was real happy for 'em. They worked their butts off, and deserved everything good that happened to 'em. I was real tickled to learn they'd recorded two of my songs. I'd always told 'em anything I'd written was fair game, and by golly, they took me up on it. I still get mailbox money from that, and a few other things I did.

"Anyways, I hung around Seattle and tried to put another band together, but I couldn't take the weather. I ain't ever seen rain like that, and I'm a big fan of sunshine. Last thing a booze-infested dope fiend like I was needed was more gloom, you know?

"The style of music that would later be called grunge was really starting to take off there. I met a few cats and we jammed some, but we never clicked, and I was running outta money. Well, that's not entirely true. I was running out of disposable income. I had a hell of chunk put away that I promised myself I wouldn't touch, and I didn't. I had myself on a tight budget, and that budget was just about gone."

"Oh, no, Slim. Do not tell me you were inclined to secure a…*gasp*…real job?"

Slim rested his chin on his chest. The look he gave me from under his bushy eyebrows made me giggle. It embarrassed me, and I cleared my throat to assume the posture of a grownup.

"Hell, no. I'd have sawed off my pecker with a butter knife before going to work for somebody. I played a few solo shows, but the acoustic clubs paid diddly squat at best. I gave busking a whirl for a couple weeks, and I was pretty good at it, but only did it long enough so I wouldn't have to get a job.

"I worked this one corner next to a pizza joint most days, and got to know the owner Angelo pretty well. I think his wife's name was Gina, and she used to sneak food out the back door to wayward folks. Angelo fed me every afternoon and let me sleep in his backroom for almost a month. I paid him, but he'd always just slip it back to me somehow.

"One afternoon, this cat snuck up to my tip jar and split with it. Just grabbed it and ran like the wind. It took me a few seconds to figure out what had happened. By the time I'd gathered my senses, he was a block away, and there was no sense chasing him.

"Maybe five minutes later, I look up this mime and bodybuilder I sort of knew was leading Mr. Thief Man by the earlobe back to my corner. He presented him to me like a cat with a bird, and handed back my tip jar. I thanked him profusely, and he silently slipped back away into the crowd to a round of applause.

"After that, a few folks in the crowd got a bit unruly, and took Mr. Thief Man down and stripped him nude. They split with his clothes. There he was, naked as the day he was born, looking to me for help.

"By this time, Gina came out to see what the fuss was about and asked me why there was a naked man standing next to me.

"'What naked man?' I asked.

"'Um, the one standing right next to you,' she said. 'What the hell's going on, for Christ's sake?'

"'Somebody left him for me as a tip,' I replied. 'Can I keep him, Mom? Please? I promise to feed him and clean up his messes.'

"'I'm calling the police,' she said.

"And then Mr. Naked Thief Man took off running again, in the same direction as before. Well, five minutes later, he's dragged back by the earlobe again by my mime buddy, who was unable to stay in character by this time and was laughing hysterically. We all were. The cops arrived and arrested Mr. Naked Thief Man on the spot."

"Ah. Now I get it. I noticed in the liner notes of one of your records you thanked Mr. Naked Thief Man. That one stuck with me."

"I can't believe you saw that. I've never read a single liner note in my life. Anyways, I told you that story because Mr. Naked Thief Man showed up at my corner about a week later to apologize. It turned out he was a down-on-his-luck guitar player who offered to play with me for the afternoon for free. I took him up on it, and I'll be dipped in donut dust if he wasn't the best damn guitar picker I'd run into in Seattle.

"We worked together on that corner for a week or so until he had enough money to stand up again. I even hooked him up with a band I knew who needed a guitar player. Anyways. Where was I, Stevie Boy?"

"The pizza joint? Angelo and Gina?"

"Angelo worshipped the ground Gina staggered on. She had a glass of wine in her hand from the moment her eyes opened in the morning until he carried her to their bed. She had a real good heart, but couldn't keep her legs together, you know? She cheated on Angelo with every guy up and down the damn block. She made a play for me one night, and I got the hell outta there. I never went back or got to thank Angelo for his kindness.

"I still feel bad about that.

"So, I decided to make my way back home to South Dakota once more. I knew I wanted to put the band back together again, but I wasn't right inside, you know? There were too many bad echoes bouncing around and such. I knew my batteries were on low, and South Dakota had always been my soul charger. The mountains and trees always welcomed me home, and the land felt damn good beneath my toes. I would spend time in my sacred Black Hills and figure things out. Might've helped the process if my mind hadn't been so polluted with chemicals, but who was I to argue with being high all the time?

"Anyways, to this day, I won't eat fish, I won't set foot on a boat of any kind, I don't trust wine drinkers or lawyers, and you'll rarely find me without a breath mint.

"Am I jumping around too much for you, Son?"

"Nope. I'm right here with you, Boss."

"Why don't you turn that machine of yours off and let's scare up some real food. You hungry?"

"Famished," I answered, rubbing my hands together.

"I've found over the years steak and eggs cures everything from cancer to melancholy. Why don't you have a lay down on the couch over yonder, and I'll call you when they're ready. You look like you're feeling much better and don't for a second feel badly about feeling badly."

"Thanks, Slim. I just don't make a habit of being emotionally vulnerable during interviews. There was a time when my anxiety was so bad I was unable to function or work. Years of hard work, therapy, and medications pulled me out of the pit and I have been doing quite well for over two years. Why it fired up inside of me tonight I do not know. All I do know is I feel much better, and I feel safe with you. Thank so much for your understanding."

"We all got wounds, Son, and most folks ain't got the courage to acknowledge 'em. I'm glad you trusted me enough to talk about some of yours. I know all about fear and pain, and what they can do to a man. I ain't no therapist and I ain't no guru of any kind to speak of…but I do know one thing. We ain't got no choice about pain. We all have it. But suffering is optional, Son. The key for me was to stop stepping in my same damn footprings when I was lost, you know? I had to try some different paths. Different roads. I had to let go of the discomfort I'd come to know so well. The thing is, most folks stay sick because there's just too damn much responsibility and work in getting well. It's easy to be a victim, and boy I wore that coat a long time. Hurt can be healed. We just can't give up before the miracle happens. No matter how long it takes. Listen to me go on. You're gonna be ok, Son, and so am I. We all got the good stuff inside of us, and God don't make junk."

Chapter Six

Following our feast, we returned to the living room, and the recorder went back on. I was back to feeling like myself again and what a relief that was. Slim started a fire in the fireplace, and with a full belly and a fire, I was concerned I would not be able to maintain consciousness. My wick was about burned down. More coffee was needed and poured.

"Maybe you could slow down on the coffee, Slim? I think your pupils are dilated, and I can see a pulse beating in your temples."

"You looking for a knuckle sandwich, Junior?"

"Thanks, but no. The steak and eggs took care of me nicely. Perhaps some pancakes?"

"I oughta pancake you. Only reason I don't is I'm old and you're probably just a little tougher than I am. Well, that and I kind of like ya."

"Don't delude yourself. I am much tougher than you are. I am fond of you as well, Slim."

"Well, now that we're in love with each other…let's get back to the regularly scheduled program."

"What was next on the agenda for you?" I asked, picking steak from my teeth.

"I had to always be doing something to keep my mind wolves at bay. Hanging out in the Black Hills was good to my insides, but South Dakota ain't exactly a hotbed for entertainment, and I developed a restlessness I couldn't shake.

"I decided I'd just go ahead and be a movie star."

"Of course you did," I said and grinned at the idea.

"Back to California I went. I worked as an extra on a couple of movies, and I even had speaking parts in a really bad horror film, but the scenes didn't make the cut. Almost got my SAG card for that one. I had some pretty good auditions, and folks told me I was a natural. I didn't see what all the fuss about acting was. Growing up in the home I did, acting was second nature to me, and I had to be damn good at it to survive. After spending time around some seasoned stage actors, I figured out it ain't as damn easy as it looks.

"Like I said, I did okay on some auditions and landed a couple small parts, but I couldn't remember lines to save my butt. I had a couple meetings with movie producers, too, but I found out those cats eat their young. And I thought the music business was full of crooks. My big-time movie career was over before it started, but my heart wasn't in it, anyways.

"I'd supported myself playing music for years, and I knew I'd get back to it. And, what the hell was I gonna do if I got a job? Serve hamburgers? Sell vacuum cleaners? I didn't exactly have a skill set, Son. My only plan was to get fabulously rich, buy a sailboat, and retire somewhere in the tropics.

"Back then I had a pal in LA named Nicholas Anton Slick who tried to talk me into going into the drug lab business. He handed out business cards to trusted customers that said: 'Nick Slick, Chemical Entrepreneur,' and his specialty was cooking speed for biker gangs. I was sure he was gonna blow himself up, but he never did. The money he made was amazing, and he kept it all in boxes in his attic. His plan was to make a couple million bucks and then get out for good.

"Slick would've made it, too, if he hadn't gotten busted. He went to prison for two years, got out, starting cooking dope again, and got popped the second time. The last time I talked to him, he was still locked up. He said he was going straight and was gonna make this product in his basement whenever he got out that would make him rich.

"He called it Mow No Mo'. He would develop a powder folks could spread on their lawns that would stop grass growth. It would keep the grass green, but you wouldn't ever have to cut it. I thought it was a great name and a great product idea. I always told him to get in touch with me when he got out and I'd invest in his idea. I knew he'd never call."

"You never immersed yourself in the drug lab business, I take it?" I wondered.

"I dipped my toes in it. The money was damn tempting, but I didn't have the nerves for it. There were too many things that could go wrong, you know? And the bikers scared the bejesus outta me. I was always afraid they were gonna kill both of us and just take the dope.

"Slick told me that would never happen. He was the irreplaceable cook with the recipe everyone wanted and would pay top dollar for. Dynamite speed was hard to come by, and Slick had it down to an art.

"Still, it was a damn scary scene, and I started noticing once in a while folks were disappearing. Cats that would come by Slick's pad on a weekly basis to buy huge amounts of speed would just never be seen again. It didn't happen often, but often enough for me to put two and two together. These weren't the kind of people who just decided to load up the BMW and move to Scottsdale, okay? They were dope-dealing bikers who handled lots of cash, lots of firepower, and lots of risk. I knew they were dead. It all made me creep lightly on the eggshells.

"One biker in particular scared me more than all the others combined. Everyone called him Rooster on the street, but behind closed doors, he was Reaper. He'd show up at the lab once a month to collect a big bag of cash, and I made a point to never look at him.

"Slick told me he was a dyslexic hit man who sometimes got addresses wrong and had, on a couple occasions, killed the wrong people."

"Holy cow, Slim."

"Yeah. If he took you for a ride, his face would be the last one you'd ever see. It wasn't his physical presence that was so damned intimidating. It was his eyes. Pale blue, totally devoid of emotion or humanity. He was a stone-cold killer. The rumor was he had over fifty kills under his belt, but I talked to a guy in the Banditos who told me it was closer to a hundred."

"Holy batcopters! Was he ever arrested for any of them?" I asked.

"Hell if I know, and I don't wanna know. For awhile, the bikers thought I belonged to 'em since I was privy to their business dealings with Slick. They had me doing everything—from driving hookers and strippers, to appointments, to making dope and cash drops for 'em. I didn't want to take their money, but it would've made them real nervous if I hadn't, so I just did what I was told, took what I was given, and kept my damn head down.

"I couldn't get over the cash involved. These guys would light cigars with hundred-dollar bills. I saw big boxes full of cash being hauled in and out of the lab, two or three times a month, and they just kept coming.

"There was no rhyme or reason to my pay. I'd make a drop and some gorilla would give me five thousand bucks. The next time I'd get a thousand. One time, I got eight thousand to drive four strippers and a cardboard box out to a cabin in Laurel Canyon. It was stupid money, Son. The most money I ever got was twelve grand, and all I had to do was pick up a large duffel bag at the lab and deliver it to a cosmetic surgery clinic in Beverly Hills.

"This cat in a lab coat met me out back and handed me a manila envelope that I brought back to the lab to give to a gorilla I'd never seen before. He reached in the envelope and pulled out three banded stacks of hundred-dollar bills, counted out three thousand dollars that he put back in the bag, then gave me the rest. He told me to keep my blankety blank mouth shut. I assured him that I would, but he still felt it necessary to stick a gun to my forehead in case I was confused about the process.

"He also told me he would peel my face off of my skull and nail it to the wall if I said anything to anybody."

"Oh, my," I said, swallowing hard.

"Yeah. Skull peeling didn't sound like all that much fun. Again, I assured him of my silence and complete ignorance of everything related to his business. Slick intervened, and got the gorilla to lower the gun and split with the cash. I stood there swallowing and sweating profusely, wondering how I got mixed up in any of it."

"I can only begin to imagine what it would feel like to have a gun pointed at me, Slim."

My observation hung heavily over the room, and a seriousness I had yet to see in Slim's face showed.

He pointed a finger at me, bit his lower lip, and leaned towards me. I could not help but cringe as his gaze bore into mine.

"Don't think too hard on it. It makes you feel pretty damn small. It tightens up every orifice you've got. I'd avoid the experience if at all possible."

"Don't get a gun pointed at my head. Got it." And boy, did I get it.

"One day, I dropped off five kilos of speed to a motel room and got a shotgun stuck in my mouth by a Dominican fella while his buddy searched me for a wire and made me snort a whole bunch of coke. When they didn't find a wire, they got all chummy with me and gave me a briefcase for the bikers—and a bag of coke and a solid gold watch for my trouble. I thought about inviting them for Christmas dinner, but decided against it. Slick apologized all over himself for putting me in that position and promised me I wouldn't have to do deliveries no more.

"Of dope and cash, that is. They still wanted me to deliver human beings, and I became the taxi driver for strippers and hookers who I was smart enough to stay the hell away from. I did that until a jealous boyfriend of a stripper broadsided me in Slick's van with his Monte Carlo and my damn head went through the side window. All I needed was another damn concussion. That was it for me, and I retired. I've still got a crick in my neck from that episode. It's something to remember why I don't hang out with such folks anymore.

"I also got outta that game because I wasn't fond of the idea of going to prison. I'd done enough county time to know that prison wasn't gonna work out for me too good. I didn't cotton to the idea of going steady with some guy named Bubba for five to seven years, you know? Slick always told me he had enough cops in his pocket to never have to worry about getting busted. Well, I guess maybe a cop or two fell outta his pocket, because he surely did run outta time."

"So, what did you do?" I asked.

"I was done having guns stuck in my face, I'll tell you that, and I got the hell as far away from the bikers as I could. I'll bet I looked over my shoulder for a damn year after I split. Thank God I wasn't a threat to them, because I'd be long gone.

"It was around that time I started to really struggle with anxiety which you know something about. No matter how much I drank or drugged, I couldn't shake this uneasy feeling down in my guts. Back in those days, I was what you'd call a chronic malcontent.

"I worried about both sides of everything I looked at. I'd worry that something was gonna happen. I'd worry that the same thing wasn't gonna happen. Depression started to creep in, too, but nobody talked about those kinds of things, and I didn't want to come off as weak minded."

"Weak-minded?"

Slim drew circles with his finger next to his right ear and stuck his tongue out to punctuate his point.

"That's what my old man called folks who had mental problems. I surely didn't wanna be that, so I kept my mouth shut and muddled through as best as I could.

"I prefer to be called strong hearted. I listen to my heart a hell of a lot more than my mind. A mind worries, but a heart always just knows. And worry is just meditating on the wrong things. Suffering future pain. The quieter my mind gets, the louder my inner voice becomes. Weak minded ain't all that bad of a deal in my book.

"I had depression and anxiety and didn't know where the hell to turn. I tried my best to reason with 'em. They weren't in a reasonable mood, I guess. Every morning when my eyes opened, I'd get hit and wonder how the hell I was gonna keep 'em at bay. I'd busy myself to keep my thoughts away, but they'd always find me. It took everything I had in me just to show up for my life. Sometimes I'd sleep sixteen hours in a day and wake up exhausted. Hell was within walking distance for me, I'll tell you that.

"I never talked to nobody about any of it. I put on the best face I can muster, wandering around with a pasted smile and overacting like I was as happy as a clam. Another egomaniac with an inferiority complex, pretending everything is okie dokie.

"In the back of my mind, a record was always playing, telling me I was being punished by God for all of my sins. It just made me turn away from Him even more than I already had. I had a choice to make: do it my way or His. I knew that if I was gonna truly follow Him, I'd have to make some big changes. Changes I wasn't willing to make. So, I slammed my mind shut and put a towel under the door to keep out any light.

"During those days, I kept having dreams starring my dark visitor. Every damn night he'd show up, whispering to me about making some kind of a deal. I'd wake up in a cold sweat and curse him and God. There were times I swore I saw that demon outta the corner of my eye during the day, smiling at me. I'd turn to face him, and he'd be gone. I think he was waiting for me to pull the plug on what sanity I had left.

"I couldn't tell anybody what was really going on. I was more invested in how I looked than how I felt. Always comparing my insides to people's outsides and losing at every turn. That's just false pride, and false pride will kill you dead.

"You know that saying about how most men lead lives of quiet desperation?"

"It's actually 'The mass of men lead lives of quiet desperation.' Henry David Thoreau. Sorry. I couldn't help myself," I said.

"Okay, Mr. Smarty Pants. Whatever it is or was, he was playing my song. When I was a kid, it was a life of quiet inspiration. Well, it grew and changed into a damn time bomb in my brain, and I never knew when it was gonna go off. The times it did, I couldn't put two days together without thinking about dying, Son, and I've never told anyone that. I rubbed up close to suicide three times in my life, and the last one truly scared the bejesus outta me. To know I was that close to giving away this amazing gift of life staggers me to this day."

Slim shuffled over to stoke the fire and add more wood. The fire backlit his form, and I thought about his dark visitor. Goosebumps covered my arms, and I blinked to make them go away.

"Around that time, I did get some relief from opiates. A pal of mine took antidepressants, and I helped myself to a bottle and took it for a couple months. I think it may have helped some, but I really don't know for sure. It's hard to know what's helping in a situation like I was in. I was constantly drunk and constantly high. My body didn't know if it was coming or going, you know?"

"I would not be surprised if the antidepressant provided measurable relief," I offered. "Even amidst the chemical barrage. I also would not be surprised to learn you were suffering from PTSD."

Slim nodded. "I thought about that. I knew some Vietnam vets who came back unscrewed upstairs, and we had a lot in common. All I know is somehow I was able to keep trudging through the abyss.

"The constants in my life back then were dope and booze by the gallon. And an occasional girlfriend, but I always seemed to pick the really wounded ones. Well, it took one to catch one. Like the old saying goes: 'The odds were often pretty good, but the goods were often pretty odd.'

"I thought I knew everything about gals back then, but I kept baking the same cake over and over, wondering why it always tasted the same. I tried to change it up. I'd only date blondes. Or redheads. For a while, I only went with women who'd never been married and didn't have kids. Then, women who'd been divorced and had kids. I drove every relationship road I could find and kept ending up at the same damn address. I couldn't see the only common denominator in the equation was me. I was as much or more of the problem as they were. Tough to swallow.

"My grandfather once told me if I kept doing what I was doing, I'd keep getting what I was getting."

"Doing the same things over and over and expecting different results. Isn't that the very definition of insanity?" I asked.

Slim laughed. "It took a long time for me to figure out I was the one shooting myself in the foot. It took me a longer time to figure out my woman picker was as broken as I was. I attracted women who were as sick as me, but you couldn't tell me that. No, Sir. I believed from the tip of my noggin down to my toes, I was there to rescue 'em. I truly did. God's very own love crusader.

"I felt so bad inside myself that the only thing I could think to do was to get hooked on something or someone else, you know? Anything to fill the hole I had. I didn't know it was a God-shaped hole. I never did read my owner's manual. I was a crib notes kind of cat.

"I should mention a gal I almost hitched my wagon to for good, who was the smartest human I ever met, and crazier than a fish taco."

"You're not fond of fish tacos?" I wondered.

"Don't interrupt me when I'm flowing, Son. Her name was Temperance King. Dr. Temperance King. She was an orthopedic surgeon at a hospital in Denver, and we met at a bar in the Denver airport. I accidently on purpose bumped into her in a book and magazine shop. I felt so bad about almost knocking her over, I paid for her coffee and newspaper. A drink led to dinner, which led to more drinks and then animal sex in her Mercedes.

"Best flight I ever missed, and I moved in with her immediately.

"Like I said, Tempe was the smartest person I ever met, and as luck or the devil would have it, she was an opiate addict with an endless supply. I never could understand how she functioned on the stuff, working eighteen-hour days, cutting and pasting folks back together. But she never missed a beat.

"She swore she never took anything when she was working, but I never believed her. She'd call from the hospital and slur her words. I always worried she'd get messed up and mess up. She was doing surgery, for crying out loud. She wasn't building model airplanes.

"One night when she was on call, she slept through her pager. She just got a louder pager. It was like that with her. She always had a quick fix for everything.

"We had these amazing talks every night, and I loved her mind best of all. She could expound on any subject in front of her, and I could never stump her. She would talk for hours, and I'd just take it in like it was a deep breath. You might find it hard to believe, but I'm usually the talker in most outfits."

"You're full of surprises, Slim."

"She was a stone-cold genius. And that's a word that gets tossed around too much, Son. But she was the real thing. Her IQ tested out at 175 in medical school, and in my book, that's off the damn charts.

"She'd go on and on about her day with her head on my chest, and I'd do my best to stay with her…but most times she'd lose me like a thrown-out rag on the road. And she had one of those photographic memories, which hurt my chances in any argument, you know?

"She knew the Bible inside out and didn't believe a lick of it. She'd spend hours disproving it to me, and then talk about the only god she believed in."

Slim rose from his chair and shuffled over to pick up my coffee cup, which I covered with my hand. His shoulders shrugged, and a loud pop from the fire caught his attention. He turned back to face me.

"What's the difference between God and a doctor?"

"What? I don't know."

"God doesn't *think* He's a doctor.

"She said she believed in a creative intelligence, but not some bearded deity sitting on a throne in heaven. And she didn't think this creative intelligence inserted itself into our lives at all, which is why she didn't believe in prayer.

"We had lots of great plans for the future. She was gonna work until she turned fifty, and then retire somewhere on an island. For a time, I thought maybe we'd tie the knot, but it wasn't long before the boat started to spring some leaks.

"She never wanted me to leave her house. Ever. It was a damn mansion on a golf course, and I had everything I could ever want there, but a guy's gotta get out on the town some, you know? I was an almost rock star, for crying out loud. My public needed me."

"They were probably suffering withdrawals," I inserted.

"You're damn right they were. Anyways, she was always worried I was up to something behind her back. She didn't have a reason to be jealous. All I did all day was take pills, smoke cigarettes, sip whiskey, and watch cartoons. I could barely find my pants, let alone the door to leave. I got so damned lazy, I pretty much quit eating. I figured if I couldn't reach it from wherever I was laying, I didn't need it. And yet she was still always convinced I was seeing other women.

"She called the house constantly to make sure I was there, and if I didn't answer, she'd sneak outta the hospital and check on me. There I'd be on the couch, stoned outta my mind, wondering what all the fuss was about. Wondering why I had a knife pressed up against the side of my face.

"She always gave me a *look*. One that said, 'If you cheat on me, I'll chop you up into tiny pieces and feed them to the neighbor's dogs.'

"Well, I got tired of cartoons, and moved my pill-popping, whiskey-sipping operation out to the pool. I figured it was better to be bored and tan than bored and bleached.

"One afternoon at the pool, I cooked up an idea I thought was gonna make me rich. I'd been trying to tan on my stomach on a foldout lawn chair, and I couldn't get comfy no matter what I did. My neck hurt. My biceps hurt. The tops of my feet hurt. My lower back felt like it was broke. Pissed me all the way off. So, I called my buddy Gizmo, who could build anything outta anything, and we designed ourselves a sun tanning chair that made some damn sense.

"It was a beauty. It had a hole at the top to put your face in like one of those massage tables. It had padded cutouts for arms and feet, and a book holder. Hell, it even had a squeeze bottle mister that ran the entire perimeter of the chair. Anyways, we were just sure it was gonna take off, and we'd find ourselves retired on a sailboat someplace in the Caribbean.

"Maybe the only thing that kept us from untold riches was the fact we were doing so much dope back then, we forgot all about it in Gizmo's garage. It was the opiates that dropped us in quicksand. Anyways, I wonder whatever happened to the prototype."

Slim's eyes suddenly narrowed at me. "You look like you got a question."

"I don't want to interrupt you while you're flowing, Your Highness."

"I'll do the jokes, Son. A couple months went by, and I was climbing the walls with boredom. It was time to put a new band together, but Temperance wouldn't hear of it. She begged me not to. Threatened me not to. Pulled knives on me. Fell down on the ground crying. Tried to seduce me into her way of thinking. Told me she was done getting me Fentanyl. I told her I didn't need her damn Fentanyl.

"Hell, there was always heroin.

"We'd always had our share of fights that got physical on her part. One night after she'd slapped me for the tenth time, I knew the fat lady was done singing. Easier said then done, Son. As I was leaving with my duffel bag, she blindsided me with the butt end of a full bottle of wine, and it knocked me ass over teakettle. Then, she hit me on the head again while I was down.

"When I finally came to, she was sitting naked in a chair, smoking a cigarette and looking right through me with these desolate eyes. On the coffee table in front of her was at least ten thousand dollars in cash and a bottle of Fentanyl.

"It was her last bribe to get me to stay."

Slim shook his head back and forth, as if sawing through a very tough memory. He gathered himself, and I watched the color in his face disappear as he gently eased back down into his chair and his story.

"Man, you won't believe it, but I felt sorry for her. I had cared for her deeply, after all. There was something about her that was so above and beyond me, and I craved that, even when things got crazy. But her wounds seemed to feed on my wounds until they grew so big neither of us could breathe. I had to be done.

"And so, I got up, kissed her on the cheek, and started to walk towards the door. She never even looked at me as she threw the dough and the Fentanyl on the floor. You know something? I about bent down to get the bottle, but I didn't. I guess I still had some pride left.

"I went back to South Dakota to retrieve my belongings and to make preparations to put the band back together again."

"When I think of South Dakota, I'm reminded of the Sturgis Motorcycle Rally. Did your band ever play that event?" I inquired.

"We played it when we were based in California a couple times. I avoided it when I was growing up—I don't cotton to crowds unless I'm getting paid handsomely. The Rally is quite a party, though. South Dakota's population doubles for about a week every year, and it's right up your alley if you're a people watcher.

"I used to call it Halloween for adults, on account of folks dress up like they're bikers when they ain't. My buddy Wheezer once called the Rally the world's largest Adult Children of Alcoholics convention. There might be some truth to that."

"Did you ever go there just for fun?"

"I got bored and curious and went there one year in a powder blue Mercedes sedan with a one-eyed parrot I'd won in a poker game that nearly bit my finger off. I remember running out of gas twenty miles from Sturgis. I also remember the reverse gear went out on the Mercedes somewhere in Wyoming, and I had to push the damn thing outta parking places. The rest of the week is cloudy, as I'd spent most of it doing whiskey, diet pills, LSD, and a green-eyed harlot I'd met at a rest stop who was impervious to the discomfort she caused me.

"After three days together, she thought we were meant to be together forever, and I thought if I had to spend another day with her I was gonna chew my own fingers off. When she blindsided me in the back of the head with her backpack, I got the notion our affair was troubled. When she almost bit my ear off when I was sleeping, I had the notion it was circling the drain.

"When she pulled a gun on me and took off with my car and my bird, I had the notion I'd made another one of my famous errors in judgment. She was kind enough to let me keep my guitar, my clothes, and my record collection. She even blew me a kiss after she'd robbed me."

"What a sweetie pie," I quipped.

"She was Satan's apprentice, Son, and she got all A's. Anyways, I befriended a group of hippies who took me to their campground, and I bunked with 'em for a couple weeks. We weren't popular with the biker crowd, so we stayed at the campground and killed as many brain cells as we possibly could. I played a lot of guitar, had a lot of sex, ate and slept once in awhile, and did enough dope to cripple an elephant. It was a summer camp for heathens. An orgy of hedonism.

"When it was all over, I joined 'em when they left for San Francisco in a converted school bus. I smoked so much pot and dropped so much acid on that drive, my hallucinations had hallucinations. I was never sure if I was too drunk or not drunk enough, so I just kept drinking. I used to drink myself sober back then. I'd go right into a blackout, keep drinking, and come out on the other end sober and wondering what the hell I'd done.

"I fell in love twice on that trip. Once with an old Gibson guitar owned by the bus driver, and again with myself during a LSD-fueled chanting session ran by the Machiavellian leader of the outfit who lived in a white robe, sandals, and a bulletproof vest.

"Everyone called him Poppa, and that cat was crazier than a drum solo in a library. I remember his eyes burned into me like branding irons, and he always wore this crooked smile that never fit his face. I never trusted him for five seconds, and he knew it. I used to stare him down, and that really pissed him off, you know? Someone questioning his omniscient authority.

"Rumor had it he was part of the Manson family, but Charlie had him kicked out right before the murders happened. Poppa had three wives who all looked and acted like they might've gotten their heads stuck in a microwave oven on high. Dazed and confused doesn't even come close. They reminded me of three feral cats.

"I tried to communicate with one of 'em after a group ceremony, and she about jumped out of her skin. Her eyes darted around, trying to see if Poppa was watching. I told her everything was gonna be okay, and if she wanted me to help her get away, I would.

"She sat down on a prayer pillow and started howling like a wounded animal. The other two pushed past me and rushed to her aid. I got the hell away from her before someone accused me of hurting her. She freaked me all the way out.

"The other two reported this to Poppa, who called me back to his sleeping quarters. I wasn't going anywhere near his sleeping quarters, and I positioned myself close to the door. If he had pulled a gun, I would've jumped out without hesitation. He just glared at me and disappeared behind a curtain.

"Anyways, my mistrust and dislike of Poppa wasn't helped after he tried to jam his tongue down my throat. I'd been sleeping on a couch when I felt my arms go behind my back. I looked up just in time to see Poppa trying to slap handcuffs on me and I fought him off. I managed to push him away and he suddenly grabbed my face with both hands and planted a slobbery kiss on my lips. I got my mouth closed before he could insert his tongue and I shoved him to the ground and stormed out of the bus. I decided then and there to split that scene as soon as possible.

"I left somewhere in Idaho, where I stayed for a couple months. That was my last Sturgis Rally experience, and I ain't been back since. Every time I see that scar on my finger where that damn bird bit me, I think of Sturgis, that old Gibson, that whack job Poppa, and who the hell got away with all my records."

"When did you put the band back together again, Slim?"

Slim reached for the scrapbook, thought better of it, and set it back down on the table. He rose from his chair and shuffled over to stoke the fire and add a couple small logs. He placed an index finger to the side of his forehead.

"I ain't real good with timelines, but I know the answer to this one for sure. It was 1980. Mount St. Helens erupted, and Mark David Chapman assassinated John Lennon. Ronnie Reagan was in office, and John Hinckley tried to assassinate him."

"And cocaine was king," I said.

"And cocaine was king. Half the country walked around rubbing and sniffing constantly, pretending they weren't doing coke. You really could buy it anywhere you went, and I mean anywhere. I can't begin to tell you how much money went up our noses in those days, Son. I used to joke around and say that every time I sneezed, I lost a hundred dollars. I wore a solid gold snorting spoon around my neck and carried my coke in a diamond-covered case.

"We'd all get coked up before gigs, and without question, one of us would be playing away on stage with blood running out of his nose. We'd just signal him when it happened. He'd turn around and wipe it off with a big grin on his face. It was a badge we wore, you know? We were fools, and then some.

"Disco was finally losing some of its steam, thank God, and then MTV launched in 1981 and changed everything. If you didn't have a video, you weren't in the game. If you wanted to be in a video, you needed a thick checkbook, and it didn't hurt to be shiny and such. All the bands we played with were obsessed with making a video and getting it on MTV. That's back when MTV played music videos, Son, and not shows about pregnant teens, transvestite zombies, and angry kids of celebrities with eating disorders and addictions to plastic surgery. Cripes!"

"How can one not be rendered nauseated by the inane elements this society celebrates, Slim?"

"It's a society based on distraction, and I'm proud to say I don't cotton to any of it. If we're not careful, greed and moral decay are gonna run the table and take us all out."

"Greed and moral decay have ruined great empires," I added.

"Everyone's running around addicted to damn cell phones, and folks are gonna forget how to communicate face-to-face. Parents and teachers can't discipline kids, and they might as well be playing porn movies on the boob tube. Professional athletes make more money in fifteen minutes than a fireman does in a damn year. Folks change spouses like they change underwear, and pay through the nose to be anywhere other than where they're supposed to be—and that's present in the moment.

"And, they changed the recipe of my favorite soda. That's beverage blasphemy, Son. When I was a kid, it would burn all the way down your throat. It could take rust off of a trailer hitch. Not today."

"It's an honest to God shame, Slim."

"It's a damn beverage abomination is what it is. You know what I think the problem is? Spiritual growth has gone backwards, and technological growth is screaming ahead. We just might be doomed if we don't get those two to line up better. Technology might tank us, Son."

"And never the twain shall meet."

"Rudyard Kipling. I'll bet you didn't think I'd get that one, did ya?"

"I am flabbergasted you scored on that play." I was truly astonished.

"Yeah, I got some skills. Anyways, I know where I'm going if the planet falls apart, and I don't get exercised about things I ain't got any control over. You can't keep the bad things out and the good things in. Sometimes the best any of us can do is to stop the bleeding. I stay in my world where I belong, doing the next best thing in front of me.

"And you wanna know something? Life is damn good. I just can't get enough of it. Hell, I'd live to be two hundred if I could get away with it. Hell, three hundred.

"I always try to expect the best. Maybe God's got a trick shot planned that none of us can see. A bank shot that comes outta nowhere and heals my favorite planet. Call me a hope junkie, and I'm hoping a whole bunch of good overtakes a big bunch of evil in the fourth quarter. There's a lot more good than evil in this world. The devil just has a damn good publicist."

Slim rubbed his hands together and slapped both knees. More animation than I'd seen for a while. He went back to the kitchen to refill his urn, and then did a bit of a dance on his return trip to the chair.

"I'm gonna tell you my favorite band story of all.

"We got stranded somewhere in Colorado during a blizzard on the way to a gig in Denver. It was right around the time I put the band back together for the second time and we all barely knew each other. Six of us crawled into one motel room to launch a clandestine chemical consumption mission, but we were disturbed by shenanigans in the room next to us. We took it as long as we could, but then I went to give 'em the business. I pounded on that door like I was gonna put my hand through it, and it just suddenly swung open.

"Well, you might be surprised to know, as I was…that the room was full to the hilt with midgets and hookers, who were carrying on something fierce.

The place was a damn wall-to-wall circus orgy, and I had to steady myself in the doorway to see if I was seeing what I was seeing.

"Caligula would have blushed.

"All I could do was stand there while the bottom of my mouth dropped like a damn anchor and my eyebrows headed north. The spokesmidget and I had words, and next thing I know, I get body slammed to the ground by five of 'em, who started punching and kicking me. Well, my screams alerted my team, and suddenly we had us an all out midget/musician brawl.

"The hookers remained neutral.

"We were just getting the upper hand when more midgets showed up, with weaponry, and the battle spilled out to the hallway. I got some good shots in, but I was taking too many blows to the crotch, and every time I'd throw one off, three more would jump me. They just kept coming like ninja oompa loompas.

"I managed to shake about four of 'em off me, and I looked around to see how my team was faring. They were all spread out on the floor, screaming like they were on fire, covered in punching midgets. For a second, I tried to remember if we'd all taken a bunch of acid. That's when I took a monster shot to the groin that put me on the ground. I looked up into the smiling face of the spokesmidget, who flipped me over and commenced to rapid-fire kidney-punch me.

"Well, I'd had enough, and I decided I would try to crawl to the soda machine in the hallway, but I had the seven dwarfs on my back, and they pulled me back into the room. We were plumb outnumbered, and those midgets seemed more familiar with the process then we were.

"All I could think to do was start yelling, 'Truce,' over and over, but that did nothing to slow the onslaught. Out of the corner of my eye, I saw all the hookers sitting together on one bed, laughing hysterically. I beckoned to them for assistance, but they didn't budge. That was when I caught a desk lamp to the side of my face and almost blacked out. You should've seen the blood. It looked like I'd been hit in the face by a helicopter. I felt four or five of 'em jump off of me at that point. They probably thought they'd killed me.

"So, I played possum while my teammates continued to suffer the brunt of the beatings. I can't begin to explain to you the surreal nature of the whole event. I'd been in some scuffles in my day, but I just never expected to get gang-jumped and pummeled by a gaggle of rabid leprechauns. There's just no rite of passage to prepare a fella for something like that.

"Thankfully, another guest called the front desk, who called the authorities, who showed up in full battle regalia to bring it all in for a landing.

"The hookers were let go, and the rest of us assumed 'the position' on various walls. The midgets were no worse for wear, but all of us were bloodied and beaten. It turned out we'd stumbled across a midget-wrestling troupe from Minneapolis, in town for an anti-violence rally and benefit.

"Go figure.

"When they searched our room, they found a few extra-curriculars, and not only did we lose the damn fight, we lost some of our dope stash. For some reason, we'd left the bulk of our dope hidden in the band's trailer, and it never got searched. Had it been, we'd have been up shit creek without a paddle or a canoe.

"Funny thing was, we all got tossed into the same cell, and when the booze and dope wore off, we all got to be good pals. The next morning, we all appeared before the judge, who laughed the glasses off his face. He told us if we agreed to immediately skedaddle outta town, we'd be released with fines.

"We thought he was a damn genius.

"The roads were cleared off that morning, and back on the road we went, still shaking our heads and nursing the cuts and bruises from the main event.

"Believe this or not, we stayed in touch with the midget's manager, who called me later with a dandy of a business proposition. They needed a band to play live at their wrestling events, and he made us an offer we couldn't refuse. To make a long story short, we did a mini-midget wrestling tour, and we played twelve shows for fabulous money.

"Come to think of it, midget wrestling and rock and roll go hand in hand.

"We called it the Midgets, Music, and Mayhem Tour. They got top billing. We printed t-shirts and everything. It was an alcoholic's dream. The most booze I'd ever consumed on a daily basis, and those midgets could drink and play gin rummy.

"And, damn, they could chase women. You should've seen all the action those little guys got. The groupies were unbelievable, and we'd seen some ourselves, you know? Women would line up backstage like you wouldn't believe. Hell, women would ride to the next show and not care how they were gonna get home. Every time I turned around, one of 'em was copulating. I got a hell of a kick outta the deal.

"We travelled in tour buses, and once in awhile I'd jump in theirs. By the time we'd get to where we were going, I'd be so sloshed, they'd just leave me on the bus to sleep it off. I couldn't keep up with 'em, and I had a black belt in imbibing. Man, we had a hell of a time with those little fellas, and they knew what they were doing business-wise. It was a top shelf operation with great, detail-oriented folks.

"The funniest part of all of it was that the midget's manager was a six-foot-eight giant who chain-smoked Cuban cigars, flew his own plane to the shows, and ran an offshore sports betting operation that made him millions. Gary Miller was his name, but I called him Shorty. How in the hell does that happen? How does a millionaire giant become the manager of a flock of fighting midgets? Shorty was also a dynamite promoter, and a joy to work with. If he'd been on board with the band early on, you and I would be doing this interview in a damn castle somewhere. He ran a tight ship and had all the angles covered.

"The crowds were some of the best we ever played for. It was a fabulous tour, and a real blast. And everybody kept the egos in check, which was a rarity for the bunch I was playing with at the time. We'd open the show and do about an hour to get the wheels greased, they'd do about ninety minutes, and we'd close the show with a short set. We sold more records and shirts than we ever had, and Shorty never took a damn penny of it.

"In honor of the motel fight we'd had, during the very last show of the tour, all the midgets rushed us while we were playing, and we had a farce battle. A couple guitars got broken in the fake mayhem, and Shorty promptly replaced 'em. It was all great fun, and I was sorry to see it end. I got real fond of the little guys, you know?

"The wrap party for the tour was epic, and I don't think I've ever seen that much booze in one place. Shorty rented an entire floor of a fancy hotel in Minneapolis, had it catered by the best barbecue joint in the Twin Cities, and gave everybody involved with the tour a very generous bonus check. By the time the fat lady sung on that one, the floor of the place looked like the Wizard of Oz set had exploded. Bodies everywhere, and some of 'em in sexual motion. Most were passed out, me included. I remember I woke up with two midget buddies of mine, one under each arm."

"That must've been adorable," I noted, placing both hands on my cheecks.

"Other than the fact they'd both vomited on me, it was borderline precious. Vito and Sam were their names. Again, it was a great operation with great folks who really knew what they were doing. Who would've seen that coming? To this day, I'm drawn to midgets. One married my wife and me."

Chapter Seven

"Woah. Wait now. You're married? You never said a word about that before, Slim."

"It's a glorious story, Son, but I don't know if I have the right fuel in the tank to tell it all. I'll give you the microwave version. As a young man, I'd reached the conclusion love was a joyous disease, curable by the act of getting married. I subscribed to the catch and release program, and I made myself too slippery to catch for very long. I always figured I was best left alone. I didn't think it was a good idea to bring a wife or kids into the whimsical whirlwind I called my life.

"I've heard it said it's dangerous to fall in love with artists of any kind, on account of they're already in a relationship. It is a sad harvest with no fruit. Are you married, Son?"

"I have yet to cross that river, but I *am* in the boat."

"Got someone real special in your life?"

"I do indeed. Her name is Marcia May Moorehead, and she is the apple of both of my eyes. She'll make a wonderful Mrs. Barber."

"Hold onto her like she's a life preserver, because she likely is one. You gonna marry her and have kiddos?"

"That's the plan. She wants to have two children, and I'm leaning towards three."

"Sounds fabulous. I never felt up for the challenge. I always figured a parent is only as happy as his most unhappy kid and I didn't wanna risk it, I guess. I was too damn selfish to be a daddy."

"You were busy chasing the brass ring, Slim. Some people are happier without children."

"Like I said, too damn selfish. Don't get me wrong. At a certain level, I adore children, but I also figured in order to be a parent, it would be helpful to be an adult. Well, I certainly wasn't one. Not until I hit my forties, anyway. Before that, it would've been me, a perpetual teenager, raising a kid. I did the math and such, and none of it added up. You seem like a well-adjusted adult. You'll do just fine.

"Don't wait for the Poloraoid to develop before you get hitched. You love her. She loves you. Time is ticking, and sometimes time can be damn unforgiving. I ain't saying you're on the fence over this deal, but if you are, jump down off it as quick as you can and make that woman your bride. That's coming from a man who lost out on a lot of good living waiting for just the right moment to get in the jump rope game. A fella can stand there his whole life. Jump in there, and if the rope hits you, laugh it off and try it again. It only hurts for a second, and it's so worth it."

"I appreciate that, Slim. I'll marry her tomorrow and we'll be pregnant by supper the following day. I'm kidding. I really do appreciate your input, and I am going to marry Marcia, and we are going to start a family."

"Now I'll just bet raising little ones is the most powerful experience we humans can have, and I missed it. By the time I'd grown up, it was too late.

"Well, jump to the spring of '97 when I found myself standing in line at a grocery store in Scottsdale, Arizona with the most beautiful woman I'd ever laid eyes on. She was so pretty, I had to look at her sideways. I cooked up the best opening line I could, but it deserted me when I opened my damn mouth. Left me standing there, verbally impotent.

"'For the life of me, I can't recall what I meant to say to you,' I said. 'But believe me, you would've liked it.'

"I stuck out my hand, and it was shaking about as bad as my legs were. Our eyes met, and mine about rolled back in my head. Man, she was shiny.

"'My name's Slim Chance, and you are the second prettiest woman I've ever seen in my life.'

"'The second?' she asked. 'I have to ask…who's the fairest in the land?'

"'Well, my momma," I answered.

"The corners of her mouth went up a tad and she stepped towards me with her hand out.

"'Well it's nice to meet you, Slim Chance. I'm Julie.'

"I don't know if the folks in line with us felt the electricity running between us, but I'll bet we could've lit up a damn football field. I crossed my eyes, fingers, and toes she was feeling it too. I'd never had an allergic reaction to a woman like that before, Son. My inner throttle was wide open, and my heart was doing jumping jacks. I got kidnapped by her eyes.

"I had a hell of a time putting words together to form sentences. My communication skills must've left to use the restroom or something. All I could manage to do was spit and sputter, but for some reason she saw enough she liked to stick around. We took a long walk together, and it's still going.

"We got married six months after the day we met by my three-foot-tall buddy, Reach, in Sedona, Arizona, standing on a bluff in a wind that would've thrown us off had God not been holding us in place. When I said, 'I do,' I let go of that tired old fear wrapped in a mess around my heart, the one both of this vow and of being alone, and a wounded relief shot through my entire body. I swear the colors around me got brighter.

"My soul never smiles like it does when I'm with her, and her love for me is the gold I've been digging for my entire life. I thank God every day I finally learned how to put this woman first. That's where the good gets great, Son. When a man loves a woman enough to put her wants and needs ahead of his own. Action. Love ain't a noun. When you love someone, you do things for 'em. And gladly."

"I'd love to meet her," I stated.

"She'd love to meet you, but she has to stay at sea level on account of her joint pain. I take care of this place, and when we sell, it we'll get us a place on the water. She's in Florida with one of her daughters—she's got two—and we see each other as much as we can, and talk on the phone every night at bedtime. I miss her horribly. She's my epic love, and I don't breathe the same when I ain't with her. Hell, I don't even walk the same. I call her my Hunky Bunky, but don't print that. I don't want my public to think I've gone soft."

Slim picked up the recorder, handed it to me, and escorted me to a small room next to the kitchen. A meditation area, possibly, with throw pillows on the floor and a potbellied stove. Simple. No distractions. Something about the room seemed to coax me in.

"She's the woman in the pictures you have adorned on your walls, right?" I asked.

"Indeed, she is. Except for my Raquel Welch poster in the garage. Raquel was my backup babe, but she never took my calls. And you know, that still bothers me."

"Hell, yes it does. Your wife is very pretty, Slim. Where was this one taken?"

"Paris. Texas, not France. The one above the fireplace was taken in Mexico, and that one beside it was taken in Hawaii, where we honeymooned. And you know something? I remember every part of every second I've been with her—because I've been sober. I gave up the dope before I met her, and I agreed to never drink in her presence.

"She's been awful damn good for me. The best teacher I've ever had, and I've had some great ones. Julie Marie Chance. She pours gasoline on my fire, Son, and she's my absolute favorite thing to do. She completes my puzzle, and helped me with a lot of pieces I could never get to fit. And she expects me to take good care of myself. She's the first woman I've ever been with who told me upfront she wouldn't lift a finger to fix me.

"She said to me, 'I'm not in your life to heal you, Slim. That's God's job. I'm here to love you exactly as you are. We both have our wounds, and I promise to address mine. That's the best gift I can offer you, my love. I will be the best partner I can be.'

"Spending time with her gives me a sense of peace I've chased all my life. She makes me want to fight everything I have stacked against me to be a better man. God loves me so very much, he sent me Julie Marie when it was time. After I'd healed up enough to make peace my priority. My life became a masterpiece when I began to master peace."

"Ah. Another great Slim Chance lyric, perhaps."

"What we have is truly beyond my reach and a mystery to me. Julie Marie calls it a delicious kind of love. I don't know if you can teach love like thatYou almost gotta learn it from the inside out. She coaxed me outta my hiding place, Son. She made me believe in happily ever after and such. For the first time in my life my heart got louder than my head and it killed my fear of fear. And man is it ever great to have a true partner. I have a teammate who I get to share everything with. I don't have to go it alone no more. What a blessing.

"The best gift Julie gave me was helping me truly find a faith I could live comfortably with. Now, I never stopped believing in God, but what I had wasn't really faith. It was maybe a long lost brother of faith. I had so much anger towards Him, but I worked through most of that in therapy. What was left was the decision I'd made years ago to not give a damn, you know? To ignore Him. The anger was gone, but the understanding and connection were mysteries to me. I had the hunger, I just couldn't open my mouth.

"Julie Marie helped me see I could just change my mind about all of it. So, I did. I made a decision to turn myself over to Him, regardless of the outcome. I couldn't help but notice the blessings in my life and how little I had to do with any of it. I chose to believe, and I chose to go ahead and get grateful. I climbed down off the big fence, Son. It's the biggest decision I ever made. Ain't nothing more important than knowing where you stand when it comes to spiritual matters. And I happen to believe everything is spiritual. God is everything…or nothing.

"Another thing she taught me is to live life now. I spent my whole life thinking about next week, next month, next year. I'll be okay when this happens. I'll get around to living after that happens. Well, today, I live it like the fuse is lit. If I wanna do something, I just do it. If I wanna go someplace, I go there. She taught me that. This life ain't meant for sideline riders. You gotta get in the game before the buzzer sounds. Life is now. This moment matters as much as I allow it to. I can't put the right words to it, so I'm just gonna quit here."

"You put more than the right words to it, Slim. It sounds to me as if you both possess the love songwriters and scriptwriters strive to represent. You have a love for the ages, if you will."

"Cupid saved his best arrow for me, Son."

"It sounds as if he did indeed. I'm happy for both of you."

"You make powerful sure you make love a verb with that lady of yours. Make Marcia your absolute priority, and what you get back will fill you to the damn brim. Pay attention, Son."

"I shall do my very best," I promised.

"We're talking about sacred love here, Son. Go ahead and do better than your very best. Anyways, where are we going now?"

We returned to the living room, where the fire had picked up steam and was roaring. We both sat back down, and I returned the recorder to its previous place. I glanced at my notes, laughed, and set them down on the floor.

"If you don't mind, Slim, I'd like to go back to when you put the band back together in 1980. Where were you based out of then?"

"No place. Every place. Son, I was riding a dope roller coaster that always had me pushed all the way back in my seat, and it's a damn miracle I remember any of it. One minute, I'm snorting speed and bouncing around like a damn tennis ball…the next I'm jamming a spike full of heroin between my toes so I can get my damn mind to stop bothering me long enough to sleep. All the while, putting on a front that I ain't doing any of that. Appearances were everything to me, and damn deceiving.

"Anyways, we somehow managed to keep the band on the road, and we got a chance to cut a record in Nashville with a hotshot producer and a great engineer. I called that one The Plastic Ocean. We didn't have record label support, and we spent a pile of money on that record.

"Hell, most of us even cleaned up some for that one. I know I did. I somehow managed to stay off the smack, and slowed down on the rest of it all. Well, not the booze, but I was what you'd call a high functioning drunk.

"There's something else I remember about that studio now. It had a basketball court out back, and we'd go out to smoke and shoot hoops when we were taking breaks. Summer was just out of bed and stretching, and the heat and humidity were like a web you couldn't shake off.

"My drummer at that time was a cat from New Jersey we called Cowboy on account of he always wore cowboy boots no matter what. Even with shorts. Anyways, Cowboy and I got to jawing about who was the best basketball player, and it led to an all-out battle on that court. Turned out, he played basketball in high school, which gave him quite a leg up on me. I knew about as much about playing basketball as I did about performing gallbladder surgery.

"Anyways, he was kicking my butt when one of his cowboy boots tripped on my foot, and I'll be damned if he didn't break his ankle."

"Oh, no," I said, wincing.

"It turned purple and black and he couldn't stand on it. He refused to get it doctored and wanted to keep recording. Our producer started to call a backup drummer into the studio when Cowboy knocked the damn phone outta his hand.

"He said, 'I got this, man! Put the damn phone away and get me some tape, some whiskey, a redhead with an oral fixation, some pain pills, and some more tape.'

"Well, Son, I ain't no drummer, but you kind of need both legs working, and Cowboy was down to just the one. We loaded him up on booze and painkillers, wrapped it as tight as he could take it, and I'll be dipped in donuts if he didn't make it through the rest of that record, without the redhead. And he did a fine job, too.

"However, it turned out we'd wrapped the ankle too tightly, and he almost lost the foot due to lack of circulation. We found that out at the hospital the night we finished the record. We'd called the oxygen squad after he'd passed out from the pain about thirty minutes after he'd put down the last drum track. He was a trooper, I'll tell ya, and he never missed a single beat.

"Our producer shopped it around to labels, but we didn't land a contract. RCA Records told us we weren't unique-sounding enough. Capitol Records told us we didn't sound enough like anyone else. Atlantic Records liked us a lot, but just when we were gonna sign with 'em, their management changed up and we got dropped. ABC Dunhill wouldn't return his calls.

"It was a hell of a week, though, and we were tickled to finally get to record in a real studio with a producer. The Plastic Ocean is still my favorite record."

"After recording, did the band get back on the road?" I inquired.

"We stayed and played around Nashville a bit, but it wasn't our scene. We did manage to see a lot of great players, though. Nashville was filled to the gills with folks that could play circles around all of us, and they were just busking the street for tips and such. We met one guy who'd been a studio musician for just about every famous country star you could name.

"We picked him up off of a street corner. He was hot, broke, passed out, and homeless. What drew us to him was this old Martin guitar case that was handcuffed to his wrist. I woke him up, and he asked me if I was an angel. We all got a good laugh outta that one.

"We took him back to our motel and cleaned him up some. Man, he had captivating stories. He played with all the legends of country music, and he was some kind of idiot savant. He knew over two thousand songs, words and everything, and would you believe I can't even remember his damn name?"

"I am beyond astonished."

"Only thing was, he got hit with schizophrenia, and it sunk him. It took his dreams and tossed 'em overboard. He told us the medication the doctors put him on stopped the voices and all, but he couldn't play the way he'd always been able to, and he couldn't live with that."

"And so, he quit taking his medications?"

"He did. He told us it was like his mind was underwater. He could still hit the chords and play the notes, but he couldn't feel 'em anymore. He couldn't feel himself. It took every ounce of energy he had just to have a conversation, and he just got too damned tired of holding it all back…so yes, he quit the meds and just let the storm come.

"He told us some folks got together and helped him out for awhile, but you know how that goes. He just let go of the raft and slowly slipped beneath the surface of the water and away from everything he knew. Lost his life. He lost pretty much everything.

"He said living in the homeless shelter wasn't for him. They wouldn't let him drink booze or smoke in his room, so he never went back. He thanked us for our hospitality and turned down our offer for him to stay with us. He said he slept better outside, and that he had a good, safe place.

"We dropped him off at a park with his guitar, a bottle of scotch, and a few bucks he'd finally agreed to take. And that guitar he had? It was his life preserver, and you should've seen the autographs on the back of it. Hell, he'd known everybody. He said he'd been offered fifteen thousand bucks for it, but it was his friend and not for sale. I'll never forget that.

"I've thought a lot about him over the years, and I've been on psychotropic medications. I've been on some effective ones, and I've been on some not-so-effective ones. I'm the last one to judge anybody, but maybe it was part his fault he was living on the street. Maybe it's part his fault he lost everything. If he'd have stayed on the meds, who knows? Maybe the music comes back, maybe it don't, but at least he'd get a shot. It didn't help that he was drinking a fifth of scotch a day.

"It's been my experience that when the student is ready…the teacher really does appear. If the student ain't ready, God can paint the answers inside of his eyelids and the student still won't see 'em.

"And forget about trying to make the student ready when he ain't. You might as well try to talk a dog outta eating meat. Most folks want you to fix it so they can drink and use like they did before it all turned on 'em. They want that magic pill that'll cure their addiction once and for all. I tell 'em I got just the pill they're looking for.

"It's called cyanide."

Chapter Eight

"Okay, Slim. When we first met, you mentioned you'd written a song about a serial killer. Dark something?"

"I wrote a tongue-in-cheek song called Dark Heart about a woman who falls in love with a serial killer who kills her during a conjugal visit in prison. It's a bluesy number and was always a crowd favorite. We even made up a t-shirt for the tune, and it was always our best seller. It had a woman in a wedding dress with a knife in her heart, with blood spilling out that formed the words, 'Dark Heart.' Horrible design, but we sold the hell outta 'em.

"The damn song even had groupies, Son. We'd show up to play a gig, and there'd be these women standing in line carrying *Dark Heart* signs and such. We'd be driving up to the venue and these crazy chicks would start yelling all kinds of strange comments at us: 'Kill me, Slim!' 'Drink my blood!' 'I want to die in your arms!' Stuff like that, you know? I guess they didn't get the joke.

"Anyways, I've always been fascinated by serial killers, and the women who want to marry 'em once they're caught and in prison. I know lots of ladies like bad boys and all, but some of these monsters kill and eat humans.

"Without catsup!"

We both considered the implications of eating flesh, recoiled, and laughed before returning to the task at hand.

"What the hell do those women see in those empty, black eyes? They must see something that reminds 'em of how they feel deep inside. If you marry a serial killer, you'd best go stand on your head, as it's obvious you ain't got enough of what you need going up to that noggin'."

"I never understood that dynamic, either," I said. "I understand the pen pal phenomenon, but a marriage?"

"There was a gal I liked for a minute, but she loved the bad boys, and I was trying hard to steer clear of drama, so I kept my distance. Emily would fall head-over-heels in love with one mean asshole in prison after another, and every one of 'em beat her up when he got out. Every damn one! She was in the hospital so much, they could've given her a parking place. By the time I met her, her heart was pretty much cried empty.

"For a while, I rode up on my white horse to save her, but I got tired of working harder on her problems than she was, you know? So, I shot my white horse, and quit trying to save folks who don't want to be saved.

"I knew this cat who loved to save damsels in distress, though. His name was Rex, and he'd done time as a marine and studied some kind of martial arts none of us could pronounce. He claimed to have multiple personality disorder and PTSD, and he was cursed with a volcanic temperament. He was real smart, but the day they handed out common sense across town, his car didn't start."

"So, you introduced them," I said and shook my head.

"I did. He didn't have anything else going on, so I hooked 'em up, knowing he'd keep busy trying to keep her alive, and she'd keep busy keeping him busy. He'd just come off a bad divorce and didn't want anything to do with romance of any kind, and she wanted to play with bad guys.

"Now, Rex was the kind of cat who'd show up at a barbecue with a flamethrower, just in case you needed something to light the coals with. The guy could do three hundred pushups with a cigarette hanging out of his mouth, and crawl under a car in ten-below-zero weather and fix the damn thing. A man's man, you know? Well, he'd turn into mush around women. You could push him over with a feather. He said he was put on the Earth to protect 'em.

"Looking back, I shouldn't have helped tie those two together. Hell, when I knew him, he was the last cat I'd ever believe would fall for such a wounded woman. It's why I put 'em together like I did. I thought they'd just be pals and such, and he'd stay in shape beating up the abusive men she'd keep bringing home."

"But he fell for her?" I asked.

"Hard. It was a recipe for a bonafide disaster, and I set the whole thing up. She initially responded in kind, and they were a happy snappy couple. Here was this gal with a voracious sexual appetite, and there was Rex, who had multiple personality disorder."

"Wow. A match made in heaven," I noted.

"Anyways, she got twisted up with another convict that threw her around some, and Rex found out about it and paid the cat a visit with a baseball bat.

"It turned out Rex also played college baseball and was quite the hitter, and that didn't bode well for the convict. Rex caught him coming out of Emily's apartment following that evening's main event, and he started with the guy's kneecaps. Then he worked his way up…slowly. By the time he'd reached the cat's face, the neighbors had called the cops.

"Rex snapped out of it and took off in his red corvette that didn't exactly blend in the neighborhood, and the cops caught up with him two miles from Emily's place. By the time the fat lady sung on that one, Rex outran everybody and pulled into his garage like nothing had happened. When the police showed up at his door, he met 'em with a grenade in each hand and both pins in his mouth.

"That got their attention.

"Rex backed himself into his house and sat down calmly to have a cigarette. He later told me he'd planned to come out guns blazing.

"There's an anticlimactic end to the rest of the story. A hostage negotiator managed to talk Rex into surrendering, and the grenades turned out to be duds. The convict survived, Rex went to prison, Emily's picker stayed broken, and I cussed myself out for years.

"I truly felt horrible about the whole deal, I really did. I visited Rex in prison a couple times, and he didn't have any bad feelings towards me at all. He told me being there was the best thing that had ever happened to him. He was getting help for his PTSD. and other wounds. But I still couldn't shake the thought I'd really screwed the pooch on that one.

"Well, Rex did his prison time and came out flashing the peace sign. He gave up fighting and fretting over fair maidens, and married a real nice gal. They had a couple kids and moved to San Diego. Last I heard, he was running a dojo for underprivileged kids, and helping 'em get outta gangs.

"I left him a phone message for him about a year ago, but never heard back. I'm probably in a drawer he doesn't want to open again, and that's okay with me. I'm just glad he's doing well. What was that question I sidestepped?"

"What is it about serial murder you found to be so compelling?" I wondered.

"First, let me sidestep it again. I lived in Northern California for a time doing so much dope, I thought I was writing songs for Johnny Cash. All I had to do was figure out how to get 'em to him. I placed so many calls to his agency, they slapped a No-Contact Order on me. I wasn't hitting on all cylinders, Son.

"I was also convinced I was going to catch the Zodiac Killer. I wallpapered my motel room with crime scene photos that I'd stare at for hours. I was just sure I'd see something all them folks trying to catch him missed. I was crazier than a heavy metal xylophone solo, and my record going without sleep was seven days."

Slim pulled his lower eyelids down for emphasis, then fell out of his chair and onto the floor. For a second, I thought he'd stroked, and I almost bit my tongue. To watch him spring up from the wooden floor gave me a sense of joy I'd not felt in a long time.

"On that seventh day I got drunker than two drunk skunks, and got arrested for chasing my main suspect through his home with a tennis racket. I'd had him under surveillance for weeks and just knew he was Zodiac. I got a couple good backhands on him before I tripped on a coffee table and knocked myself out. Lost a tooth on that one. I also peed my pants, and you ain't really drunk until you pee your pants."

"Okay, Slim, I'll bite. How many times have *you* been really drunk?"

"Just that once. Anyways, I woke up when the police stormed the place and carted me off to the hoosegow. I slept the next two days in my cell.

"I guess I needed the rest.

"As luck would have it, I was a drinking pal of a drinking pal of the boyfriend of a gal who clerked for the judge assigned to my case, and I only got six months in county with a one-year probation to boot. That episode got a puck past my goalie, and I quit drugs and booze for good.

"For one week.

"I did give up on my Zodiac Killer chase, but I gave some thought that my butcher was The Night Stalker in June of '84. One day I was picking up some bologna, and I just asked him if he was a serial killer. To his credit, he told me he was, and that he'd had his eye on me for some time. We both got to laughing so hard, I about tossed my cookies. I crossed him off my suspect list and got some free bologna outta the deal.

"Anyhow, my detective days were done after that."

"I guess I continue to be curious regarding your preoccupation with serial murder."

"Serial killers intrigue me on account of they cross a sacred line, and I guess I wanted to know why. Believe me, I get the whole addiction gig, but these monsters get high on murdering human beings. What has to happen to someone as a child to get their wires crossed up enough for them to become a cannibal? How do they have a conversation with themselves and decide it's okay to murder people and eat their flesh?

"Or have sex with a dead body? If you're having sex with a corpse, you need to be electrocuted as soon as possible. I mean, how're you gonna rehabilitate that? Can you imagine a therapy group for necrophiliacs?"

"I'd rather not if I don't have to," I answered, laughing.

"Five spooky monsters sitting in a circle with a therapist.

"'I'm Joseph, and I'm a necrophiliac.'

"'Hi, Joseph,' says the group.

"'I haven't had sex with a dead body for nine months.'

"'Way to go, Joe,' says the therapist.

"'My name's Leroy, and I had sexual feelings for a live woman the other day.'

"'Way to be, Lee.'

"'My name's Huey, I'm a necrophiliac, and the medication I take makes it impossible for me to have sex with dead bodies now.'

"'Good for you, Hugh.'

"'I'm Royland, and whenever I feel like killing a woman and having sex with her, I snap my wrist with this rubber band.'

"'Atta boy, Roy.'

"'Well, my name's Lawrence, and I killed a cheerleader yesterday and had my way with her. I have her on ice at home, and I can't wait to get out of here.'

"'That's really scary, Larry.'"

The laugh that escaped my lips came from a part of me I usually keep hidden from others, and I was suddenly rendered self-conscious. Slim seemed to sense all of this. He slapped me on the back and ruffled my hair.

"Thank you for that disturbing scenario, Slim."

"You're welcome. The thing is, it all makes sense to them. One man's logic becomes a horror for society. Bottom line is, you ain't gonna rehabilitate a psychopathic killer, and they need to be put down. None of these damn death row appeals for fifteen years. No free health and dental care. I used to be against the death penalty. I changed my mind on all of it. I say, if there's incontrovertible evidence someone is a stonecold psychopathic killer, it's time for 'em to take a dirt nap.

"You want any hope of deterrence of any kind? I say, fry 'em fifteen minutes after the verdict. Hell, do it pay-per-view, and use the money collected to fund the damn trials and prisons. That'd make one hell of a reality show, now wouldn't it? Have it on three times a week. We just need a name for the show."

"How about Zapped? Or Electric Justice? I don't know. I'll have to ponder it."

"Now you're cooking with gas, Son. I could see pay-per-view public executions happening in the next ten years. Wouldn't surprise me a bit.

I used to be against the death penalty.I changed my mind on all of it.I say, if there's incontrovertible evidence someone is a stone cold psychopathic killer, it's time for 'em to take a dirt nap.

"Look. I ain't no saint, Son. I've done some things that make me cringe. But I always knew right from wrong. I always had a conscience.

"I remember being eight or nine, standing in a grocery store, thinking about pocketing a candy bar. I knew it was wrong, tried to talk myself into it, and put the damn thing back. I remember the feeling of relief that went through me as I left the store.

"That's what separates the monsters from the rest of us. Lack of conscience. They're in reptilian brain mode where the only thing that matters is what's gonna get 'em high. I'll bet every one of 'em is haunted by a ghost. Every killer.

"You may not believe in evil, but like I told you, it breathed on me and whispered in my damn ear. I guess it's as real as you want it to be. I did some dancing with the devil, and he stepped on my toes real hard."

"Do you truly believe a Satan exists?"

"I dated her for awhile in the late 70s. She could light candles with her tongue, and silver bullets bounced off her like cotton balls. Seriously, in my way of thinking, you can't believe in one without believing in the other. Good and evil. Simple math, Son.

"One night in Los Angeles, I was really raining inside. I was in a bad depression that wouldn't lift no matter what I tried. And by tried, I mean I took the usual chemical combinations I'd always counted on before, and they didn't take. I'd done some praying, but it felt like I was talking to the wall, you know?

"All I could think to do was drink myself to sleep, so I started on it. The more I drank, the deeper down I went. Then the rage showed up, and it brought friends. I screamed at God. I'd had enough of the pain and enough of the empty prayers, and I did some talking to the other team to see if he had a better offer. I ain't making this up, but just then we lost all power in our band house. Everything went black, and all I could hear was a storm moving in.

"A film of fear covered me, and the hair on the back of my neck about jumped off my head. I was sweating, but chilled to the bone. I had this split second where I knew what I was playing with was as dangerous as it gets. It scared the hell outta me, no pun intended, and I spent the next hour under blankets.

"I half expected that demon that visited me as a kid to show up, but the evil force I felt that night was bigger and more powerful. It terrified me, and I was powerless to fight it. All of a sudden, this howling wind rose up outside that sounded like a freight train, and just like that, it was gone.

"The lights came back on, and the first thing I saw was a crucifix we had hanging on the wall. In my eyes, it was ten feet tall. I decided then and there no matter how bad things got, I somehow would try to trust God, even though I wasn't close to Him. That even though things didn't make sense to me, I was gonna believe that somehow I was gonna be okay.

"A calm came over me, and I slept like a baby for ten hours straight. When I woke up, all I could think about was how foolish I'd been. And then it occurred to me how lonely I really was on the inside. Hungry for a faith I could hang my hat on. I thought of the demon I saw as a kid, and the hovering, powerful force I'd encountered that evening. I tried to put it all together and couldn't.

The puzzle pieces kept falling off the table.

"It wasn't long after that I started some therapy, and worked myself through some of the rain. You see, it was time to unlearn a whole bunch of stuff I'd learned from wounded folks. The best therapists hand you an eraser, and it's up to you to do the rubbing."

Slim finished the coffee and shuffled to the kitchen for more. He brought me back a tall glass of water that tasted better than any water I'd ever had. For some reason, I suddenly really missed cigarettes. I'd quit over a year ago.

Slim returned to his chair.

"It's really about hitting bottom, and you don't hit bottom until you get done digging. There were times in my life where I thought I'd hit my bottom, but I still had a shovel in my hands. Down the road, I was finally able to toss my shovel into the pit I'd just climbed out of. Filled the damn thing up with dirt and moved on.

"I've had my share of emotional earthquakes in this life, Son, but I ain't never veered toward the other team's path. Evil is real, and I've seen and felt enough of it to both hate and respect it. Scares me to this day to think I almost opened my door to it all. Let's have another question."

"Storytelling comes so easily for you, Slim. I've always admired people who could spin a captivating tale with seemingly no effort. Where do you think you picked up this ability?"

"The best story tellers are the ones who don't let the words get in the way, and I ain't there yet. The best storyteller I ever knew was a fella by the name of Shrug, who was from too many places to name just one. I met Shrug through my grandfather, as they were epic pals. Shrug rode the trains back and forth across the country for twenty years or more, and he knew more about sizing folks up and down than anybody. It's what kept him alive and friendly with everyone.

"He was as peaceful as a peach, but nobody crossed him on account of his skill with the blade he always kept near. He could read you like a book in fifteen seconds and give you what for in thirty…and then tell you a five-minute story that'd take most folks an hour to tell.

"He always said, 'You don't need the vegetables and potato on this one… only the meat.'

"Shrug only loved one woman his whole life, and she never knew a bit about it. She was married to a paper hanger who was in and outta prison their entire marriage. When Shrug would talk about her, I swear his eyes would change color. It was like he kept that certain color just for her, you know? I felt so sorry for him about it, but he set me straight on that like he did just about everything else.

"'Don't cry for me, Slimster,' he once said to me with his gravelly voice, while cooking us dinner over a campfire. 'Some people just do better on their own, and I like being with me. I was married once, but I got tired of always being in the doghouse. When it came to that woman, there was no such thing as a misdemeanor. They were all felonies.'

"Half the stories I ever tried to tell him were stopped by his raised hand, and he'd always say, 'Just the meat, Slimster. Just the meat.'

"Everything I ever knew about storytelling, I learned from that man."

I cocked my head to the side. "Was that his real name? Shrug…?"

"I think it might have been Susan. No, Brenda."

"More of your undeniable humor," I countered.

"To tell you the truth, he never told me what it was. Everyone just called him Shrug because that's what he was always doing.

"He once told me, 'Life isn't easy for anyone, Slim, but it can get pretty darn simple. It's all about accepting things as they are. Acceptance can be the answer to any problem. There is no fight in acceptance. Just peace.'

"I asked him once, 'Shrug? How do you find God's will?'

"'I get up and ask for His guidance, and then I start moving around to see what happens. When I hit a wall, I turn left.'

"Meanwhile, I was the kind of guy that would come to a wall and do everything in my power to get over it, around it, under it. You name it. I'd fight that damn wall with all the vehemence I could summon. If I run into a wall today, I simply turn left. Because of this, I end up where I was meant to be in the first place."

Slim spread his arms out wide, then raised them above his head. A yawn, then another. Fatigue hovered over both of us. Slim threw me a jacket and invited me to join him on the porch to let the cold slap our cheeks a bit. Two rocking chairs. I could see my breath.

"Was Shrug a drinker?"

"Hell yeah, but he gave it up. When I met him, he hadn't had a drop in twenty years. Believe this or not, Shrug was a pilot in the United States Air Force, and flew the big jets and such. He told me he had to either give up the booze or flying. He retired sober. I asked him why he never took an airline job when he got out, and he told me he found life exceedingly more compelling on the ground, and that he'd always planned on drinking again.

"'But you've been sober for over twenty years,' I told him. 'You really think you might drink again?'

"'I don't know, Slimster. That's why I keep moving like I do. I never know if a town is gonna make me thirsty.'"

"That's a great way to look at sobriety for anyone. I feel badly that I made the assumption Shrug was a hobo, and a drunk."

"Shrug was both. He just loved his lifestyle, and I loved him for it. I was never sure what he did for money, but he always had it, and always shared it with folks who didn't. A guy he travelled with told me Shrug walked away from huge family money. He told me Shrug's daddy owned a whole bunch of oil wells in Texas. I started to ask Shrug about it once, and he stopped me with just a look in his eyes.

"'A man's history is his to tell if he feels like it, Slimster, and I don't feel like it,' he said.

"I can still hear his raspy voice in my head. I can smell the cheap aftershave he always wore, and see the non-filter cigarette always tucked in the corner of his mouth. This may sound strange, but whenever I was with Shrug, I felt I was sitting on my momma's lap. He made it all seem so simple, and like everything was already okay. Even the stars burned brighter when I'd sit by his fire, and I don't know how he managed it, but the smoke always drifted my way.

"I've heard it said a man is lucky to be able to count his good friends on one hand. Well, whenever I counted mine up, old Shrug was always my first finger.

He died riding a train some years back, and I heard he left a pile of money to his estranged daughter who missed out on so much by shunning him. Shrug carried a smothering regret regarding his lost little girl. It pushed down on his shoulders.

"He was definitely one of the wealthiest men I ever met, and I ain't talking money here. He had a peace inside of him that warmed any room he was in, and when his eyes twinkled, you knew you were in the presence of something sacred and holy. I used to stand real close so I could absorb him.

"'If you want a hug, Slimster, all you have to do is say so,' he'd say.

"To say he was an enigma is to aim way too damn low. He was something else, and I miss him very much. That's enough of a chill for me. Let's go back inside and warm us up some cocoa."

Chapter Nine

"You look deep in thought, Slim."

"For some reason, I got this gal on my mind. You ever hear the phrase 'Half hellfire and half holy water?'"

"I don't believe I ever have," I answered.

"Well, that was my gal pal Donnita. She divorced a doctor from Lawrence, Kansas and moved to Los Angeles to be 'discovered' with the rest of us miscreants. Her first job was a substitute teacher at a grade school. Then she dealt cards for the Hells Angels. After that, she learned how to cut hair and got a gig in Santa Monica. When that bored her, she ran a brothel in Laguna Beach. When that fell apart, she took up street preaching, and that led her back to school to be a therapist.

"She called herself a mind mender.

"I met her around 1981 during one of my treks into madness. I was court ordered to see her by a lady judge who took pity on me. I went into that situation kicking and screaming. I was back in court due to bad luck and an unfortunate series of misunderstandings. I thought I was doing so well on my own. Never mind the fact I'd been up for four days snorting speed and wrote a suicide note to my agent at the time.

"Anyways, she was good to me, and it took a long damn while, but I trusted her. I trusted her enough to share how much pain I was really in, and the fear that raced through me like electric blood. I decided I was done being a victim. I was done running from the fear and pain. I went to war with it. I became a wound warrior. I decided to be bigger than it was, you know? I started doing what she told me to do in between sessions, no matter what my nay saying noggin' thought about it.

"Then I started learning from her, and just when I felt like we were really onto something, she cut me loose after I went sweet on her."

Slim sipped his cocoa, and I picked up my steaming cup from the table. He had a little boy grin on his face that morphed into a full-blown face party.

"I couldn't help myself. She was the first woman I ever knew who called me on my bullshit. It was simple as that. She backed me into a corner I finally couldn't talk or think my way out of, and got me in touch with a whole mess of anger I'd been hiding from myself."

I leaned forward. "I've heard it said depression is anger turned inward."

"Let me tell you, when I finally uncorked that anger pressure cooker, it about blew my chest open. Rage I could never put words to. It's the kind of poison that eats folks up from the inside out and kills 'em dead. No matter how much booze you throw on it, it keeps burning. She put me face-to-face with it, and after it cooled down, it became one of my best teachers.

"I've heard it said change happens when the pain of staying where you are becomes greater than the pain it takes to change. I never changed things up when I thought it was a good idea to, you know? I changed when my butt was on fire.

"I can't begin to tell you how much I hated emotional pain, and I ran from it my whole life. Donnita helped me see that though the ups always feel better, the downs are way better teachers. She taught me there is no pain in growth and no pain in change. The pain comes from the resistance to the growth, and the resistance to the change. We do inherit our parent's shadows, but we can also give 'em the slip.

"She hooked me up with another mind mender, but it didn't take for me, you know? He was this Ichabod Crane-looking cat, who was always blowing his nose and looking at his damn watch. He'd roll his eyes at me when I'd talk about my dope and booze habits. I was just being honest. He was just being judge and jury on me. You can't pick your parents, but you can sure pick your psycho…therapist, and I fired Ichabod after the second visit. He blew his nose and looked at his watch.

"Besides, I'd managed to climb outta the hole by then, and was feeling a whole lot better. I'll tell you, it was the anger work that lifted the depression. I would've never believed it if I hadn't gone through it myself. It was like I could feel it lift, layer by layer as I put words and motion to the anger inside.

"Donnita and I ran into each other some years later, and we sort of became pals. Just pals, as she had a half-brained, half-baked protective brother who could bench press a Buick. His name was Francis, but I called him Cocoa, on account of all he ate was Cocoa Puffs, and he was cuckoo from head to toenail.

"Cocoa took me aside one night, pushed me up against a wall and whispered in my ear, 'I like you, Slim. You want me to like you. If you mess around with my sister, I won't like you no more.'

"That wouldn't have bothered me as much if he hadn't held a carpet knife to my throat and jammed his knee in my crotch. Romance was contraindicated, Son.

"Cocoa never could keep a job, but decided one day to get into the banking business. So he robbed one. Then two. Then, he got so damned confident about the process, he robbed two in one afternoon. Well, he got caught, and last I heard of him, he was in San Quentin and could bench press two Buicks.

"Donnita and I almost had our time, and we circled each other like hungry wolves. It would've been part epic love and part Greek tragedy, but we both somehow knew better. Looking back, I wouldn't have been ready for a strong woman in my life, and I had some heavy lifting to do before I'd get anywhere near healthy enough for a go at love."

Slim rose from his chair and shuffled over to the fireplace to add two small logs, dancing to a song only he could hear. He was animated. Charged by some ancient battery. I wanted some of what he had.

"She taught me to stop calling 'em nervous breakdowns, and start calling 'em nervous breakthroughs. She told me it's a breakdown only if it doesn't lead to positive change. The pain that leads to breakthroughs is really a gift, and the admission price to true freedom. It gets us to make changes we wouldn't normally make, and to take roads we wouldn't likely travel otherwise. It's a down and dirty momentum grabber, Son.

"She also taught me how important it is to be in the here and now, where the magic is. When you think on it some, it's really the only place for the mind to be that makes any sense. Man, I used to meditate like a maniac. Two, three hours a day, and the only thing keeping me from healing…was the dope, and I knew it.

"She told me the first step to enlightenment is to lighten up. And to somehow get to a place where I was grateful for everything I had and had been through. I knew that to be true, but drunk and high I couldn't get there. And I always knew sober was the way to go, Son. Let's be clear on that. I knew what I was, and I paid a hell of a price protecting my medicine.

"When I heard she'd passed, I dropped to my damn knees and I could barely get air down my throat. I kept blinking, but it wouldn't go away. Our movie together started playing in my mind, and it didn't shut off for a couple weeks. I don't do funerals and weddings unless I'm forced at gunpoint, but I attended her service and watched her disappear into the ground after the family left. I felt so guilty I was still there, and she had to go. She took impeccable care of herself, and I was a damn nightmare. I was mad about her passing for some time, Son. Mostly at God."

"What happened to her, Slim?"

"She died from a bee sting. Anaphylactic shock. The most powerful woman I ever met got killed by a bug. Lady Achilles. I still can't believe it to this day. She was unshakable, you know? One look in her eyes and you just knew you were gonna somehow be okay. That woman backed every inner demon I had into a corner, and I still hear her words when I need 'em most.

"'Change the way you see things and the things you see will change. Your reaction to the problem is the problem.'

"She had a million of 'em. Well, ten that helped save my life anyways."

"I see on your face that much of this is painful to talk about for you," I noted.

"It just gets me raining inside, Son. Opening up these drawers reminds me how important these folks were in my life. Sometimes I wish I could go back and tell 'em how much they meant to me. I wasn't in the habit of doing that, and I never ever expected to run outta time. If I've learned one thing in this life, it's that you gotta grab the hand of life when it offers it to you. I walked right past a lot of handshakes in my life, Son, and today I grab that hand without hesitation.

"Let's lighten things up again."

"You go wherever you want to go, and I'll be right there with you, my teacher."

Slim opened the scrapbook and beckoned me over as he flipped through pages. He landed on one, spun the book to me, and my eyes were drawn to a thin, full-bearded man holding a heaping plate of steak and potatoes. My mind drew a smile on his face, hid by mounds of facial hair.

"My favorite songwriter is where we're going now. You ain't never heard of him. Scooter 'The Shooter' McManahan is what he called himself. We called him Coon on account of he ate everybody's food and then some. I first knew him as a Jesus chainsaw sculptor in Nashville, and he couldn't play a lick of music, but tunes popped in his head like fireworks, and he could fit words together like nobody.

"'The Empress of Soul' herself, Gladys Knight, tried to hire him to write songs with her, and he told her thanks, but no thanks. He said he couldn't take that kind of pressure, and that he was happy just where he was.

"Man, we all wanted to slap him upside the head, but it wouldn't have done any good. When Coon's mind settled on a price, dynamite wouldn't move it an inch. I once tried to talk him into marketing his sculptures, and I might as well have been trying to move tectonic plates. He liked to make 'em for folks for fun and for free. I didn't have an acquaintance with that kind of thinking back then.

"He could write melodies and hooks that would haunt you from hell to breakfast. I'd be working on a song, getting nowhere, and he'd be on the couch watching television. I'd just about give up on it, when I'd hear these words coming outta his mouth, riding on a habit-forming melody I couldn't have found if I'd driven over it.

"Then he'd forget it and move on to something else. I finished a lot of songs like that, and got credit for a whole bunch of his ideas. I listen to some of those songs today and smile and shake my head at his words and melodies. He never cared a lick about any of it. He loved his chainsaw, cigars, and fallen women. Not in that order.

"Coon died September 26, 1992, and we never got the full story on that one. All anyone could find out was he went with a chainsaw in his hand and a cigar hanging outta his mouth. And he never took a drink of alcohol his entire life. But he smoked weed. Weed he grew in his basement and cross-pollinated with peyote buttons. The first time I tried it, I got so high I spent three hours in a state of paraplegia, Son. My brain and legs couldn't conjugate.

"Then he just quit. He threw everything away, and he was done. He said it was time to lower his landing gear and meet life on life's terms. I admired that, but not enough to go off unhinged and give up my medicines, you know?

"Man, he was a cool cat. He once told me he helped Jim Weatherly write 'I'd rather live in his world then live without him, in mine' in Midnight Train To Georgia after I told him it was one of my favorite lines. I was never sure if he was pulling on my leg or not."

"He composed songs for other artists?" I asked.

"He wrote all kinds of songs that artists recorded, but he was what you'd call a ghostwriter, and his name stayed off paper of any kind. He wrote a handful of country hits, but he'd never tell me which ones.

"I know he made a pile of money on account of the house he lived in. It had eight bedrooms, a movie and game room, three living rooms, a kitchen you could raise chickens in, and a six-car garage. He was always taking wayward folks in and letting 'em stay on for a while. The band lived and rehearsed there for a few months. We did nonstop drugs and booze, played a lot of great music, and got intense tans beside his cross-shaped pool.

"Oh, another thing about Coon. He had a wood shop where he did his chainsaw work…in the nude."

"You have got to be kidding me." All types of mental pictures flooded my mind.

"God's honest truth. Naked as a drunk prom date after midnight. His work was fascinating, but I could never watch for long. I'd get to laughing, then he'd start laughing, and it would mess things up for him. He said cutting in the nude like that helped him think.

"Well, it plum worked, I'll tell you that. He could carve out a highly-detailed Jesus statue in no time. I was always scared he'd get slivers in his pecker, or cut it off. He wielded that damn saw like it was a paintbrush. Unbelievable is what it was."

"I cannot imagine operating a chainsaw with protective clothing, let alone naked."

"I've never understood how folks can draw, paint, sculpt and such. I can barely draw stick figures, and Coon put emotion on wood…with a damn chainsaw.

"He'd always compliment me on my guitar playing and singing, and I'd just wave him off. He called me an artist and told me to be proud of my talents. That meant a whole lot to me, coming from him.

"He taught me a lot about looking differently at folks. He'd look at a piece of wood and see Jesus underneath it all. He did the same thing with people, and I'll never forget that about him.

"He once said to me, 'Slim, you gotta look past what folks are saying, and pay attention to what they're doing. People tend to talk a lot tougher than they really are. Everyone has an epic battle going on, so don't judge people if you can help it. You never know what someone's going through on the inside.'

"Anyways, he was another angel that helped me grow and spread my wings."

Slim stood, brushed something off his t-shirt, stretched his arms and back, and excused himself to the restroom. We'd both been so engaged, our bladders had remained silent out of respect. He returned, and I followed suit.

I looked out the window. The sun would be rising soon. One hell of a night.

Chapter Ten

"Okay. Where do we go from here?" I asked Slim. I so wanted to ask him about the story he refused to tell me but just as words were to escape my mouth, his burst through the door.

"Lake Tahoe," he said. "I can't recall the year, but the band was busted up after touring non-stop for five years, and I was on fumes again. I was with a cat we all called Squish after he had a two-ton retaining wall collapse on him and survived. Never mind the fact his spine was crooked and his skull was caved in on one side. When he walked, he looked like he was stepping over things with his right leg. I admired him—he never let any of that slow him down, and he never felt sorry for himself for a damn second. He was just glad to still be in the game, you know?

"Squish tried to talk me into a gambling binge after he told me he'd come up with a card counting scheme for black jack. I told him he was nuttier than a weasel with a wheelbarrow, and I wouldn't give him one single dime.

"And then we snorted some coke and had a little rum. We snorted more coke. Had some more rum. He gave me his pitch again, and I shot him down. There was no way I was gonna risk my hard-earned money on some half-baked gambling scheme. No way.

"We snorted more coke. Drank more rum. Smoked a joint. Popped a couple white crosses to really wind things up. Then, about fifteen minutes later, all the chemicals hit maximum potency like a giant cerebral gong.

"The next thing I knew, I was sitting in the parking lot of the High Sierra Casino, counting out the cash I had on hand. He had a few thousand dollars on him, and we strutted into the joint with ten thousand bucks. We were gonna teach that place a lesson, Son.

"We came out of the blocks strong, and pretty soon we were up eight grand. I told him that was good enough and we needed to split before our luck turned. He waved me off with this wide-eyed look and dug in deeper. His plan was to make fifty grand, and like a damned fool I thought he might get there. Squish played for twelve straight hours. At one point, he was up twenty thousand, at another he was down five. That's how it went. Up and down, up and down. And then, way down.

"For most of the time Squish played cards, I had myself glued to an electric cocaine machine."

"Electric cocaine machine?" I asked.

"A slot machine. I started with a hundred bucks, and at one point had it up to a couple grand, but I'd get bored and start feeding the damn thing again. Next thing I knew, I was back to a hundred, and I lost that playing roulette. It ain't surprising these billion-dollar casinos keep getting built, huh?"

"Their odds are very good, and our odds, for the most part, are very bad," I managed.

"He lost it all, and we ran outta everything. One of us got the bright idea to sell the car to buy some dope to sell and to hitch down to Phoenix. The entrepreneur spirit was alive and kicking in us. We figured when we got to Phoenix, we could make about five grand on the dope, buy more dope, and triple our money.

"We made it to Phoenix with $500, a lot of dope, and nowhere to unload it. So, we bought a $400 car and left for New Mexico where Squish had a girlfriend we could stay with. The whole time, we snorted coke and speed, and drank enough booze to float a raft. We weren't exactly on our game, Son, but we knew if we could get to New Mexico, we knew a cat who could unload all the dope and set us up in business to make some serious dough. All we had to do was get to Santa Fe."

"Were you really that broke at the time?"

"Hell, no. I had piles of money in a bank in LA, and an investment portfolio you likely wouldn't believe. I was along for the ride and the adventure of it all, Son. I wanted to see how far we could get with only what we had on us. It was a game to me, and Squish had no idea I was awfully damn flush at the time.

"To make a long story easier to digest, we got caught speeding with two unlicensed handguns, a couple hundred hits of LSD, a pound of marijuana, a big bag of speed, and a hitchhiker with a federal warrant hanging over her pretty little head for grand larceny. I was the damn driver. When we got popped, Squish and Ms. Grand Larceny were naked in the back seat, fogging up the windows and such.

"We were in deeper than the periscope would reach, Son.

"We got damn lucky with the lawyer we drew, and he got most of the evidence thrown out on account of a Miranda technicality. The judge shook his head at us and asked us if we wanted to go to chemical dependency treatment in Santa Fe instead of jail.

"We thought he was truly on to something.

"So, we got clean and sober for the justice system. I spent the first week in paper slippers, shaking like a pissed off earthquake, under medical supervision while I detoxed. The next three weeks I was with the group, and I gotta tell you, everything the counselors were telling me made a whole lot of sense. But that didn't stop my mind from swatting away their feedback like tennis balls.

"The whole experience gave me twenty-one days to rest up and get ready for another run. We did yoga, got massages, lifted weights and ate like kings. They even had a sauna and indoor pool. I got physically healthy and gained twenty pounds. Hell, I even quit smoking cigarettes for a bit, I felt so damned good.

"My counselor was an ex-marine who'd went belly up in Vietnam over dope, and he and I hit it off real well. The day we were introduced, he bear-hugged me and showed me five bullet wound scars he had in his belly. He told me he was a walking miracle, and that the same God that saved him was watching out for me. I thanked him kindly not to hug me again, and he laughed and did it anyway. He was a splendid human being, and gave his all to teach me the good stuff.

"And, I fell ass over teakettle in love with a fortune telling gypsy junkie from Seattle named Lilly Bean, who took one look at my palm and broke down in tears. I asked her what had her all exercised, and she told me she saw a very dark presence hovering around me. I stopped breathing, and searched her face for a hint she might be kidding. She wasn't."

Slim stared down at his palm. He stretched and flexed his fingers, as if to change the existing lines and alter his future. He laughed, closed his fingers into a fist, and pounded it on his knee.

"'A dark presence?" I asked. 'What kind of dark presence?'

"'The worst kind,' she whispered. 'The kind that wants to destroy your will and take everything you've got inside.'

"'It must be a female then,' I said, halfheartedly.

"'It's nothing to joke about, Slim. You have someone…or something, floating around you. It feels like a very dark energy, and you should probably see a priest. Do you have a strong belief in God?'

"'I have a strong belief that I need a cigarette, and a stronger belief that you and I need to shed some clothes and get acquainted,' I answered. My attempt at levity was likely diminished by the look I must've had on my face.

"'I'm serious, Slim! Do you believe in God?'

"'I do, but I seem to have misplaced His contact information.'

"Lilly Bean was adamant I get my prayer life in order, and was convinced I needed to rid myself of this presence before harm came to me.

"I again assured her I would be okay, and calmed her down. In the back of my mind, something stirred and tried to make its way into my consciousness, but I shoved it back down like I'd always done. Was she talking about my night visitor all those years ago? I didn't wanna know. I didn't want any of it to be real. The child in me shuttered.

"She also told me I was her hubby in a previous life, and she'd been looking high and low for me in this one. She also told me I wasn't long for this world, and that I would probably die in a plane crash.

"I liked her immediately."

"How could you not?"

"She was my higher power in that treatment center, I'll tell you that much. We couldn't keep our hands off each other, and got caught having sex twice. We were told if it happened again, we'd be thrown outta the place, which I knew wouldn't happen to me as I was court ordered there. Well, it happened to her when we got caught again, and my distraction from everything going on inside me was gone. I was stuck with me, Son, and I wasn't good company back then.

"I jumped through their hoops, played their game, and said all the right things a born again addict is supposed to say…and they cut me loose after spending thirty days in the joint. Hell, the judge even bought it, and I got off with a suspended sentence and time served. Squish signed on for another thirty days. He truly liked the taste of sobriety, and wanted some more of it.

"Silly bastard.

"Well, I beelined for Lilly Bean once I was free, and we spent the better part of two years chasing each other's mental illnesses around Seattle. We were like two giant pistons. When I was up, she'd be down, and vice versa. We never seemed to be okay at the same time. She did manage to stay off heroin, and probably the only reason the yoga, the meditations, and vegan diet didn't take for me was…that I didn't.

"About two years in, she really went over the falls. She sat nude at the dinner table for three damn days, and didn't say a word. She even peed in a bucket so she wouldn't have to move too far. I did all the songs and dances I knew at the time, but I couldn't get her to budge. I knew it was way past dangerous when I tore a mouthful of tranquilizers from her mouth. I called the oxygen squad, and they took to her to a psychiatric facility.

"I felt bad about abandoning her, but that's just what I did. I packed my things and hightailed it down the road. I don't even remember where I went, but I couldn't stay, you know? Watching her decompensate like she did was too damn close for me. I had to get the hell away from her before I caught some of what she had.

"I still carry a charm she gave me, and I ain't never been on a plane since the day we met. I sure hope Lilly Bean's doing well these days. She was a dandy, and she danced all over my heart and stole it one winter. I finally got it back, but boy did it have some dents."

"Would you say you have a love/hate relationship with drugs and alcohol?"

"I loved 'em, Son. They were my medicine. My religion. I took pride in being a dope fiend, and I was damn good at it. I used to think they saved me from going batshit crazy, you know? Saved me from the fear that was circling my soul. Maybe they did, I dunno. What I do know is they were my solution for just about everything, and in the beginning, the solution seemed to work awfully damn good.

"For a very long time I couldn't go ten minutes not being high. I couldn't stand being sober, Son. Life bored the hell outta me. Everything was in black and white and I was a Technicolor kind of cat. I didn't go anywhere or do anything unless I was properly polluted, you know?

"But along the way, they just quit working the way I needed them to. The fear the dope and booze had held at bay was suddenly front and center in my mind, and I couldn't shake it. Next thing I know, the drugs are giving me anxiety attacks, and the depressions are unbearable. So, I'd decide to quit everything.

"When you get past the detoxing, getting sober is as simple as a pimple pop. Staying sober is an entirely different donkey. Dope is just a symptom of a much deeper disease. Take away the symptom, and the disease gets real mad. It fires up and shows up in other areas of your life.

"The key to getting sober is to not pick up the damn drug or drink. I think the key to staying sober is you gotta find another solution. For me, it had to be spiritual. And you gotta listen to the body when it's whispering to you. If you don't, it will start to scream, and by then, sometimes it's too damn late.

Simple, not easy.

"Another thing I know is that sobriety gives you everything that dope and booze promises to give you but never does. It just takes time and effort is all. That one was a tough pill to swallow for this wounded warrior. I'm an immediate gratification kind of cat."

"Do you believe drugs and alcohol are inherently bad?" I asked.

"I got no beef with either, and I don't judge folks who might imbibe. Most folks don't have a problem with either. It's the ten percent who are addicts who get destroyed by the stuff. For me, dope and booze weren't my problem, just how I coped with it. They flip a switch inside of me that most folks don't have, and as long as my switch stays on the off position, I'm a happy cat."

Slim stared into the fire, and it was apparent he had gone somewhere else and arrived back in the living room. After a time, he turned to face me. He spread his arms wide, and a serious look flowed across his face.

"I don't mean to turn this thing between you and me into some sobriety pitch, and I ain't no expert on any of it. It just wouldn't be right if I didn't talk about the very thing that saved my life, and if I didn't honor the angels who helped me along the way. I guess I feel pretty strong about giving folks a rope to climb outta the pit with. The only reason I'm here talking to you today is somebody threw a rope down to me, you know?

"For some reason, I've got this cat on my mind and I can't shake him, so I guess he's up for discussion. I was good at doing drugs and such, but the best at it I ever knew was a fella we called Skuzz, who never showered or changed his clothes. Back when I first moved to New Orleans, Skuzz was the go-to guy for dope, and he popped LSD like some folks pop breath mints. I once saw him snort a line of cocaine the size of a garden hose, slam ten shots of tequila, and casually light a joint on his way out the door to go do his laundry.

"We all just stood there while our eyebrows disappeared over the top of our heads.

"Skuzz used to say, 'I have a PhD in chemical abuse. Just call me Dr. Dope.'

"The first and last time I dropped acid with him, I got stuck in a bathroom at a house party—the door kept moving. They found me curled up in the fetal position in my underwear, trying to cut through the wall with a bar of soap. I was damn glad the search party had arrived.

"I later found out I'd been in there for four hours. Then, I spent a good part of the rest of the evening and early morning convinced demons were in a van in the driveway, and that a house cat was reading my thoughts. I might've been right about the cat, but Skuzz and I checked that van from bumper to bumper, and there wasn't a demon to be found. I did, however, become convinced my lungs were on fire, and tried to smoke an ice cream bar to put it out. Skuzz got quite a kick outta that one. Hell, he even lit it for me.

"Skuzz finally managed to bring me in for a landing with some smooth talking and a Quaalude. I'll bet you diamonds to donuts, I drank thirty beers and smoked a hundred cigarettes that night. When I was tripping, I couldn't get enough of whatever my body wanted.

"Sounds like big fun, huh?"

"Thankfully, I've never enjoyed that particular brand of fun," I commented.

"Yeah, some of it was a real blast. Like the time Skuzz and I had a rum,

LSD, and opium smoking contest, and then went golfing. We played pretty well the first two holes until the acid kicked in, and the next thing we knew, we got kicked off the golf course and arrested for skinny dipping in a water hazard close to the clubhouse.

"I have no recollection of being body-slammed and handcuffed, but I was. I have no recollection of soiling myself in the back of a police car, but I did. I have no recollection of screaming and crying like a baby in a jail cell, but I saw the tape. I also have no recollection of being shackled to a bed for making suicidal gestures and comments at the top of my lungs, but again, I saw the tape.

"Skuzz was real proud for breaking the previous blood alcohol level record for that police precinct, and he had a pleasant stay playing cards and sleeping. Hell, he even liked the food. He talked me halfway back to sanity in our jail cell, and time took me the rest of the way.

"He always knew how to handle someone's dope trip when it went south, and he was inordinately patient. I think he got a kick out of it. It was like a sport to him. To see how messed up he could get folks, and then try to figure out how to walk 'em through it all. It was like a chess game with human pieces.

"One of the things I remember about Skuzz is whenever you'd ask him how he was doing, he'd answer, 'I am fabulous. But don't worry, I'll get better.'

"Skuzz never had a hangover or a bad trip as long as I knew him. He'd crash on our couch once in a while, but he'd always bounce up in the morning like it was nobody's business. The rest of us would wander around in a stupor until we got medicated properly.

"Sad story about Skuzz, though. He went on a formaldehyde and PCP trip, and only purchased a one-way ticket. They said he walked through a plate glass window at a convenience store carrying a display stand full of sunglasses.

"Hell, I guess you can never have too many pairs of sunglasses."

"Shades for all occasions, I always say," I offered.

"Skuzz took five bullets and wound up in a wheelchair."

"Tragic," I noted.

"The thing I'll always remember about Skuzz was a time he pulled me aside after a gig with a sad song playing in his eyes.

"'Slim,' he whispered, 'I need to say something to you.'

"'Well, you'd better say it,' I said.

"'I haven't been thinking right lately. I just can't seem to pull it together, man.'

"'Maybe you could slow down on the dope some,' I offered. 'Quit breaking world records and such.'

"'Yeah, I know. I spent five hours trying to think my way out of this sadness, man, and I can't shake it. I just can't change my mind with my mind, man.'"

It seemed to take Slim a few seconds to return to the room. Highly caffeinated, I broke the uncomfortable five-second silence.

"You can't change the mind you've got with the mind you've got. My father used to say that to me."

"Ain't that the God's honest truth, Son? Trying to fix a sick mind with a sick mind is like trying to pick up a rug you're standing on. And I've never been able to think my way into better action. I've always had to act my way into better thinking.

"Nowadays, whenever I got a big decision to make, answers come from two places. If an answer comes from my head, I ignore it. If it comes from someplace deep inside of me, that's the one I pick. Sometimes it takes time to figure out where they're coming from. My mind's usually got an agenda based on fear. The voices deep inside me have an agenda for my highest good. Just a peaceful, simple path, you know? I dunno if that made sense to you, but it sure rings my bell."

"It makes perfect sense to me," I said. "I think you're speaking of the difference between conscious and unconscious thought, and how different they can be."

"I hear you clucking, Big Chicken. You've got a good way with words, Son. Maybe you oughta think about starting your own religion. Make a hundred million bucks and buy an island."

"I'd have to come up with a southern accent and really bad hair."

"That's all doable. You gotta come up with a catchy name, though. The Church of the Open Wallet. Something like that.

"You are a very twisted man, Slim Chance, and I'm quite fond of your erratic rhetoric."

"I ain't exactly sure what an erratic rhetoric is, but I'll go ahead and take it as a compliment."

Slim stared up at the ceiling and mouthed some words.

I squinted as if that would help me hear them. Was it a prayer? He took a deep breath, closed his eyes.

"I hope wherever Skuzz is, he's doing okay. I hope he's got somebody in his life he can put first. Maybe he got clean and found peace. Maybe he found someone to help him change his mind. Someone to push his chair.

"We all need each other in this life, Son. It ain't supposed to be a solo flight."

Chapter Eleven

I leaned back in my chair and asked Slim, "Do you consider yourself to be a religious man?"

"I consider that to be none of your damned business!"

"Whoa now, I didn't mean to…"

"Ease back on the freak throttle, Son, I'm just having some fun with you. I usually make a point to avoid discussing religion or politics with anyone. One thing I can say about politics is, I'm for term limits. If a politician can't steal enough money in eight years, he ain't fit for office.

"I consider myself to be spiritual, not religious, and I don't make judgmental comments on none of it. Folks need to be free to believe what and how they want without me eyeballing 'em. I ain't no expert, and neither are they. As far as I'm concerned, nobody still breathing sees the entire picture."

"My father explained the difference between religion and spirituality to me this way. He said, "I can go to church and spend the entire time thinking about fishing, or I can go fishing and spend the entire time thinking about God.""

"Yeah, that about sums it up for me too. I do my best praying with birds, bees, and trees around me. And praying is simple for me. I start with a thank you. I ask God to help me be of maximum service to Him, and for knowledge of His will for me. I don't ask for nothing specific for me or anybody else. I figure God's got a better handle on that, you know? It's a daily practice for me. And I gotta take good care of myself. I feel closest to Him when I'm closest to me."

"Do you consider yourself to be a Christian?" I wondered.

"What I am is a distant relative to being the type of Christian most folks identify with. Jesus and I have an understanding, and I love His style. It seems to me, and I ain't no expert, Christ shows up in nearly all world religions to deliver good, orderly direction. Then folks took what He said and bastardized it to fit their own agenda. Like I said, I ain't no expert."

"It sounds as if you have little to no trust of organized religion," I noted.

"I don't trust anything that claims to be the one right way. That's tyranny, Son, and that ain't what my God's about. My God is a big enough umbrella for everyone on the planet to stand under. We're all God's kids. If one of us is His kid, then all of us are. If one of us ain't, then none of us are.

"I will tell you, I finally found a God I could live with after I ditched the one that folks told me acted like my old man. I changed my mind. I threw away everything I'd ever been taught about Him and started fresh by just talking to Him like you and I are now.

"And I found out I wasn't mad at Him—that's just where I had it pointed. My whole life, when things went right I blamed myself, and when things didn't go my way, I blamed Him. I finally decided to do what was put in front of me and trust the damn process. I got the hell outta the way. It took practice, but I started getting mad at the right things, at the right time, for the right reasons, and I didn't have to carry it around no more. I just dealt with it and moved on.

"Then, I started to practice being grateful. Before I knew it, I had a tank full of thankful, and like one of my favorite songwriters says, 'A thank you in a whisper beats a bottle full of please.'"

"I know that line. I've heard it recently. Is it yours?" I asked, curious.

"That it is, Son."

Slim seemed pleased to learn I knew his lyrics, and I felt like a student receiving an A from his favorite teacher. He rewarded me with more cocoa as the first sign of the coming sunrise scratched on the window.

"Anyways, for the first time in my life, I really tried prayer. I don't know if prayer changes God's mind, but it sure changes mine. Things started happening. Stuff that smelled like miracles. It was the beginning for me. He'd always been there, I just picked the wrong damn higher powers."

"Alcohol and drugs," I quickly offered.

"And money and women. I gave up the dope in 1994. I tried to cold turkey everything, but I got too sick and had to check into a detox unit. What almost killed me was coming off the damn booze."

"Yes. I know alcohol withdrawal can cause heart arrhythmias, kidney and liver dysfunction, and can be quite lethal."

"I found that out the hard way when I went into delirium tremens and a couple seizures. Heroin hurt me too, but they limped me off that with methadone. The rest of 'em sort of fell off, you know? I've been clean ever since."

"What was the hardest for you to quit?" I asked.

"Hmmm, I'd say it was a redhead named Billie Jo Barnhart in 1979. She had one heck of a classy chassis, and lips as soft as a velvet pillow."

"I'll rephrase," I said. "What is the toughest drug you ever quit?"

"The toughest drug to quit is without question nicotine. I was a heavy smoker from the age of fifteen up. I quit 'em a ton of times, but I'd always pick 'em back up whenever something pulled my tail. So, I came up with this idea I'd switch to chewing tobacco, thinking how disgusting it was would make it easier to quit.

"Well, quitting chewing tobacco was harder than quitting cigarettes, but I finally got it done in 1997. I got it done again in 1998, 2000, and hopefully for the last time in 2006. They say once you get past the first couple days, you got it licked. They are wrong.

"Only thing I take today is an antidepressant on account of it keeps me outta the pit I've been in too many times before. I don't know what to tell you about the booze, and I don't expect you or anybody else to understand my lifetime experiment with it."

"You continued to consume alcohol after you gave up illegal drugs?"

"Yeah, I did. But I found out no matter how careful I pet it…it will still bite me. Bottom line is, we have an understanding, and I ain't had a drink in quite a spell. It's a day-to-day deal, Son. As long as I do what I know to do, I don't get thirsty. It's simple to keep it in remission, but not always easy.

"I got a buddy who studied chemical engineering and physics in college. He's got himself two master's degrees and a PhD. He's an alcoholic. He's damn proud of it. He's always working on a chemical concoction that will cure it. A pill he can take that'll let him drink normally.

"He once announced publically he'd discovered a cure for alcoholism, and he'd been restored to a social drinker. He even wrote a book, was invited on television shows, and got newspaper coverage. Everywhere he went, folks patted him on the back and wanted to know more about his magic pill.

"He got some traction, and the investment dough really started to roll in. He was selling his book like water bottles in the desert, and he told me once his drug got approved by the FDA and his company went public, he'd be on the cover of Forbes Magazine. All that was left was to wait for the fiscal feast.

"Until he got stupid drunk and drove his Jaguar through the window of a jewelry store in Van Nuys with a intoxicated thirteen year-old naked prostitute, a couple ounces of weed, an assault rifle, a big bag of crystal meth, and an ounce of Peruvian cocaine.

"That hurt his book sales.

"He's drunk himself outta jobs and marriages, houses, and children, and he still thinks he's the smartest guy in the room. That's the difference between him and me.

"I know I'm full of shit."

Slim belly-laughed, and I nervously joined him.

"Do you *really* think you're full of shit?" I asked.

"Naw. Hell, I used to be, Son, but I've been rehabilitated. There was a time when even I didn't know if I was telling the truth. You get so far away from yourself, you can't keep stories straight. I'd be standing behind my mouth, wondering what was gonna come out of it next. I don't miss those days. Trying to remember what I said and to who. Now, I tell the truth and I don't have to worry."

"In almost all situations I can think of, the truth is the preferential choice," I offered.

"That it is. I had to start telling it to myself before I could tell it to others. Since then, I've had a much easier go of it all. Like they say, KISS—keep it simple, stupid. Unnecessary complexity should be avoided at all costs, and telling lies is most certainly an unnecessary complexity.

"I did have a pal who said a certain amount of lying to oneself is crucial for survival. In my lifetime I've deluded myself about many things, and maybe it saved me for a time. I dunno? Some say we're only as sick as our secrets.

"I do get one hell of a kick outta this life, Son. My goal has always been to break as many happy records as I could, and that included doing some things most folks wouldn't think to do. I guess I had what you'd call uncommon sense.

"I also had a slight case of impulsivity."

"For example?" I asked.

"For example, I spent some time in Taos, New Mexico, and one day I was driving to the store when I saw this scantily-clad, shiny gal on the side of the road, holding her thumb to the sky. I pulled over beside her, rolled down my window, and gave her my best smile.

"'Where you going?' I asked her.

"'Utah. Can you help me?' she answered.

"'Well, I was just going for milk and cigarettes…but what the hell, I'll take you to Utah.'

"The next thing I knew, she had me living in some nudist colony just outside of Provo. It wasn't the best idea I ever came up with, since Margie gave me a venereal disease I couldn't get rid of, and I sunburned my private parts something fierce. Let me tell you, when your penis peels, it itches so bad you walk around on your damn tippy toes for a week.

"I felt weird enough as it was walking around nude like that. I spent the first three days covering up my little buddy. Some of those guys were hung like mules."

"Penis envy. We have all had it at one time or another," I noted.

"It wasn't penis envy, it was *penis pissed!* As if that wasn't bad enough, it was a dry county, and it was damn near impossible to get booze.

"Damn near, but not impossible.

"The colony was run by a married couple, and they squeezed every cent out of the others and lived like royalty. James and Maxine. Maxine was a pretty woman who had lots of body piercings and tattoos. She was a tortured gal who worshipped James. She spent most of her time sun tanning and following James around like a tail.

"And Maxine had a mouth on her. She worked in obscenities like an artist. If it had more than four letters in it, she didn't have much use for a word. My diagnosis for her was a sexual addiction, codependency, and a borderline personality. The reason I know about borderline personality disorders is I dated a couple gals with 'em, and man, can they stir the soup. One day they'll die for you, the next they'd just as soon tear your damn eyeballs out.

"Anyways, Maxine was a piece of work, and carried on like she was in some beauty pageant all the damn time.

"She hit on me once, and I about threw up in my mouth. I was standing in the kitchen eating an orange, and the next thing I know, someone's shaking hands with my pecker. I turned, and there she was, standing behind me wearing this maniacal grin. I told her that would never happen, and she asked me if it was on account of her being heavy and all. I told her it was because I had pecker problems, and she offered to help me through that.

"That one backfired on me. She kept telling me not to be embarrassed, and that many men have erectile dysfunction sometime in their lives. She told me all I needed was a patient woman to help me get over my sexual slump, so to speak. I thanked her for not judging me, and I got the hell outta there. Every time I saw Maxine from then on, she'd give me this understanding look and try to hug me.

"James was a very fit control freak who snuck cigarettes and booze behind the mess hall and wore a pistol and holster real low on his hip like a gunslinger. Nothing looks goofier than a pecker and a pistol hanging down off a cat, you know? I used to fight back chuckles like you wouldn't believe. What a clown he was. What the hell did he need a gun for? I mean, who was gonna attack a nudist colony? Were they gonna steal our lettuce and tomatoes?

"James was burned as a teenager, playing with matches and gasoline. It got his face real bad, and they had to do a whole bunch of skin grafts and such. They even took grafts from his groin to refashion eyelids for him. I called him Cockeye when he wasn't looking."

"That is borderline fabulous," I proudly stated.

"Anyways, the plastic surgeons had done a damn good job on him, but you could still tell. He didn't pay it no mind, though, and walked around like he was some kind of movie star.

"Nobody knew about his smoking and drinking but me, on account of I had nothing better to do than secretly tail him. The others thought he was some kind of monk. A spiritual guru they followed without question. He knew that I knew he was full of shit, though I played the part of a dedicated follower in front of his dutiful disciples.

"We sort of had an unspoken arrangement. I didn't mess with him, and he didn't mess with me. As long as he left Margie and me alone, everything was copacetic. I found out later he'd tried to seduce Margie once, but she told him, 'I will cut off your balls and feed them to you if you touch me again.'

"One thing about Margie was she never minced words, and she wasn't scared of anybody or anything. I always admired her for that. She believed in what she was doing. Believed in the whole nudist thingamabob and living off the land. She didn't pay no mind to all the shenanigans going on around her. She just kept her head down, did her work, and chased me around the damn place.

"Cockeye had sex with as many different women as he could, sometimes two or three in the same day. As near as I could tell, everybody was having sex with everybody else except for Margie and me. She worked in the garden every day, and constantly helped Maxine with the cooking and cleaning for the group. I hid out and drank and smoked hash all day. You know, pacing myself.

"There were strange things going on around that place. I mean, above and beyond the nakedness, the group sex, and the goofy burn-scarred, gun-toting guru running the joint. I couldn't prove it, but I swear some children went missing at one point. I wasn't exactly conscious for most of my time there, but I sort of had a count on the little ones, and I swear to God, the damn number went down a couple."

"And you suspect foul play, I take it?" The room got quiet and I waited for his answer, silently hoping the kids were all ok.

"I dunno," Slim continued. "I talked to Margie about it and she thought I was off my rocker, but I saw something in her eyes that gave me concern. Like she knew something she didn't wanna know. Like I said, I was so high all the time, who knows what was true and what wasn't. I just hope I was wrong about it. But the longer I stayed there, the more I needed to get the hell away from what I was seeing.

"One day, I walked around a corner and found three naked women going at it with each other with a damned summer sausage. I'd just had a summer sausage sandwich about an hour earlier, and I about launched it."

"That is horrifying on several levels."

"They asked me to join 'em, but I was so damned nauseous, I couldn't even politely decline. I just gave 'em a horrified expression and backpedalled around the corner like I'd just seen three women going at it with a summer sausage. To this day, I won't eat summer sausage."

"Nor will I from now on. So, you didn't fit in with the others?"

"No, I wasn't exactly part of the team. One thing I learned about my nudist colony experience is, they are filled with some folks you do not want to see naked under any circumstance. There were days when I wanted someone to glue my damn eyes shut.

"There was one woman, God bless her, who had to weigh over three hundred pounds. Everyone called her Moonlight. She'd been a successful watercolor artist in Sedona, Arizona who flipped out and tried to eat herself to death. She somehow ended up at the nudist village, and seemed happier than all get out to be there. She was a walking fanatic, and had lost over a hundred pounds in just under a year.

"We were both night people, so she and I would take late walks, and one evening she told me her parents had both been murdered in their home when she was a teenager. What do you say to that? It sure dropped some perspective in my lap about my growing up. I was operating under the impression I'd gotten a damn raw deal as a youngster, but all you gotta do is throw a rock and you'll hit someone who's had it worse, you know?

"Whenever I greeted her, I'd ask, 'How's life?'

"'Taking forever,' she'd say, and we'd laugh.

"Moonlight was a real nice gal, and never complained about anything, which encouraged me to follow suit. She was a good friend to me, and I was glad she'd found a comfort zone for herself.

"Margie and I lived in a hut, grew our own food, and just when I'd have myself talked into leaving, she'd sexually hypnotize me again, and I'd keep wandering around like a naked fool. This went on for three months, and by that time, I felt like I was peeing razor blades. The colony's herbalist told me I had a bladder infection, and she treated me with horrible tasting teas that made me have to pee about every twenty minutes.

"I ain't never felt pain like that before or since, Son. It was like trying to pass a penny through my pecker. When pus started to drain outta me and one testicle swelled up to the size of a plum, I decided medical attention was in order.

"Anyhow, Margie and I parted company, and I made my way to California for some peace and penicillin. It turned out I had a nasty case of gonorrhea, and the doctor told me I'd waited so long for treatment, I was likely sterile. I sent word to Margie and told her to get treated, but I never heard back from her.

"Soon afterwards, I put the band back together."

Chapter Twelve

"That was one impressive segue. You went from nudist colony, to sterility, to rock and roll." I laughed, looking at Slim.

"What can I say, I got skills to burn. It wasn't long before we got some momentum back, and we opened for a couple of heavy hitters. That put us back in the game. We ended up playing for some nice crowds, and started to really roll in some decent dough. Hell, it was like I'd never missed a step. With the band buzz we had going, once in awhile we had some labels sniff our butts a bit.

"One night, a guy from Capital Records came out to see us. After the gig, he showed up in our dressing room, and told us he was gonna get us a deal. He poured out a bunch of cocaine on the table for us, and was talking outta both sides of his mouth, you know? He had us nodding like bobble heads. This was the guy who was gonna make our dreams come true.

"He told us he'd gotten ahold of one of our demo tapes and had to see if we were as good live as we were on tape. He said he saw everything he needed to see that night, and would talk to his boss in the morning about signing us. Man, my goosebumps had goosebumps, Son. It's what we'd been working so hard for. It was right there, and we could taste it like it was a pill sitting on the tip of our tongues.

"Well, that got blown all to hell after a drunk drove his pickup into Mr. Capital Records' sports car behind the club. A red Jaguar, if I recall correctly, and he didn't take too kindly to the fact his steering wheel got pushed to the backseat. Good thing he wasn't in it at the time.

"He said it was an omen and that we were bad luck. Can you believe it? He wouldn't take our calls the next day."

Slim shook his head for what seemed like a minute as I sat silently, waiting for words that never arrived. The sunlight lit his gray hair like a halo. Sadness bubbled inside of me. I didn't want this to end.

"I do not know what to say to that, Slim. Wow."

"Anyways, we went back to banging away in the clubs, looking for that record deal that was gonna skyrocket us to fame and fortune. Around that time, we hooked up with a guitar player that was pretty shiny, and he got us some extra attention around Los Angeles. He'd do all these stage moves and spin his guitar around his head. Play with his teeth. Stuff we'd never seen before, you know, and the crowd ate it all up.

"Steve Fingerett, also known as Showtime, was one hell of a guitar player, but as strange as they come. He lived on rice and chocolate pudding, and washed his damn hands about a thousand times a day. I think he must've had the worst case of obsessive-compulsive disorder in the history of California. There were times when we'd have to wait to start the show on account of he couldn't leave the dressing room until he'd performed about twenty rituals. If one ritual went wrong, he'd start the whole damn thing over again.

"I'd be standing there, yelling, 'Showtime, it's show time.'

"He wouldn't budge until he was good and damn ready. It drove us all up a tree, I'll tell ya, but he was worth the wait. Guitar players from all over would come and stand in front of him, trying to soak up what finger magic they could.

"Once we got him on stage, all eyes were on him. He had the kind of charisma and talent that oozed out of him like maple syrup. There were nights where he'd rip out a solo and I'd lose my damn place in the song from watching him. When that cat decided to take a room over, he'd just rare up and do it. Star quality, Son. He had it by the gallon.

"Any momentum we'd lost in the past, we made up around that time. Things were really looking up for the band, and we were all getting along famously. We were working with a manager named Russ Wilson at the time, who got us great gigs for fabulous money and a damn fine tour bus to travel around in.

"And just when things were about to get better than we could handle, we found out Russ didn't want to be a man no more, so he stole every red cent from us and hightailed it to North Carolina to have his plumbing redone.

"I ain't making this stuff up, Son."

I leaned forward. "Cripes, how could you?"

"Well, Showtime got a better offer from a band that had just gotten signed to Sony Records, and we limped on and on and on and on. And that brings me to the most interesting, brilliant, frustrating, inspiring, and heart-busting musician I ever met.

"We were the house band for an upscale club in San Diego for a bit, playing mostly for college kids and trust fund hippies. We got finished up one night, and I noticed this cat sitting at a table, staring me down like he was gonna jump me. Well, being the level-headed guy I was, I strolled over to him and asked him just what in the damn hell he was staring at.

"'I want to play something for you,' he said. His eyes darted around like a snake's tongue, and his head shook back and forth repeatedly. I was about to dismiss him, but something in me guided me to a chair.

"'What do you play?' I asked him.

"'Everything,' he answered. 'Well, everything you have on stage right now.'

"I invited him up on stage, handed him one of my guitars, and then almost lost my eyebrows over the top of my head when he started playing the most amazing piece of music that guitar had ever kicked out. It was so good, our lead guitarist at the time came outta the dressing room to see who the hell was playing. They came out, and we all sat around while this cat brought out sounds we'd never heard before.

"By the time the sun came up, he'd played every instrument we had like they'd meant to be played all along. We were all dumbfounded by him, and from then on, he used to hang out with us all the time. Hell, I stole tons of song ideas from him, but he never cared a lick. And he never wanted to join us on stage on account of what I thought was stage fright.

"I later learned he had a mental illness, called paranoid schizoaffective bipolar disorder. Don't know if that's what it was, but it sounds right. Anyways, you never knew what you'd get with Repo. We called him Repo because he kept getting repossessed by a darkness nobody understood.

"It seemed like he only had two moods: elated or desperate. One day, he'd be bouncing off the walls happy, tossing around ideas faster then we could catch 'em. Next time you'd see him, he'd be suicidal and wouldn't stop crying. Hell, you'd sometimes get both in one day. In the morning, he'd be full of energy and hope. Ten hours later, you might find him curled up in a fetal position, shaking fiercely.

"Man, I didn't know how to take him. I'd had my share of mental problems, and I knew a thing or two about mood swings. I fought some wicked demons over the years, but this cat had something inside of him that was clawing at his damn soul. He was freaky talented, and freaky tortured.

"And I gotta tell you, sometimes his freakiness was funny. One time he and I were driving around, and he just dove under the dashboard. I about wrecked the damn, it scared me so damn bad.

"'What in the hell are you doing?' I asked him.

"'See that car in front of us?" he asked. 'It's following us. It's an old CIA trick.'"

"That *is* hilarious."

"One time he got to smelling so bad, we couldn't take it no more. It took four of us to strip him down to shower him. Turned out he was covered from his neck down in tinfoil so he could send signals to the mother ship or something. He even had this little tinfoil hood for his pecker."

"That is hilarious to the second power," I quipped.

"He was another one who just wouldn't stay on his medication, and he was a different cat when he was taking it. Level. Cool and calm—and he hated every second of it. Repo didn't cotton to low-key.

"I'd say to him, 'You're doing so much better, man. Just stay on the meds and give 'em a chance.'

"'The highs are worth the lows, Slim,' he'd tell me. 'I don't want level. I'm not meant for level. I want the buzz that comes after the storm. I want to ride the biggest wave of the hurricane. I want to reach up and scrape the bottom of the clouds with my teeth. I want to be in the center of the tornado. I've got to have my mania.'

"So he medicated himself, and he suffered horribly. Hell, we suffered just watching him. There wasn't one of us who could play like him. He'd go places musically the rest of us never even thought up. He was on a different level with everything. He even cooked better than any of us, for crying out loud. And he taught himself to do all of it.

"His dad once told me Repo tested out at a genius level, and that he'd had a full scholarship at MIT for engineering. He could do numbers in his head like you wouldn't believe. He had a memory that never missed, and he could draw you a picture that you'd swear was alive on the page. He was one amazing cat, and an unbelievable talent.

"He used to talk to me about throwing in the towel, and I never knew if I had the right words to tell him. I knew all about the suicidal shuffle, Son. I'd played it in my head a hundred times. But it was my big secret, and I couldn't tell him about it. All I could do was to try to talk him down and out of it.

"'Do you think people who commit suicide go to hell?' he asked me once.

"'Nope. I think they go right to God's lap,' I told him.

"'You really do? You think they get to go to heaven?'

"'God knows they've had enough of hell already.'

"'I've seen Satan. He doesn't look like they say he does. He looks like you want him to look. Everyone sees him differently. He wants my soul, Slim, and I'm scared I might give it to him.'

"'That's just fear talking, Repo. You gotta fight this. Be a warrior. Get mad if you have to. You're bigger than it is. Way bigger.'

"'Are you close to God, Slim?'

"'I'd be lying if I said I was, Repo. But I do know one thing: I believe in Him in my heart, and I don't want any part of what the other team has going on. You and I are on God's team, whether we feel like it or not. We're His kids. Brothers from the same Father. You ain't alone in this. You're gonna find your way to some answers. You just gotta hold on and make the best decisions and moves that you can.'

"'I don't want to have this anymore, Slim. I'm tired. So damned tired.'

"'I know, buddy. I wish I could take it from you and carry it for a bit. I wish I could get that brain of yours to make friends with you.'

"'You're a good friend, Slim. Thanks for always liking me no matter what. If I don't make it through…through all this…I want you to know the time I spent with you was the best time of my life.'

"'You will make it through this, and learn to live with what you got, just like I do, Repo. Life ain't easy for anybody, and you gotta take the good with the not so good and focus everything you got on the good because you got a pile of that. You got dealt a tough hand to play, I know, but there are plenty of cards left to draw, so let's hang in there and see what happens around the bend.'

"'I don't have to do this alone? You'll walk with me?'

"'I'll walk with you through the fire if I have to. You ain't alone in this.'

Slim rose, shuffled to the kitchen, and returned with two glasses of orange juice he set on our tables. He got more wood for the fire, then opened the window shades. He looked out the picture window and started to say something, but stopped. He returned to his chair, sipped his juice, and continued.

"Like I said before, I've been down in the suffer hole a time or ten, and we all know a lot of folks don't make it out of that kind of pain. They end up crazy or dead, and that's a fact. You see 'em and they have tombstones in their eyes, and you ain't surprised when they finally murder their pain.

"Repo did the best he could with what he had to work with. He was in and out of hospitals the entire time I knew him. He'd get back on the meds, say and do all the right things, get released…and then eat a handful of downers, smoke a joint, and drink himself silly. He'd wake up the next day, way behind enemy lines, and wonder if he should keep going. It was an abysmal existence, and none of us would've faulted him for taking the big nap. Trying to help him was like putting a puzzle together without the box cover.

"He finally found himself a shrink who went the extra mile for him, and she found a medicine that gives him middle ground to stand on. He ain't cured, but he's better, and doesn't lose himself in the process. He's clean and sober.

"He told me, 'Slim, I once was a hopeless dope fiend, and now I'm a dopeless hope fiend.'"

"I love it. A success story emerges from the morass of mental illness," I managed.

"I'm tickled for him, and my heart goes out to all wounded warriors with minds that take 'em hostage. I used to tease Repo some about how his head would twist back and forth like it did. He'd do it when he was on an upswing.

"One time this cat I knew said to me, 'It looks like he's saying 'No!' when he shakes his head back and forth like that. Why does he do that?'

"'Repo was a ping pong referee for twenty-five years and he can't help it,' I said.

"This fella looked at me, then at Repo, back at me, and then at Repo again, chewing on what I'd just said to him. He never did get it swallowed."

Chapter Thirteen

"Anyways, what you wanna hear about now?" Slim asked.

"I most certainly do not want to hear the story you refuse to share with me. No way. That's the last thing I want to hear about."

"You're like a mosquito with a memory, Son."

Slim swatted imaginary bugs away from his head. He turned to face me with a weary warning in his eyes.

"Ok, I'm serious, Slim. I know you warned me about this, but maybe you need to tell it."

His words stung me like a hornet straight to my heart.

"Don't you fucking tell me what I need to tell and don't need to tell, Junior! This is my life. My story, and I've repeatedly told you this is none of your God damned business. What do I have to say to you so you'll drop off of it?"

The look on my face, I'm quite certain, did no justice to the horrible feelings cursing through me. I felt I'd just fumbled the ball on the goal line. I'd let him down. Hurt him deeply. I'd been warned and could not help myself. My mind began to backpeddle and no matter how hard I tried, I could not make the situation go away. I proceded with as much caution as I was able to muster.

"Man, I'm sorry, Slim. I screwed up. Again. It's just the journalist in me wants the whole story. I feel horrible that I…"

"I thought we were clear on this."

"I know. I am sorry. I'm an idiot."

One corner of Slim's mouth rose up. It was almost a smile.

"Naw, you ain't," he offered. "You're just a newspaperman and you can't help yourself. We've come this far and we're gonna keep on keepin' on. I'm sorry I raised my voice again and used the Lord's name in vain. That ain't like me. Temper takes me to places I never want to visit again, Son. So please. As a favor and out of respect to everything we've shared together tonight. Do not bring this up again."

"You got it, Slim. It's a done deal with me. Lesson learned and my lips are sealed tight on this. I'm not one who normally bathes in obscenities, but son of a bitch. I fucked up."

"It's ok, Son. It truly is. You're just doing what you've been taught to do. Like a trained monkey."

I nodded. I deserved that.

"I'm just pullin' your chain a little bit. Look. All you gotta know is it's just something I've been carrying around and ain't ready to set down yet. I want to, but I just can't…yet."

Slim's eyes seemed to tear up as he turned his face away from me. Whatever it was he was carrying was awfully damn heavy, and more than anything I wanted him to be free from its weight. I took a deep breath and waited for his next move. It was all I was able to do.

"Well, how about we talk about my angels? I ain't told this story since I last told it. That was humor, Son, laugh amongst yourself."

"I am laughing inside."

"Let it out, Son. This is as good as it gets."

"Slim?"

"That would be me."

"Are we ok? I mean, you are ok…with me?

"Everything is copacetic, Son. Don't go getting all gooshy on me now. Let's just get this buggy back on the road where it belongs."

"I would like that very much, Slim. Very much."

"I'm a big believer we are visited by angels all the time. Looking back on my life, I've been touched in major ways by folks I believe were angels, though I couldn't see it at the time. I think they choose to remain anonymous, but there are some angels on this Earth who you can't miss if you're paying attention.

"I used to sort of believe God uses angels to keep Him informed about his kids, and to help us along. I've since come to believe God is all present and all-knowing, and I believe angels come to us in human form all the time and we never know it until later. Maybe they're just hanging around to help us turn left when we hit the damn walls, you know?

"What I'm talking about here are some folks that have blessed my life repeatedly, and have been some of my very best spiritual teachers. Some folks call 'em special needs people. Others call 'em developmentally disabled. I call 'em angels, and I ain't got any doubt about it. I'm a blessed man to be able to call so many of these spirit-touched folks friends of mine.

"1992. Spearfish, South Dakota. The Queen City of the Black Hills.

"I was back home to lick wounds and play a few shows in the Midwest. The band was limping badly, and it wouldn't be long before I'd shut it all down for good. My drug and alcohol use was off the charts, and I was giving some thought to getting clean again. I just didn't wanna deal with withdrawals, you know? Coming off that much dope and booze is a full-time job for about two weeks, and then what? I'd stopped before, but I could never stay stopped.

"Anyways, I was helping out at a Special Olympics track meet in order to burn up some court-ordered community service hours for another harmless, legal misunderstanding. To tell the truth, I had no idea what to expect, and was shaking in my boots, partly from fear, and partly on account of I hadn't had my medicine yet that day.

"So, I'm standing there waiting to talk to one of the organizers, looking as uncomfortable as a flute player at a hoedown, when I feel someone grab hold of my hand. I looked down into this angel's face and she says to me,

"'You've got earrings and girl hair. You're a mangirl.'

"Made perfect sense to me.

"I squatted down to meet her eye to eye, and she tells me her name is Karen, she's forty years-old, she'd just gotten a new apartment, she loved horses, she was running in three events that day, and was working on her Christmas list for Santa.

"Again, it made perfect sense to me.

"I was tickled by everything about her, and began to relax immediately. She introduced me to her friends, and the next thing I know, I'm having the best damn morning I can ever remember. They put me on the starting line for the races to help them line up, and I'd never seen joy like that before. I'd never been to an athletic event where every participant won.

"Karen stuck close to me that day, and she had all kinds of things to teach me. Like when she saw the protruding vein that's always on my forehead.

"She reached up, touched it with a finger, and asked, 'Why do you have this?'

"'It's because I'm too serious all the time.'

"Karen thought about that, touched my forehead, looked up at me and said,

"'Maybe you should be one serious instead of two serious?'

"Boy, that was a truth from the mouth of that angel. I'd been two serious my whole damn life, and that evening I decided to try to someday get it down to one."

"I am down to around three serious."

"And people feel sorry for folks with developmental disabilities. Man, do they have that backwards. Those folks have something most of us never get close to. They are present in the moment, and fully awake. They ain't fence riders, I'll tell ya that. They get passionate about something, and they go after it. They follow where their desires lead 'em. Innocent desires.

"Karen and her angel friends were my special guests at an outdoor gig we played later that summer, and to watch them dance put smiles on us that about swallowed our faces. I make it a point to attend two Special Olympics events every year, and I've been a student of developmentally disabled folks ever since. I ain't down to one serious yet, but sometimes I get pretty close."

"You mentioned the band was on fumes again at that time. When did you retire from playing live?"

I thought I caught some sadness in Slim's eyes then. He rubbed it out, sat straight up in his chair, and took a deep breath. Then, all at once, everything about him relaxed, almost as if he'd climbed a hill and reached the top.

"It was 1993, I was forty-four, and I played my last show in a big club in Detroit. I remember like it was Tuesday. There was a blizzard like you wouldn't believe. Anyways We showed up to set up, and sound check and the overly-intoxicated club owner started in about us about keeping our volume down, and what type of songs we should play—then blamed us later because the crowd was light that night.

"We played the gig, and when we were tearing down, this gorilla of a bouncer called me into the back office. The owner was sitting behind this big damn desk with a big bottle of scotch and a pistol laying on it. The owner handed me half the money he owed us, and told me we were lucky to get that. I took a look at the gun. I took a look at the gorilla, and the empty look in his eyes.

"Some folks would say I had two choices on that deal, but I really only had the one. We took our money, somehow made it outta town through the storm, and I knew I was done. And we'd had way worse things happen to us over the years. Way worse. I don't know why that piece of straw broke my back, but it did. I guess I hit a wall and turned left. I was tired. Strung out on powder, pills, and booze.

"I was six foot three, and weighed one hundred thirty pounds. My cheeks were sunk in, and I had circles under my eyes that looked like caterpillars. I'd been swimming with sharks for so long, and I was plum out of bandages, Son. I called our booking agent and band manager and told them we were done, and that was that. It all went out with a whisper, really."

"Do you miss it? The fanfare?"

"You know, playing live was great, but my favorite part of all of it was recording. In the beginning, playing for folks was what we all lived for. We didn't know squat about writing songs, but we started doing it anyway. We also didn't know squat about making records, and if you didn't have a lot of money, you didn't get into a studio. That's why we all were running around trying to get a record contract. They had the money, the radio stations, the distribution outlets, and they had the promoters eating outta their hands. They held all the cards, Son.

"Nowadays, folks can record with computers in their damn basement. Hell, they don't even have to sing on pitch—they can just adjust it. Pick a chorus they like, and drop it in the rest of the song. It doesn't have to be about the performance anymore.

"And talk about worldwide exposure in seconds. Folks can record themselves and…what's it called when they put it out there on their computers?"

"It's called posting and streaming. Some of today's biggest artists started that way."

"I guess they can get millions of fans and never have to leave their damn bedroom. That's a hoot and a half, ain't it? I say, more power to 'em. They bypass the corporate clowns and do it on their own terms. I'll bet you diamonds to donuts, the record companies didn't see the computer revolution coming. They weren't ready for artists and bands being able to become famous on their own.

"In the early days, most of the bands we rubbed shoulders with played their own music and looked down on cover bands. But the cover bands got most of the local club gigs, so we all had to give in some and find a recipe we could live with. As we gained a fan base and quit playing the small clubs, we had more leeway on what we could do and play. Folks came out to hear our music, and they wanted to buy records.

"The first time I got to record in a studio changed everything for me. After that, it was all I thought about. Getting back in there to do another song."

"You recorded first in Los Angeles?"

"Yeah, with The Codefendants. A tiny studio in Santa Cruz, which we all called the Devil's City back then. It must've been around 1973 or so. This biker named Mack Zander owned it, and had a small label called Panhead Records he was shopping bands with to the big dogs. He saw us at a club and invited us to come to his place to do a six-song demo, which we jumped at. He told us if it went well, he'd sign us to his label, which we later found out was a money-laundering front for his dope business.

"But by golly, we got in the studio.

"And it was heaven. I loved everything about the process, and never wanted to leave. Mack Z produced everything, and for a dope dealer, he was real good at arranging tunes. He had this cat working the board named Mickey, who was a damn fine recording engineer—when you could keep him awake through the heroin he slammed into his arm.

"We'd finish a take and just know we'd nailed it, and Mickey's voice would appear in our headphones: 'Aw, shit, man. I'm sorry. I didn't get that one. Let's do it again, dudes.'

"We'd all look at each other and shake our heads and play it again. Mack Z would scream at him, and sometimes would slap him around. He kept Mickey on because when he was on his game, he was one of the best recording engineers in southern California. A sober Mickey could've worked for any of the labels or major studios. The thing was, Mickey worked for heroin, room and board, and Mack Z lived with his…idiosyncrasies.

"We all chain-smoked pot and cigarettes back then, and the place had this blue haze that covered everything. Lava lamps and mood lights were everywhere. It was eerie, really, but a great creative atmosphere. Anyways, we all set up together and played everything over and over until we got a take Mack Z liked and that Mickey stayed awake for. No overdubs. We did everything live with three microphones for the drums. Simple and organic, you know.

"One thing I recall was Mack Z had the best speed we'd run into in a long time, and Puck kept starting the songs too fast. Once Puck slid into a tempo, you couldn't budge him. Mack made him play with ankle weights strapped to his wrists until his arms got tired, and then we tried it again and it worked. Pretty creative.

"It took us two days to record, mix, and master six tunes, and we were tickled beyond belief with the end product. Hell, even Morti and Rev were happy with the recordings and they were never satisfied. I remember Flash disappeared before the record was mixed and I never did find out where he went. I think he was mad about the fact he'd written a song for the record that didn't make the cut. I do recall it had an identical chord progression and melody structure as a song I'd written, but I didn't say nothing on account of I didn't want to hurt his feelings.

"Anyways, Mack Z promised us he'd press the songs to record, and we got fifty cassette tapes to hand out to clubs, label people, and such. Mack Z signed us to Panhead Records, and promised us all kinds of things that never happened. We didn't care. We were recording artists.

"Once we realized Mack Z wasn't gonna have our record pressed, we had it done ourselves. We called it *Passion Fence*. When that first box of records arrived at our band house, we all about pissed ourselves. Everybody took one out and just held it in their hands like it was pressed gold. So many years listening to records, and suddenly we had our own.

"I'll tell you, there's something magical about holding your music in your hands and being able to share it with folks. And the first time I heard it played on the radio, I felt vindicated. For us, that was proof we were on the right track."

"What was the first song of yours that received radio play?" I asked.

"A Slim Chance and the Codefendants tune off *Passion Fence* called "Love You Right" and it charted nationally on college radio. We'd show up to play on a campus, and they'd already be asking for it as soon as we'd set up our gear. Sometimes, we'd play it three times in a night.

"We rubbed up against greatness back in those days, Son, but every time we went to shake its hand, greatness would turn and slip away. I'm gonna dust off that turntable one of these days and take a spin down Memory Lane."

"Let's put a record on now. I would love to listen to some great Slim Chance music."

Slim chuckled. "Well, now you're playing to my ego, and I'm powerless to resist you. I'll throw on a record, and let's take us a break. Don't be surprised if you're suddenly inspired to dance around like a monkey with a boner. This music I'm about to play you is powerful stuff, Son."

"Though I have never seen a monkey with a boner dance, I have been known to cut a rug on a rare occasion. I might want your autograph afterwards if that's permissible."

"I normally don't sign autographs, Son, but I'll make an exception for you. Just call my people and they'll get back to you eventually. They'll probably send you a signed photo and such. Just make sure you tell 'em I told you to call, and give the code words so they know it's really me."

"The code words?"

"'I'd rather have a bottle in front of me, then a frontal lobotomy'.

"You are a demented mammal, Slim Chance. Do you think I could possibly get a Slim Chance coffee mug?"

"Don't get your hopes up. Those mugs are a precious commodity, and hard to come by. I might be able to get you a used one. I know I can get you a keychain and a t-shirt, but you gotta pay for shipping and handling."

Slim shuffled over to a pile of records, dug through it, and removed a dusty record jacket. He placed it on the turntable, and as he lowered the needle, a loud whistle escaped from his lips. We were going for a ride, back to when time was spread out like an endless blanket and pregnant with glorious dreams.

Chapter Fourteen

"When did you record the record you just played for me?" I asked.

"The Spring of 1974," Slim said. "San Francisco. A cat named Nevada Robinson who worked for Warner Brothers for a bit started a small label and built a studio down near the wharf. Right-On Records. Can you believe it? We cut eight songs in just under a week and had ourselves a self-titled Slim Chance and the Codependents record.

"We shopped it to every radio station that would let us in the door, but back in those days, payola was alive and well, and it took lots of dough to get played. The kind of dough none of us, including Nevada, had at the time. He had some great connections, but they all had their hands out, too. We got regional radio exposure, and folks really responded well to our stuff, but the song didn't break nationally, and we lost our momentum.

"So, we focused again on college stations, and that paid off for us. Based on our strength on college radio, we did a real nice tour. We went out for a bit with a band that had a huge following and had just signed to a major label called Johnny Diamond, and that got us in front of lots of folks.

"That was about the time we got on board with our merchandising. Nevada knew that's where a band could really make money, and he forced us into that world. And what a profitable world it turned out to be. We sold t-shirts, sweatshirts, hats, bandanas, coffee mugs, and a hell of a lot of records. We made more dough on merchandise then we did for the gigs, and that was good money in those days.

"Nevada had his hands in everything, especially the cookie jar, you know? We paid him a percentage of everything we made, and he basically promised to get our record played on radio stations that counted. He handled booking the band, promotions, transportation, hotels, expense budgets, and investments. He designed all the merchandise, and even helped us pick set lists. He'd travel with us sometimes to keep his eyes on everything. He was a hands-on cat, and he really got us kick started in many ways.

"Nevada's drug use turned on him, though, and he got real paranoid. One night, he ripped my shirt open and asked me if I was wearing a wire. Then he put a pistol barrel between my eyes and started laughing hysterically."

"Don't you hate it when that happens?" I noted.

Slim gave me a sideways glance. "I ain't fond of it, that's for sure. It was the most scared I've ever been, before or since. Everyone froze up, and nobody said a word. When he cocked the hammer back, I thought I was a goner, but then he just turned and walked out. I think it took me three hours to get my butt unpuckered after that one.

"Next time I saw him, he told me he was just testing me to see if I was a cop. I screamed at him and told him he was losing his marbles. He got this foggy look in his eyes, and I got the hell outta there before he could do anything crazy.

"And the more paranoid he became, the more dope he did, which led to more paranoia. There were times when I just knew he was gonna shoot somebody, but as far as I know, he never did. I used to take the bullets outta his gun when he'd pass out. He was a real handful.

"One night, Nevada threw a cocaine and cognac party at his house, and ordered hookers for everyone there. I was terrified of catching a sex disease, and me and my hooker spent most of the night snorting dope, playing cards, and watching movies in the basement. We actually hit it off.

"I remember she told me she had a bachelor's degree in biology, and had toyed with the idea of medical school, but dope took her. Legal dope. Prescription medication for a back injury is how it started for her. So much for the dreams she had before the chemical storm hit. She had a sadness surrounding her like an angry fog, and I couldn't look into her eyes very long without feeling sad myself. She was powerfully wounded.

"When I told her I didn't wanna have sex, she asked if I was gay. This gal was a looker, Son, and wasn't used to being around cats that didn't have their tongues wagging. I told her no, I was not gay, but that I had a girlfriend I was committed to. Well, that turned her on, and she really went after me.

"I was higher than a kite in a spaceship, and that gal peeled off her clothes and I caved. She was the only prostitute I've ever slept with, and if I could've used five condoms at once, I would've. All she had was three.

"We were on the couch together, sharing a joint, when we heard gunshots upstairs. I got dressed and snuck slowly upstairs. I knew Nevada was behind it, and wasn't sure what I'd find up there. I poked my head around the door, and three cats had tackled Nevada and were trying to get the gun away from him. It went off again before they finally wrestled it outta his hand.

"It turned out Nevada wanted to switch girls with another cat who didn't want any part of it. So, he took a couple shots at the cat's feet to shake him up some. What I remember most about that night is how calm the prostitutes remained through it all. They didn't even blink when the shooting started. It wasn't their first rodeo with Nevada.

"I grabbed a bottle of Hennessy and as much dope as I could carry, and we got the hell outta there. We ended up at her place, and talked for hours. I never knew what else happened at Nevada's, and I didn't care. I had enough coke and speed to last me for days, I was with a beautiful woman, and I had a really good record under my belt.

"I remember the look on 'my gal's' face when I asked her when I could see her again.

"'You bring $500 with you and you can see me tonight,' she answered."

"Ouch. I'll bet that smarted, Slim."

"Yeah. I broke up with her on the spot. So much for the warm fuzzies I had going that night. I thought we'd connected, you know? She was a great damn actress.

"It wasn't long after that Nevada shelved the record—just when it had started to get wings. For the life of me, I still don't know why he did that. Some damn paranoid control freak move, I suppose. He owned the master tapes, and it turned out I'd signed some papers in a drunken stupor that gave him ownership of the songs and publishing. Without the master, we couldn't make more records, and we sold out of what we had.

"Remember that cat named Rufus that hung with us and helped out some?"

"I do indeed remember Rufus."

Slim had started to reach for the scrapbook. My answer to his question stopped him. He nodded, and headed to tend to the fire.

"Well, he didn't take too kindly to Nevada's treatment of us. One night, he got all jacked up on crank and whiskey and decided to talk some sense into Mr. Robinson. He told me what he was gonna do, and I didn't believe him. I thought he was just being Rufus, and nothing would come of it. Then, Rufus called me from Nevada's house and told me he'd stuck a gun in Nevada's mouth and had him tied to a chair.

"We decided maybe an intervention was in order, so we all loaded up in Rufus's VW van and rushed over there.

"During the drive, all I could do was picture all of us wearing prison orange for the next twenty-five years, swapping spit with some gigantic cat named Earle. We pulled up to the house, and there was Rufus on the front porch, having a cigarette and an adult beverage, real casual like.

"'Where is he?' I asked.

"'He's in the living room. Tied up. He pissed himself.'

"'Rufus, have you misplaced your damn mind? Where's the gun?'

"'In my boot, where it always is.'

"'You mean when it ain't in Nevada's mouth? How am I gonna fix this one now?'

"'You don't have to fix anything. Nevada and I have reached an agreement that benefits both parties.'

"'What kind of agreement?'

"'He gives us the master tapes and your song rights back, and we don't tell the cops about the pot he's got growing in his basement, or the automatic weapons and explosives.'

"'He's got pot growing in his basement?'

"'He's got about a half acre of it, and a damn arsenal. I'll show you.'

"We followed Rufus into the house, and there was Nevada, gagged and tied to a chair as reported. He tried to make a sentence to me using his eyebrows as we went by him to the basement door. Sure enough, it was a damn marijuana plantation, with grow lights and a fancy irrigation system. It was one hell of a set up, and then some.

"Rufus then led us to a room with about fifty machine guns, boxes of ammunition, and a whole pile of government-issued explosives. We looked at each other and smiled. Maybe we could cut a deal.

"We cut Nevada loose, he grabbed the masters from his safe and tore up the papers I'd signed, and agreed to all the terms we presented for our new record deal…and we promised to keep his dope farm and little weapons collection a secret.

"He picked up our record again, but he didn't exactly run with it. It was more of a limp. I think he made some calls and pretended to be busy, but Nevada's money came from peddling dope and side deals with other artists. We never had a shot at getting much further than we did with him. Nevada was a master orator. Tons of great motivational speeches for us, but very little follow through.

"Nevada went to prison for tax evasion about a year later, and we were out a record label and a manager. But, we had the masters and could press more records, and we had a ton of gigs and merchandise to keep the show on the road."

"That was some negotiating technique. I trust your next recording process was less dramatic?"

Slim shrugged. "They all had their drama, and their fun. The story was pretty much the same, Son. We went in and played the songs and had the time of our lives. There's an electric pulse in a studio that everyone feels and responds to. It bounces back and forth between the players, and takes the tunes to places they normally wouldn't be able to go.

"So much of it depends on the recording engineer. A decent one can make a band sound real good. A great one can make a band sound spectacular. Then, if you've got a producer with a vision for the songs, who can coach you to those new places…you got a shot at making a record to be proud of.

"And there are momentum shifts, just like in a football or basketball game, when the team comes together like one heart beating. It's really something to be a part of, Son. The songs get recorded, mixed, and mastered, and then pressed on vinyl, and only then do you feel like you are finally done with the process. And then, you realize they never belonged to you. They are bigger than you.

"Then, the folks who have all the money keep all the money, and they work the band like dogs on the road. Bands that sign with major labels get pennies on the dollar for record royalties, a bit more if they are lucky. They really get screwed when they sign away their publishing rights, and that's where the real money is. They end up selling their damn souls for a shot at the title, and many of 'em end up more broke then when they started. Always been that way.

"I probably made more money on my records than some artists did who had major hits on account of their record deals.

"That's the truth, Son. I knew guys who had hit songs on the Billboard Charts who were making $300 a week, begging their A&R guy for an advance to buy booze and cigarettes. Somebody's gotta pay the label back for the tour bus, the tour equipment, the tour staff, the studio time, distribution, merchandise, the video… You get the picture. Millions of dollars floating around, and the artists have their hands tied behind their backs and can't grab 'em.

"The other side of that coin is, the labels can take a record to places I never had access to. They were a necessary evil, you know? They fronted for the big money projects and covered the band's expenses while they were being developed. They got the records played. They got the videos shown. They got the venues for the tours, and had the distribution outlets for the records. There was a time I would've crawled across fire to get a deal.

"I made four records in my career, and we made a pile of money on all of 'em. The best one I made was in Nashville, when we had a real producer and a state-of- the-art studio."

"And a drummer with a broken ankle," I inserted.

"And a hell of a jump shot. That was a dandy of a studio, with million-dollar drum and vocal rooms, and a mixing board that went on for miles. I really thought that record was gonna do it for us. I really did.

"You know, it was almost as if I pulled the tent down on myself every time something really good would happen. I mean, we sold thousands of records on the road, and that kept us in the game, but we were always one break away from really making a splash.

"One story I will tell you. I made the third record—called *Take It Higher*— in Minneapolis, and had to use studio musicians on account of the band was broke up. This multi-millionaire named Roscoe Winter was a big fan of mine and had a nice studio overlooking the Mississippi River, and he promised me the moon and stars to come record there. Roscoe had made all his money the old-fashioned way. He inherited it from his daddy, who owned rock quarries all over the country.

"I showed up at the studio, and Roscoe met me at the door with a line of cocaine and a contract to sign. I did both. Then, I met this talented group of musicians he'd gathered up, and we listened to demo tapes of the songs we were gonna record. They all seemed to dig the tunes, and said it would be no problem learning 'em.

"It took us four rehearsals, and those guys had the songs down tighter than an ant's ass. Great players and good guys, but the best part of the sessions was getting to play with a horn section. Man, that was like stepping into the sunshine for the first time for me. I thought I'd died and went to God's cabin.

"We'd start a tune and slip into a nice groove, and I'd get to thinking, 'Yep, we got it going on this one.'

"And then the horns would kick in, and adrenaline would shoot from my crotch out the top of my head. They were dazzling. Four college kids who moonlighted for Roscoe for studio time, and every one of 'em was a monster player. I didn't even care if the songs called for horns. We just spread 'em on everything like peanut butter. And I love peanut butter, Son."

"As do I."

"We got along real well. They called me Hillbilly—which, after hanging out in Hollywood, I took as a compliment. I was so damned tickled by it all, I didn't drink the entire time."

Slim's chin dropped to his chest, and his eyebrows lifted like two garage doors as a grin poked out of his beard.

"Well, that's a lie. I didn't drink in the studio, is what I meant to say.

"But boy did we snort cocaine, and Roscoe got the purest stuff you could get. I'll never forget—one night, we were mixing a song, when three uniformed police officers came through the door. One carried a shopping bag, and the three of them and Roscoe disappeared to his office while the rest of us sat there hyperventilating.

"Five minutes later, the cops casually strolled by and left without glancing sideways. Here comes Roscoe with an ashtray full of the purest blow I ever did, and he says to us,

"'Enjoy, gentlemen. And by the way…they were never here, dig?'

"We dug.

"We finished those songs in record time, as we never slept or took breaks. Roscoe kept feeding us coke, and we kept doing the next thing in front of us. It was quite a week, and I don't think my pulse went below a hundred-fifty once. I never did coke that pure again, and if you listen to that record, you'll notice the tempos are a tad faster than they needed to be.

"My voice has a different timbre on the record, too, and that was all the damn coke and cigarettes. I actually like the raspy sound of it, though I had a hell of a time hitting high notes.

"'Grab your damn balls, Slim,' Roscoe would yell through the studio intercom. 'You've got to reach up and hit that note, man.'

"Roscoe threw a record release party at his home for us, and that was a doozy. Lots of folks showed up, and Roscoe introduced me to a round of applause. At first, it was a pretty calm event. We all grazed around the catering tables, chatting about this and that and trying to act like we were famous recording artists. Roscoe put the record on, broke out some champagne, and brought out a mirror with a pile of cocaine the size of a toaster on it. It seemed like a record release party to me.

"I may not be the sharpest knife in the drawer, but I surmised Roscoe and his fifth wife were swingers when she had sex with two of the horn players on the pool table while he videotaped it."

"Oh, my."

"That's what I said. It turned out everyone at the party other than us musicians were swingers, and it turned into an orgy. His wife made a play for me, but I was so coked outta my mind and paranoid about the whole deal, I hid in the garage with a bottle of scotch and four sports cars.

"Roscoe and I parted ways over a misunderstanding or twelve, and the record never got the promotion I was promised. The last time I saw Roscoe was at a show we played in Minneapolis, and he was in the process of his fifth divorce.

"Maybe the swinger's lifestyle didn't cross over real well into marital stability, but who am I to judge?"

"Well, a happily married monogamous man, that's who."

Slim pointed an index finger at me and winked.

"Good point. I do remember how damn tired he looked, and he kept apologizing for this and that. I think he knew we had a great record that didn't get the attention it deserved. It was good to see him, though, and it brought back some potent memories.

"There was a rumor going around he died of AIDS, but I don't know that for a fact. Another story I heard was he caught MS and was in a wheelchair. I was always gonna try to contact him to see how he was, but I could never dial the damn phone. What I do know is he helped me make a great record, and I'll always be grateful."

"So, you had a record and no band."

"Yeah, and my mental health was unraveling like a ball of yarn in a hurricane.

I can't remember where I went first after that, but I ended up back in LA to try to get the damn band's engine running again. Just when I'd found some great players, I got locked up when I couldn't snap out of a real bad depression. That one nearly tanked me, Son, and I stared at a handful of pills for a week before I decided not to take 'em."

"Thank God you didn't. I take it you pursued professional help?" I wondered.

"I ran for cover. My mind was firing at me like a machine gun, and I hadn't left my house for a month. I had a gal pal at the time named Feather, and I called her. She drove me to a crisis center, and they forwarded me on to the looney bin.

"Pardon my damn self. Looney bin is disrespectful to the patients and the good folks who operate 'em. Let's call it what it is: a psychiatric hospital. I was in one in New Orleans, one in Minneapolis, one in Miami, the state hospital in Yankton, South Dakota, and the last one in Los Angeles. The four previous were court-ordered stays, and the latter was a three-month spin dry where they got me off dope and loaded me up on pharmaceuticals and therapy.

"I don't remember much about my stays in Minneapolis and New Orleans on account of I was withdrawing so bad, and they had me on so many psychotropics, I could barely operate a fork and spoon. I mostly slept and wandered the halls. I don't remember even seeing a counselor either time. It wouldn't have helped anyway, you know? I was still bulletproof, and didn't need any help from anybody. I was merely suffering another series of bad luck and misunderstandings.

"What I remember most about my stay in Miami was getting a really good tan hanging out in a garden area, and smoking about three packs of cigarettes a day. I was also placed on anxiety medication, which I would cheek for a couple days, and then take all the pills and really get relaxed. The food was fabulous, I had my own room with a television and bathroom, and I couldn't have been more comfortable. What I didn't do was tell the truth about how I was really feeling inside. I had a mud storm going on in there, and it was raining hard.

"They cut me loose with a pat on the back and a six-month supply of depression and anxiety medication. It was recommended I seek out a therapist, and I found one when I got back to LA. She wouldn't have known psychological pain if it had run her down in the street. She was a nice gal and did her very best with me, but you can only take someone as far as you've personally gone…and as far as I could see, she hadn't left the driveway.

"The things I remember most about that state hospital stay was my oriental shrink who barely spoke English and kept calling me Shim instead of Slim.

"She'd sit me down in her office and ask, 'How are we feeling today, Shim?'

"'How are we feeling? Well, let me think on that some. You seem happier than a teenager with a two-day hard-on, and I'm about ready to run head first into that concrete wall over there, Doc. The medication you have me on makes me feel like I'm a record playing on the wrong speed, and my mouth tastes like copper and sand. I guess one of us is fine.'

"She'd just smile and nod her head, but she had no idea what I'd just said or how to help me.

"To add to my delight, I had a roommate named Ronnie, who was a compulsive masturbator and snored like a bulldozer with a bullhorn. He'd pull on his pecker so hard, I was afraid he was gonna do a damn back flip. He followed me around like a hungry puppy, and talked my damn ear off. He left masturbatorial DNA samples all over our room, and I didn't get relaxed until I got transferred down the hall. My next roommate never said a word, and slept the entire time I was there. That was fine by me. I later found out he'd ran off the rails after backing over his infant daughter in his pickup. Poor guy killed her, and how the hell do you recover from something like that?"

I pursed my lips together a moment, then said, "It would take an inner strength and personal forgiveness I cannot begin to imagine."

"It would take a miracle, and then some. I remember another patient who sold me cigarettes and some of the pills he pretended to take. He'd be calm one minute, and throw chairs the next. I think he liked the shots they'd give him. The cat was impervious to pain, and one day I saw him stick a sewing needle through his hand. When I asked him why he'd done it, he smiled and told me physical pain helped him focus. He also told me he was a paranoid schizophrenic who castrated himself with a fishing knife after nearly choking his mother to death with her underwear."

"That is a conversation stopper," I noted.

"Yeah, it was a real Hallmark moment.

"The dayroom was the only place we could smoke, so that's where you would find me. Playing gin rummy with Poker Alice. She was my good buddy who shot her hubby three times accidentally. She'd managed to convince a jury of her peers she was legally nuts at the time, and she was sentenced to the hospital until she was cured.

"I asked her, 'How will they know you are cured?'

"She winked at me and laid her cards down with another gin. She was quick as a whip, and I could never beat her at cards. She was also a cheeker, and saved up her really good meds for rocket trips. She acted like she was plumb loco, but she was a damn fine actress.

"The sad part about the state hospital was a lot of the folks were lifers, and weren't ever gonna get out. They wandered around the joint like tired ghosts, and their eyes had no hope or light behind 'em. I felt real sorry about it, I truly did, but I was busy trying to pull my own head outta my ass.

"For those who have never struggled emotionally, there is a tendency to unintentionally minimize. "I've been sad, too." "Everyone goes through ups and downs." "We all get depressed." Things like that."

"Yep. It ain't about being sad. I can swat sad off of my shoulder like a damn mosquito. I'm talking about a soul storm that inhales you from the inside out, and all you can think about is making it stop no matter what. For some folks, that's suicide. For others, it's dope and booze. Shopping. Gambling. Maybe it's cutting. Eating and purging. Exercise. Or sex. They'll do anything to stop it because it hurts that bad."

Slim shuffled around uncomfortably in his chair before rising. He glanced at the kitchen, then the fire, then outside the window. There was nothing to attend to. Nothing to distract him from whatever had shown up inside of him.

"Major depression and anxiety are diseases of the mind, Son, and fighting 'em ain't about smarts or strength. Therapy and medication saved my bacon, pure and simple. I couldn't fight it alone. I required adequate representation to defend me in the court of my mind, you know?

"Anyways, the hospital stay in Los Angeles did me some good. Like I said, all the others were court-ordered, and didn't do me a lick of good. In LA, I knew I needed help and I was gonna die without it. When I went in, I was pounding booze and dope as fast as I could get it. The only thing I knew for sure was I had to fire Dr. Chance and find me a good shrink.

"Well, she found me. I had this lady shrink who was so damned shiny, I had to look at my shoes when I was in her office. I think she thought it was on account of my depression, but it was really so I could hear what she was saying. She was one fine-looking woman, and damn smart to boot. She reached down and pulled me outta the hole.

"I'd been in the dark so long that when I started to see some light, it about scared me. That's one thing about pulling out of a depression. There's responsibility in getting well. Nobody expects things outta you when you're that sick. It's easy to sit on the bench and do nothing perfectly. You start to get better, and life expects you to get in the game again.

"Let me back up. I remember the day after I checked in—I was sitting in the dayroom watching television, and this cat sat down next to me. I never looked beside me, as that would've taken some effort, and any effort at all was beyond me at that point. I was way down there, Son, and my hope had given me the slip."

"'Hello, Slim. How's it hanging?'

"I looked sideways, and I'll be dipped in donuts if it wasn't an old bass player of mine from the early eighties. We called him Pork, on account of he was a vegeterian. He wasn't with the band long, maybe six months or so, but he and I became good pals."

"'Pork?' I asked.

"'In the flesh,' he answered with a sloppy grin.

"'Holy sheep shit! I ain't seen you in forever. What in the hell are you doing here?'

"'I work on the adolescent floor. I happened to be glancing through the adult patient roster and saw your name, so I thought I'd check on you. How are you doing?'

"'I'm breaking all kinds of fucking happy records here. I weigh about a hundred and thrity five pounds, I ain't slept in three nights, I'm out of cigarettes, my roommate thinks he's Jesus, and I can't even get the gumption up to kill my damn self. At least the food sucks and my shrink has the personality of a strangled snake. How you doing?'

"'Man, I'm sorry, Slim.'

"'I used to be able to climb outta the pit, Pork. Lately I can't get a grip on anything, and I'm raining inside something fierce.'

"'I'm sorry to hear that. You might not believe this, but I was sitting where you are five years ago with a major depression that wouldn't lift. I wanted to die, Slim.'

"'You made it out. And now you're gonna tell me I'm gonna make it out too, but I won't believe you, so save your damn breath.'

"'That's up to you, my friend. If you're willing to stand up and face your feelings head on, you'll make it out, and that means giving up the sauce and the drugs.'

"'Please don't give me the happy, joyous, and free speech, Pork. I've heard it all.'

"'And yet, here you are. Look, maybe part of this is you haven't been following directions. I read your chart, and you and I both know you're a drug-addicted alcoholic with a chemical imbalance in your brain. I've got to get back to work, but listen to me. Dr. Stephenson is a miracle worker, so give her a chance. I'm serious, Slim. You have to get out of yourself, and in order to get out, first you have to get in.'

"'That's really deep, Pork.'

"'Deep is where you need to go, Slim.'

"'Please, don't give me psychobabble bullshit!'

"'I just want you to get better.'

"'Oh hell, I'm sorry. I'm just in so much pain, and I can't pretend my way out of it anymore. I know I gotta give up the booze and dope, but every time I try to get sober, it's like giving birth to a porcupine. The last thing I need is to feel sorry for myself. I got a battle ahead of me, and I gotta keep my head up. It's good to see you, and please come back when you can.'

"'Not to worry, Slim, and of course I'll be back. I'm serious about Dr. Stevenson. Give her a chance, and she'll evict you from your hiding places. The hiding places that keep you sick and in the dark.'

"Well, I didn't exactly take his advice to heart overnight, but I eventually got there. And he was right on the money. She was a miracle worker, and got a couple of pucks past my goalie. She saved my life, Son. And Pork visited me every day, and we got to laughing about old times and new times ahead. Who knew he was an angel.

"The day I was released, Pork walked me out through this garden area. We sat down while I waited for Feather to come pick me up. We both got quiet, and then he put his hand on my shoulder.

"'I've heard it said that mind-altering drugs put us in touch with a reality we haven't earned yet, Slim. You can get to those places sober, and that's when the great mysteries all start to truly make sense.'

"'That's always been my problem, Pork. When I'm sober, nothing seems to make any sense. I mean, I feel better and think clearer, but eventually the anxiety gets too damn loud, and I have to shut it up any way I can. That's always been booze and dope.'

"'I get it. I felt the same way, Slim. Anxiety is a bitch, but it will always pass, and it can't kill us. In a way, I made friends with mine. It all just takes time. And some work, too. I believe in you, and I know you have what it takes to get to the other side of this. But it all starts with sobriety. Without that, you can't get to the peace you're looking for.'

"'Did you get evicted?' I asked him. 'From your hiding places?'

"'I've shed most of them. I like it a lot better now that I have keys to this place, but this building and Dr. Stephenson saved my life. Hokey as it sounds, I learned to name it, claim it, blame it, but not to frame it. I learned to coexist with some of the problems I haven't worked through yet, and I'll always be a work in progress. I still have bats in my belfry, but at least they are now flying in formation.'

"Here's to keeping the bats in formation. Here's to getting evicted from our hiding places. Here's to solving the great mysteries, and the miracles we trip over on the way there."

Chapter Fifteen

"Do you miss performing?" I asked Slim. "And what did you do when you knew you were finally done playing music?"

"That's two questions, Son. I only got the one brain, you know."

"Sorry, your majesty," I offered. "One question. Got it. How did you feel when you stopped performing?"

"Well, that was the biggest bite of humble pie I ever took. To know I wasn't gonna reach my lofty music goals, you know? But when I got it swallowed, it was a damn relief. No more promoting this and promoting that, driving sixteen hours, and living outta a suitcase. No more firing and hiring musicians or hanging my head when things didn't go like I wanted. No more dealing with jaded and jagged folks in the music business. I bowed out of the rat race, Son, and it felt good to pull over and turn off the damn engine.

"And I was given perspective from an old pal who said, 'This might be a case of be careful what you wish for because you might just get it, Slim. If someone would've handed you a million dollars in your twenties, you might not have seen your thirties.'"

"Boy, is that not the truth. So many of our most revered musicians died so young. Perhaps too much was given to them before they were prepared," I pondered.

"Honestly, the way I was running and gunning and doing dope, if I'd have had unlimited funds, there's no doubt in my mind I would've been dead before thirty. I still had folks in my life who told me the truth and spanked me when I needed it. You get to a certain level of fortune and fame and there's nobody to tell you the truth. There's nobody to make you face the person staring back at you in the mirror. There's nobody to save your damn life.

"And, what do you do when you make it to the very top of the mountain and you still feel empty? What then? How do you fill that hole? I think that's what happens to a lot of really successful folks. They get to a point where they have everything they ever wanted except peace."

"Peace is priceless. So many do not even have an inkling," I noted.

Slim placed both hands on his chest above his heart, closed his eyes, and inhaled deeply. Maybe thirty seconds passed by, and I tried to put words to his posture. His words pulled me back to the room.

"We both know peace can't be bought. I believe gratitude and humility go hand-in-hand, and lead to a faith that really works on all our problems. A lot of folks can't get there, and many celebrities seem to have a really difficult time. They're trying to fix a spiritual problem with material solutions.

"I guess it's tough to learn to worship when you're worshipped, you know?"

"Well said, Mr. Chance."

"I don't believe money is the root of all evil. I think greed, pride, and ego are part of it, too. I call 'em the Fatal Four. Pride might be the worst of all of 'em, and to my knowledge, nobody ever choked to death swallowing it.

"This reminds me of a cat I knew in the music business—you've heard of him, but I ain't gonna tell you his name. He was a big star and had over eighty million bucks in the bank. Eighty million. And that was after a couple divorces.

"This cat would buy a new car whenever he flew into a city, drive it for a week, and leave it at the airport when he flew out and forget about it. He had six homes and his own jet airplane. Anything he wanted, he bought. Then he'd just lose interest in it and go find another check to write.

"He bought and named a yacht after me.

"'Folklore says water never forgets' he said to me. 'If you have a boat named after you, you'll live forever.'

"'But why name it after me?' I asked.

"'You're the only person in my life who doesn't want anything from me. Since you're my only friend, that makes you my best one.'

"I remember a time I got picked up by a limousine and driven to the private airport where my friend parked his plane. We flew to Paris for dinner, and came back when we were done. Paris. For a damn dinner. This is the kind of life this cat lived every day. He never even carried money. Not a single penny. He had a guy who travelled with him and took care of all expenses, as he couldn't be bothered with such trivialities.

"He was the most miserable human being I think I've ever known. Tortured from the moment his eyes opened until they closed at night. And, he was a non-stop drinker. After I got clean and found the handle on some peace, he'd come find me and we'd talk for hours. I guess he liked me on account of I always told him the truth. He called me his zen master, and I'd just wave him off. One day, we were flying around in his jet when he was hurting. He always seemed to feel better in the air.

"'Why can't I get it, Slim?' he asked me. 'Why can't I have what you have?'

"'Who needs God when you've got eighty million bucks?' I told him.

"'I'd give you everything I have if you could make me happy,' he said. 'Everything…I have.'

"I didn't have the heart to tell him he didn't have one damn thing I wanted.

"I went on to tell him all about what I had to do and what I had to let go of, and he really listened, you know? He tried to get it. But he couldn't, because he couldn't get past his image to the person he was created to be. He was poisoned by his persona, Son, and no matter how tall his life got, he couldn't reach the God he craved so much. The God who was waiting for him down on the damn ground.

"The last time I saw him, he gave me a big hug and said, "I think I've got it, Slim. I'm going to AA meetings, and I really think I'm starting to understand what you've been talking about.'

"Two months later, he jumped off a chair with a rope around his neck and finally found some peace. I helped carry his coffin the day they put him in the dirt. All these famous folks were at the funeral. I could tell they weren't there for him. They were there to be seen. There were no tears shed over his grave that day by his supposed loved ones. Only whispered prayers they'd been remembered in the will.

"The papers said he'd died of natural causes at home. He had a hell of a publicist. And about sixty cars spread out across the country nobody knew what to do with.

"I felt real bad about him dying like that, but I know there was nothing anybody could've done for him. His eyes and ears were closed by pride and ego, and you can carry the message, but not the alcoholic. And there's nothing more deadly than a head full of AA and a belly full of booze. Anyways, where were we before I jumped up on my soapbox?"

"I asked you if you missed music, and what you decided to do when you were done."

"It was a relief to be done, and I started seeing things in a different way. I had my time, and I loved the whole shooting match. Knowing what I know now, I would've spent the money for a video and pushed the records to radio harder than I did. And, I would've done it all sober.

"I know if I hadn't been doing dope and booze the way I was, I would've gone a lot further. That's just simple math. We had the tools to take it all the way. I just never released the reins and let the horse run like it could've.

"And I didn't think I could go to the places creatively I wanted to go to without chemical assistance, Son. I know a lot of cats who felt and believed that way. I've known some real heavy hitters in the music industry who killed themselves with dope they couldn't let go. They believed it was their magical muse. For some, they'd rather die than lose a creative step.

"I tried to write music after I cleaned up, and it was like trying to start an old lawnmower. The harder you pull, the quicker you snap the damn cord. I couldn't force it. It wasn't time. I didn't have a grasp on myself, and creativity wasn't in the cards yet. A few months down the line, song ideas started to creep in, and it was enough for me to know they were still there. But by that time, I didn't want to be a part of that game anymore, and that was fine by me. I knew it would always be waiting for me if I chose to pick it up again.

"I still love picking on that old guitar, but it's all coming from a different place now. I haven't written a song in years, and not because I decided it would be so. They just quit coming.

"No, that's not true. It's not that they quit coming—I just don't let 'em sit on my lap anymore."

"Perhaps you are simply on hiatus, Slim. Taking a creative holiday."

Slim shrugged nonchalantly, pointed to a shiny black guitar hanging on the wall and hugged himself with his arms.

"I dunno, maybe. What I do know is I wrote a lot of songs, and they're all like kids to me, but I was an alcoholic parent. One day, I was a loving father, and supportive of all aspects of my career. Maybe the next day I wouldn't care as much. Some days I wouldn't care at all, and just wanted to get high and turn the volume down. It was like that for years, and likely the true reason I never got to that next level. I put a governor on my motor.

"I do know that for a while, I thought my creative juices dried up along with the dope and booze. I don't look at it like that today. I just think I got to a peaceful place inside where it's no longer important for me to 'be someone,' and today I have different creative outlets. I don't know if it's a good thing or a bad thing that I'm not writing songs. I only know I'm not writing songs."

"You mention having different creative outlets."

"I got a strip tease act and I perform exclusively at polka festivals."

"Gives a whole new meaning to roll out the barrel, I suppose."

"You ain't gotta one up me every damn time now, Son."

"Seriously now. What creative outlets have you developed?" I asked.

"Well, my marriage, for one. I'm in love deep, Son, and we reinvent our relationship all the time. I've written a lot of short stories, mostly mini murder mysteries. I really pay attention to my friendships these days. They are sacred to me. I tried painting, but a monkey with a toothbrush could make better pictures than I can.

"My spiritual life is always a work in progress, and I also fell in love with carpentry and working with wood. I get a lot of practice keeping this place up. Hell, I even took pottery and dancing lessons with Julie Marie, and we really enjoy cutting a rug now and then. How's that. Enough for you?"

"Indeed. I'd really love to read your short stories, if you'll allow it."

"I'll have to think on that some, Son. Julie Marie is the only one who's seen 'em. She tells me I'm pretty fair at it, but I dunno. I just love the process. I take off on my typewriter and I never know where I'll end up. The stories tell themselves, just like my songs did. That kind of writing seems to come from a different part of me. It's using a different muscle entirely.

"The bottom line is, I'm proud of how I picked the right side of the fence for me and didn't just sit there on it like so many do. I didn't pick the side with plush grass and a cushy trail to walk on. I picked the side with rocks and hills, snakes and wolves, wind, snow, and rain. Music gave me a ton of adventures to dance and smile to.

"And yes, sometimes I miss it, but not for the reasons you may think. I miss the camaraderie. Going to battle night after night with teammates. Watching a piece of music bounce around from player to player like a ball of energy and become something bigger and better in front of your eyes.

"But then you bring in the personality conflicts, addictions, chronic fatigue and egos, and the boat starts to spring some leaks. Crazy girlfriends who wanna play tambourine and sing in the band. The drummer wants to be the lead singer. The bass player wants the band to do all of his songs. The manager steals all the money. The producer shelves the record. Disco takes over the planet and nobody likes rock and roll anymore. That's when the movie gets interesting. When the band gets to see what it's really made of. You find out which leaks can and can't be patched."

"Again, when you knew you were done, what did you do?"

Slim gave me the best grin of the night, rose from his chair, and placed his face inches from mine. My breath caught in my chest and I braced myself for come what may.

"Whatever the hell I wanted."

Slim turned and began to pace.

I took a breath. Smiled to myself.

"I never lost the travel bug, so I took some of my money and bought me a gigantic, fancy RV. I went back and forth across the country maybe ten times before I landed here for good. I had to put my finger on America's pulse, Son, and it's real strong.

"You meet all sorts of folks in campgrounds, and I had me some adventures. I remember a place in Nebraska where a family from somewhere down south camped next to me. They had these teenagers who were always up to no good…sneaking cigarettes and booze and such. I caught 'em in my camper one night when I came back from a stroll, and thought I'd teach a lesson.

"Back then, I always had a pistol in my boot, and you should've seen their faces when I produced it.

"'You boys lost?' I asked.

"'No, I mean, yes, Sir,' one of 'em said.

"'Well, which is it? You're either lost or you're in here looking for something to steal. Maybe I oughta shoot one of you in the leg.'

"'We're sorry, Sir,' the other one said. 'We were just looking for some alcohol is all.'

"'Were you now?' I thought on it for a minute, then decided on a course of action.

"I had some moonshine I kept for special occasions, and I figured this was gonna be one of 'em. I sat those boys down and proceeded to fill two cups with a concoction that would melt your tongue. They were coughing and sputtering and carrying on, but I made 'em drink just enough of it to get the message. And to speed things up, I made 'em load their cheeks with some chewing tobacco.

"Maybe twenty minutes into the deal, they were both out behind my camper, projectile vomiting. By the time they'd finally finished, I grabbed 'em by the arms and delivered 'em straight to their parents."

"What did you tell their parents?" I asked.

"Only thing I could tell them. The truth. I told 'em what happened exactly as it did. Their momma was horrified, and looked at me like I'd put 'em in a guillotine. Their poppa slapped me on the shoulder and profusely thanked me for my efforts.

"Funny thing was, when I was sitting in my camper later that night, I heard a knock on the door. There was Poppa. He'd come by to see if I had any of that shine left. I did, and we almost finished it.

"Turned out he'd been a college football coach for forty years, and six of his players went on to play pro ball. They named their stadium after him, and he was damn proud of that. He'd played football in college as well, and he walked like he had concrete blocks tied to his feet. Maybe on account of he'd broken his back twice.

"I'll tell you another thing, Son. I drank a ton of booze with a lot of different folks, and there weren't many who could outdrink me. Poppa showed me how it was done that night. I kept up with him until the fourth quarter, and don't hardly remember much after that.

"I talked to him the next day, and he told me I'd given him quite the concert. He said I played some dandy guitar until I'd tossed my cookies on it. I went to check it, and sure enough, I'd put it back in the case covered in booze ooze. I dry heaved the entire time I cleaned it."

"Now there's a Kodak moment." I mimicked taking a picture.

"Yeah, the makings for another Hallmark card. Another time in Missouri, I was sitting outside my buggy, staring into a fire I'd made, when this old boy showed up and asked if he could join me. I pointed to a chair and he took it. We introduced ourselves, and got to jabber jawing about this and that, upping each other on stories and such. Then, he went and told me a doozy.

"He was an ex-lawman from Texas who'd taken a bullet chasing down a gang that had just hit a bank in Laredo. He'd shot one down before he'd passed out, and the others got caught trying to cross into Mexico. He showed me the bullet hole in his right shoulder, and I got a kick outta the fact he'd tattooed the word 'ouch' below it.

"He retired from law enforcement, and learned how to make cowboy boots from Charlie Dunn himself in Austin. You don't likely know it, but Charlie Dunn was known as the 'Michelangelo of cowboy boots.' The most famous boot maker in the world."

"I have heard of Charlie Dunn from the Jerry Jeff Walker song."

"Well, ain't you the cultured cat. Anyways, he pointed at my boots, and I'll be dipped in donuts if he didn't tell me he'd made 'em. I'd won the boots in a poker game, and I could tell they were real expensive. I told him he was plum full of beans. He insisted I take one off.

"'Just peel that left one off, and there'll be some initials on the inside that are mine,' he said.

"Well, I pulled off my left boot, and he leaned over and pointed at three initials: WSB.

"'Wilbur Smith Boots,' he said, with a grin stained with tobacco. 'Thousand bucks a pair. Where'd you get them?'

"I told him how I'd won the boots and a gold watch from a cat named Fletcher Williston in a poker room in New Mexico.

"'I knew his daddy well,' he said. 'Arrested him in Arkansas in 1952.'

"I didn't know whether to laugh or spit on that one. I cocked an eye.

"'You knew Fletcher Williston's daddy?' I asked.

"'Naw, I'm just tuggin' on your tail. But I made them boots. Yes, Sir, I did.'

"We shared stories and laughed like hyenas that night, and I remember Wilber Smith's voice and presence like it was Tuesday."

"That is a great story. You still have the boots?" I asked.

"Lost 'em in a poker game."

"Oh, no. Sorry to hear that." Then I gave him a look. "Are you serious?"

"Naw, now I'm just tuggin' on *your* tail. They're in my closet, too worn to wear, but I can't bring myself to get rid of 'em. Julie Marie bought me the ones I got on. They're Charlie Dunn specials. Look at the leatherwork. It's like wearing masterpieces on your feet.

"Wanna take 'em for a spin? What size do you wear?"

"I wear size ten tennis shoes, but ten and a half in boots."

"Well, ain't that a peach. These are ten-point fives. Peel off them sneakers, and I'll show you what some real footwear can do for you. Take a little spin around the room and tell me what you think."

I slipped my loafers off of my feet and pulled on Slim's boots. They fit surprisingly well, though I felt silly in them. I stood and began to stroll around the room.

"Oh, my. These *are* comfortable. I've never worn cowboy boots in my life. I could get used to these."

"Handmade boots such as those are a tad spendy, but worth every penny. My grandfather taught me to always spend good money on footwear, and I always have. After I healed up a broken back, I've never had feet or back problems. That ain't a coincidence, Son. What we put on our feet can make or break us.

"You get what you pay for in this life. It took me half of my life to start buying good clothes. I always wore thrift store clothing, and never paid no mind to quality. Why spend a ton of money on a shirt or a pair of jeans when you can get both for ten bucks at a Goodwill store? Well, a gal I was dating way back when showed me the error of my ways. She was always buying me clothes and dressing me up real fancy like. At first, it drove me crazy, and I hated it. And then, I started noticing something.

"The good clothes felt great. They wore better. Fit better. Lasted longer. They were more comfortable, and I'd look forward to wearing 'em. Folks started complimenting me on my appearance. Why didn't I think of that? I was busy wearing five-dollar jeans and two-dollar shirts. Wearing cowboy boots from the damn Civil War. I stepped up my game and felt better about myself."

"You became a fashionista. A purveyor of fine music really should adorn himself with haute couture."

"Don't try to confuse me with them twenty-dollar words, Son. If you said what I think you just said, I'll agree with you and move on. But first, give me my damn boots back."

Chapter Sixteen

"What is the worst thing that has happened to you on your sojourn?" I asked.

"Hmmm, it would have to be the time I ran outta coffee creamer in Mississippi."

"Again, I am cracking up on the inside."

"You're a tough crowd, Son. Let's see now…the worst thing that happened to me. I'll tell you what the scariest thing was, but again, you might not believe me."

"Try me."

Slim's eyebrows raised, then he asked me, "You ready for this?"

I nodded and said, "Yes, I am."

Again, his bouncing eyebrows moved and he asked, "Are you *really* ready for this?"

I tilted my head to the side and pursed my lips. *Come on. Tell me.*

"I was driving an all-nighter somewhere in Arizona, and my eyes were getting mighty heavy. I was doing what I could to stay awake. You know, blasting the music with the windows down. I tried to get some praying done, but the Almighty and I weren't exactly on the best terms at the time, and my words were glued to the roof of my mouth.

"I was just getting ready to pull over for a nap when the hair on the back of my neck rose up and fear gripped my throat. I suddenly felt like I was falling off a cliff. Thirty seconds later, I saw this shadowy figure standing just off the shoulder of the road.

"He scared the bejesus outta me. I'm in the absolute middle of nowhere, Son. I'm looking around for a vehicle and there ain't one.

"I pulled to the shoulder, thinking maybe he needed help, but more fear rose up in me, so I grabbed my pistol out of the glove box and set it on the seat beside me. I sat there for a bit, trying to catch my breath and figure out why I was feeling the way I was. I could hear my heart beating in my damn ears. I was on red alert, Son.

"I looked in the side mirror and there he was, watching me watch him. When he didn't walk towards me, I took a deep breath, opened my door, and stepped out onto the pavement.

"Now again, I'm fifty miles to the next town, and it was so dark, the stars looked like Christmas lights on a tree. He had no business being out there. I stepped around my buggy and yelled.

"'You okay?'

"He didn't move an inch, and neither did I.

"'You need a ride?'

"Nothing. I remember thinking it was strange I couldn't see any of his face. Almost like he didn't have one. We both just stood there facing each other, and I remember thinking how calm and quiet the night was. All I could think to do was say a prayer and to keep my eyes on him in case he moved.

"All at once, I heard a voice in my head that drowned out everything. It said, 'Where's your God now?' Everything in me tensed up, and I remembered that voice and his breath on my skin all those years ago. He was there.

"'Be still, and know I am God,' I repeated several times.

"My breath caught in my throat every time I said it. And maybe I was seeing things, but the figure seemed to move slightly every time I said it. The voice in my head got louder. 'Where's your God now, Boy?'

"I closed my eyes and took the deepest breath I could take. Somehow, I knew I had to swallow my fear and face this thing. I opened my eyes and yelled at the top of my lungs, 'I BELONG TO GOD! I BELONG TO GOD! I BELONG TO GOD!'

"Well, I watched his yellow eyes light up, and he let out a screech that hurt my ears and could've been heard miles away. I half expected him to come flying across the road and take my damn head off, and I tried to yell again, but I couldn't get words out. Couldn't move. I was nine years old again and absolutely paralyzed.

"Several voices ran through my head, but they were too quiet to make out. They were chanted whispers that ran over the top of each other, and I plugged my ears and yelled at the top of my lungs. The figure tilted its head to one side and raised its hands to its ears to mimic me.

"Every ounce of strength I had available rose up inside of me, and I started walking towards it. I was done being scared, Son, and for whatever reason, I needed to see its face.

"Just then, the wind came up outta nowhere, and dust and debris started flying around. I had to shut my eyes and cover 'em with my forearm. I don't recall what I said, but I know I whispered another prayer.

"Then, just like it came, the wind was sucked back into the sky. It took me a while to get the sand outta my eyes, and then I looked back to where he was standing.

"I'll be dipped in donut dust if he wasn't gone. Disappeared. The hair on the back of my neck felt like it went clear over to my face. I looked on both sides of the road and in all directions, and he wasn't there, Son. Before I even knew what I was doing, I was in the cab of my buggy with my pistol in my hand. I half expected him to grab me from behind. With my finger on the trigger, I glanced in the rearview mirror. Nothing.

"I turned the lights on in the camper and checked everywhere. Normally, I would've felt silly for acting this way, but seeing this guy lit me up inside like a Roman candle. It took me quite awhile to shake all the fear off of me."

"Excuse my mouth, but holy shit," I stated.

"See these goose bumps on my arms? All these years later, and he's still got me chased up a tree."

Slim brought his arms to me, covered in emotional moguls. He pointed to several of them as if I couldn't see them. He was lit up like a beacon, inside and out.

I ran my hand up my own arm. "I have goose bumps as well. Why do you think it picked you?"

"I dunno. In a way, he'd been with me in my dreams since the age of nine, you know? There were times in my life when I'd forget about him, but I think he was always close by. Waiting for me to drop my guard and let him back in.

"Maybe I'll never know why it picked me. I was no threat to evil. I wasn't a preacher or a teacher, and I certainly wasn't a prophet. For whatever reason, it had designs on me. Maybe I was low-hanging fruit. I was vulnerable, and ripe for the picking. I do know it woke me right up, and I again picked my side and decided to stick with it come hell or high water.

"Maybe that's what it was all about. Finding a passion for the right side of the big fence. It's a puzzle I still ain't put together yet, Son. I was visited by an evil being on three occasions, and the third time really got my attention. In fact, since that night on the road, I haven't seen or felt any evidence of him. I finally picked God with all my heart, and that sent him away.

"As I look back, that happening led me to a freedom inside I'd never felt. When I saw that thing again, it shook me enough to open my mind to praying again. And praying led me to some open-mindedness and gratitude, which led me to Julie Marie."

"A happy ending to a disturbing story," I said.

"Yes. She came along when I was finally healthy enough to meet her head-on. Any other time in my life, a powerful woman like her would've had me hiding in the bushes. I had to get to a place where my insides matched my outsides and I could let the great in. In the old days, I just swatted it all away. I was always ready to snatch defeat from the jaws of victory.

"All the crying and dying I did from the inside out paid off in spades, Son. It scraped all the bad stuff outta me. I had to find my joy in that storm. So many folks don't stick around long enough for the joy to evict the pain. I just didn't give up and quit before the miracle happened.

"I found out the world is really a good place, you know? The best thing I learned from being on the road was that most folks are damned fine people. It restored my faith in humanity is what it did. I befriended everybody I could, and for a compulsive introvert, that's saying something.

"I think what surprised me the most was that you can really count on people when you need 'em. I must've broken down or got a flat tire five times, and folks were standing in line to help. Snow, rain, or shine.

"One time I tipped the RV over on its side in a blizzard. When I climbed out and jumped off, I bounced off a snowbank and did a headfirst swan dive through some ice and into water. Ten below zero, Son, and I didn't know what I was gonna do. Just then, an old couple drove up in a big Suburban, and next thing I know, I'm in the backseat getting wet clothes stripped off me and being covered in blankets. They even had cocoa to boot. They saved my bacon and gave me a ride into town.

"A tow truck flipped my buggy back on all fours, towed me to his shop, slapped two tires back on the rims, and I was back on the road in under two hours. Only thing damaged was my pride."

I leaned forward. "Slim, you could have *died* in that situation."

"Those folks came along in the nick of time, and for a couple years, I sent 'em Christmas cards. I met a lot of angels on the road, and a lot of 'em were in Alcoholics Anonymous meetings. That's a spiritual program that came straight from the Almighty, Son, and I learned a hell of a lot sitting in those rooms. Now I ain't saying I'm a member of AA. If I was, I'm not supposed to talk about it at the level of press, radio, or film. Let's just say I'm an ardent advocate for the program."

Slim covered his chest with both hands and gave me an animated wink.

"I met a cat at a meeting in Santa Fe who'd spent ten years living on the streets. Before that, he was a therapist. Booze thumped him good, but he crawled into a meeting after being sick and tired of being sick and tired, and AA took for him. He'd been sober for fifteen years, and was a supervisor of five homeless shelters in New Mexico after he'd gotten clean.

"He was the cat who told me he would never say he was done drinking. He just wasn't gonna drink that day. He told me putting the plug in the jug is a small part of sobriety, and alcoholism is a disease of the mind and an allergy of the body. You can only take someone as far spiritually as you have gone yourself. He spent all those years trying to help folks with an empty tank.

"And he was real big on getting rid of resentments. He thought resentments were a luxury not meant for alcoholics. Having them was like drinking poison and expecting the other person to die—it was deadly to sobriety.

"He told me whenever I am upset with somebody, I have two choices. First, if I owe an apology to somebody, I make it without hesitation. Second, if I don't owe an apology and they are at fault, I forgive 'em without hesitation. That's it. No middle ground. Just action. It's a prescription for good health and low blood pressure.

"I've always thought of alcoholism as a soul sickness. Once alcohol enters the body of an alcoholic, it triggers a craving more powerful than a hurricane. It's said one drink is too many, and a thousand is never enough. And just because an alcoholic puts the plug in the jug doesn't mean his thinking gets better overnight. You see, the monkey's off my back, but the circus is still in town."

"The circus is still in town. That is fabulous. So, every sober alcoholic is just one drink away from the disease process starting up again."

"One drink or drug away from insanity, institutions, or death, Son. I'm alive today because I got sober, and if the dope and booze hadn't killed me, I certainly would have. A person can only take so much darkness before he shuts it all down for good. I know what a gun barrel tastes like.

"Another gal I met in Baton Rouge said she'd been locked up in a mental hospital and they threw away the key. Nine years she was in that place, and all she could do was babble on account of they said she had alcohol-induced dementia.

"An angel took her to AA meetings in the hospital, and I'll be damned if she didn't come out of it. She said her psychiatrist was so tickled, he wrote a paper on AA for a medical journal. She went on to be clean and sober for five years, then went to college to be a teacher at forty-four years of age. Stories like that fell off the trees in and around those meetings, Son. Just when I thought I'd heard the best, a better one would come along. Sort of gets your attention when you're grinding metal on metal emotionally, you know?

"Seems like every time I went to an AA meeting, I met someone who had something to say I needed to hear. Too many coincidences start to taste like a miracle.

"It's really sad when you see folks fall of the wagon, though. I knew a guy with over thirty years clean who started up again and blew his brains out, three weeks after he sat right next to me in a meeting. Another gal I knew took herself out with a hose hooked to her exhaust pipe. She'd sponsored and helped a ton of women, but she stopped doing what she was teaching, and it killed her. They got real thirsty, and for some reason, had nothing or nobody to knock the glass out of their hands."

"Do you still go to AA meetings?" I asked him.

Slim puckered up his face, then said, "You're kinda nosy, ain't ya?"

"I'm incredibly nosy."

"Yep. Those meetings are the closest I ever get to going to church. Everyone's welcome, and there ain't no rules on what you gotta believe. Hell, you don't even have to quit drinking to go. If you have a desire to quit, that's good enough for them. And, you get to pick a Higher Power of your own understanding, and nobody gets to judge that. It's a big enough umbrella, you know?

"That's the damn genius of it all. That, and sick folks helping other sick folks for fun and for free. For many, it's a recipe that works when nothing else does, Son. Heaven sent."

"Not to be pejorative, but I've heard some say AA is like a cult."

The anger in Slim's eyes filled them with moisture, and he pointed at me like I was a misbehaving child.

"Some say you only live once, and they're wrong about that, too. I've heard it all, and I'm not gonna dignify such nonsense with further comment. It would be best if you kept any AA criticisms to yourself in my home."

"You got it, no problem, Slim. I have nothing but respect for Alcholics Anonymous and all the good work the organization does. Seriously, you won't hear a negative peep from me."

"I'll say what I always say to folks who don't like AA. If you find something else that can get and keep you sober, my hat's off to you and I wish you well. You ain't gonna hurt AA's feelings none. But don't poison the water for those who might want to taste it for themselves.

"And don't knock something you haven't yet tried. AA calls that contempt prior to investigation. The bottom line is, it has worked for millions of folks, and I just thank God it's there for all the wounded warriors out there who can't kick booze alone and who are open to trying it.

"Today, if I ever get thirsty, I get that butt of mine to a meeting. I go there to give, not to get, and by the time I leave, not only am I not thirsty anymore, I'm filled to the gills with enough good stuff to last a while. The highest I get these days is from helping somebody else dig out a bad emotional ingrown nail. No question. When my tank's on empty, I find me an alcoholic to help. I gotta keep my faith fed, Son. That's what keeps me on the road when I overheat."

Chapter Seventeen

"Speaking of respect, Slim—I'm curious to know what you think of today's popular music."

Slim looked away before his eyes met mine. "I'm out of touch, Son. I don't listen to music much anymore, and when I do, it's usually older jazz. My bottom line when it comes to music of any generation is, I admire anybody doing it. Good for them, I say, and I wish 'em all the best. I admire anybody who does art of any kind, you know? You may not get rich but creating will make you wealthy on the inside—where it counts."

"That's it? No critique of any kind?"

"One thing I will say is music today sounds the same to me. It's all written, arranged, and recorded with the same formulas. Back in the old days, you could tell an artist the second you heard his or her voice. You could spot a band when the song kicked off. I don't know if the same is true for today. I know it ain't for country music—or what they're calling country music today. It sounds like classic rock with a twang to me, and I can't tell one singer or band from the next. Maybe there's some good ole traditional country around, but I doubt it's getting much play."

"Are there any artists you really enjoy or admire?"

"I'm a front man junkie. I always thought cats like Freddie Mercury, Mick Jagger, Bowie, Rod Stewart, and Robert Plant were dazzling. I'm a huge fan of Steven Tyler. I tried to get a message to him through his management people about a Chinese cooking show he should host called Wok This Way, but I never heard back from them."

"That is an incredible idea."

"I thought so. Steven has got more damn talent in his little finger than most of 'em. He's my all-time favorite.

"Michael Jackson was amazing. Then you have Springsteen, who spills out his soul every night. The best of 'em all might be Prince."

"And female artists?"

"Rock and roll mommas. The Wilson gal from Heart could really belt a tune. Stevie Nicks has a stage presence you can't deny, and I liked Aretha Franklin, Janis Joplin, Tina Turner, Crissie Hynde, Linda Ronstadt, Debbie Harry, and Grace Slick. A more current singer I really enjoy is Annie Lennox. Sheryl Crow is something special."

"How about bands? What are your favorite bands of all time?"

"My favorite band is the Eagles on account of their songwriting and vocals. Bands that come quickly to mind are Led Zeppelin, The Beatles, The Rolling Stones, The Who, Queen, Aerosmith. And this might surprise you, but I think the best driving beat in the history of rock and roll came from AC/DC."

"Bon Scott is my all-time favorite singer. I'm also a Guns N' Roses fan. Have you heard of the Foo Fighters? I like them a lot, too."

"I've heard of 'em, but I don't know their music. Julie Marie played me a band called Radiohead I liked. She also likes a group called Pearl Jam, and another called Oasis that reminded me of The Beatles. She's also a big fan of Lady Gaga, and I gotta admit she's a huge talent and can sing anything."

"You are full of surprises, Slim Chance. You have impeccable taste, in my humble opinion."

Slim stood, took a bow, and shuffled out to the kitchen, tossing words over his left shoulder.

"I left out some singers and bands that should be on the list, but I hit most of the nails I was swinging at."

Sounds of pots, pans, and dishes crashing rang out from the kitchen. Was he looking for something? Preparing something? I was hungry and hopeful again. He appeared carrying a plate full of brownies, and I almost forgot my question.

"Bob Seger says today's music ain't got the same soul."

"Folks do the best they can to get ahead in the game. I think artists who write and perform music with essence and soul have a more difficult time than the candy-coated, 'get rich quick and look good' ones do. Back in my day, we spent more time crafting. We tried to make music that would stand the test of time. I don't think a lot of the musicians and producers of today approach their work with that attitude, and a lot of those artists and bands I mentioned likely wouldn't get off the ground if they were starting today."

"I agree with that. It seems the music of today comes off quickly on a conveyor belt filled with more of the same. Assembly line production is what I'd call it, Slim."

"There's a truckload of talent out there, like there's always been. That'll never change. And it seems the real stars of today are multifaceted, you know? They can sing, dance, write, act, produce, promote. They do it all, and I really appreciate their talents. Back in my day, the only ones doing all that were on Broadway. Like everything, that's all changed.

"And I'll tell you one thing: I miss the days when a disc jockey or program director could play a record because they liked it. With corporate radio owning everything, I'm pretty sure those days are gone. And then, a lot of folks are bypassing all of that using the internet, and that fascinates me.

"Supporting yourself by playing music is a damn fine accomplishment. I supported myself a long time, and I'm awful proud of that. When you work for yourself, you wake up every morning unemployed. You have a choice whether you want to create work or sit on the couch. There were some lean times early on, and some really fat ones later. I guess it all balanced out, and I did okay in the scheme of things.

"Anyway, I probably don't even know what the hell I'm talking about here. I'm a dinosaur, Son. I don't even have a cell phone or cable television."

"No cell phone? My God, how do you survive, Slim?"

"Lots of prayer and medication."

"You mean, *meditation*?"

"That, too."

I laughed. "I believe you are the only person I know who does not have a cell phone."

"Or a computer."

"Holy batcopters! You cannot even Google."

"The worldwide gaggle of Googlers doesn't need another member. All bent down, staring at their damn phones while life passes 'em by. Can't be good for their spines, staring down like that. Some folks think all of this technology is progress. I think it's one hell of a big pain in the neck."

"I would imagine with the advent of digital technology the entire recording process has evolved."

"Some say it's devolved, and I'm with 'em. Technology being what it is, anyone can make a record and a video in their bedroom. Folks are shooting movies with their smart phones. I know we're in the digital age, but I'll take the sound of an analog record over a digital recording any day of the week, twice on Tuesdays.

"And don't get me started on that damn device that corrects your pitch for you! What the hell's it called?"

"Auto-tune. It measures and alters pitch in vocal and instrumental music."

Slim rolled his eyes and pounded his knee quite hard with his fist. A musical purist, still chasing windmills in his rusted suit of armor.

"I know what the hell it does, and I don't cotton to any of it. Fixing mistakes with a computer? Whoever heard of such a thing? We got it right or we played it again until we did. Nobody went in afterwards with a digital wand.

"Singers could sing, players could play, and producers coached the performance outta you. You had to reach higher than you thought you could. That's what made the magic.

"But I doubt *Rolling Stone* Magazine is gonna call me anytime soon for my musings regarding today's music and such. I had my time, and we did things differently, I guess. I'm just an old school junkie who needs to mind my own business and keep this place up."

"I have to ask. Growing grapes in Ohio? How did you get into that?"

"Folks have been growing grapes in Ohio since the early 1800s, Son. Vinifera are the most challenging to grow, but they produce the highest quality wines. It's a labor of love, I'll tell you that much. I won't bore you with a grape-growing diatribe. Let's just say we do just fine, and the land is worth over ten times what I bought it for.

"Wow. That turned out to be a great investment."

"Other than sobriety and Julie Marie, it's the best investment I've ever made. Ain't nothing like owning a piece of land. It'll be hard to let this place go. I bought it from a real character I'd met in a diner I used to go to. Kind of like the way you and I bumped into each other.

"We got to know each other over coffee cups and pieces of fruit pie, and he'd just lost his wife to cancer. I could see her waving at me inside his eyes. They were married sixty years, and there were too many memories painted around the place. He'd listed it with a real estate agency, but for some reason he really wanted me to have it. I told him I didn't know squat about growing grapes, and I thought he'd want two fortunes for it, and I only had one. He put his hand on mine and said something that melted my damn heart.

"'I've got a real good feeling about you, Slim, and it would do my heart a lot of good to know you were taking care of it for Patty and me while I'm still alive. At my age, the last thing I need is more money. What I need is to spend time with my grandchildren and great grandchildren. I'm going to Arizona. You can pay it off. I'll show you the ropes, and a younger man can make a real go of it here. You'll do fine, and you're buying the pie and coffee.'

"We penciled out a deal I thought was a crime on my part, but he wouldn't have it otherwise. I promised to not sell it as long as he was alive. I gave him a pile of money up front, and by making double payments, I got it done in just under eight years. It hurt me deeply when his daughter called to tell me he'd passed, but he went with a room full of folks who loved him, and he made it ninety-five years."

"Sixty years of love with a good woman, and ninety-five years on the planet. I would have to say he had a good run."

"I'd call it an epic run. I'm hoping for thirty more years with my Julie Marie. Why the hell not? I want to live long enough to believe in fairytales again, Son.

"I think the secret to longevity is lack of stress. Stress kills folks quicker than anything. The body is an astonishing machine and heals itself daily from what we throw at it. If a fella can keep his stress level down, the body can do what it needs to take care of itself. That's why I refuse to get myself exercised over anything these days.

"Like I said, the land and cabin are worth over ten times what I paid for 'em, and we'll have enough to buy a house on the ocean in Florida real soon. Though, honestly, I'd live in a cardboard box as long as I'm beside her. Everything I've been through, all the sad and bad times, I'd do all over again, as long as I ended up where I am right now. I have everything I need, and one hell of a lot of what I want. I'm a very wealthy man."

"That's inspiring to me, Slim. It's more important to want what you have than to have what you want. It's a place I hope to reach someday."

"I hope you get there quicker than I did, Son. I took a lot of bad turns back there, and I was always looking too damn high or low for my answers. They are at eye level. Right where they have always been. We're here to learn from each other, and the best teachers on the planet are the ones right in front of you. We draw to us what we need to learn the most. You gotta keep those ears open and those eyes peeled on, as you never know when the next lesson is gonna happen.

"We are the music makers, and we are the dreamers of the dream, Son. We've all got a lot to be proud of."

Chapter Eighteen

66 **Y**ou have lived an epic life, Slim Chance."
Slim grinned. "I have lived a charmed life, Son. Filled with the best and the worst life has to offer, and more blessings than I could possibly count. Regardless of what I did right or wrong, I stood on passionate ground.

"It would've been easy for me to spend my life in a small South Dakota town with a good gal and a house full of kids. And there ain't nothing wrong with any of that. I just had a whole lot of affection for something, and I was lucky or blessed enough to have followed where it led. What else could be more important? What else would make God smile more than to know his kid lived a life filled with passion?"

"The road less travelled. Do you have any major regrets? Unfinished business?"

"Regrets are for folks who like the taste of tears. I'm just glad I figured out long ago I'd rather be happy than be right. Serenity at all cost. That's the kind of sugar Poppa likes.

"Now there were times when my body wasn't big enough to hold all the pain. I've been to hell and back and I like back much better. I truly believe the reason I've had so much joy in my life is on account of having so much pain. For me, pain has been the admission price for the great movie I call my life. A bliss-blessed adventure I've truly treasured. The band years are priceless to me; gave me more joy than I could spend. And then there was the delicious pain."

"Delicious pain? Those are two words not often used in conjunction."

"Without the pain, I wouldn't have had the breakthroughs. Without the breakthroughs, I wouldn't have had my path lit up to see where I was going wrong. For me, pain has been the admission price for the great movie I call my life. It saved me, but I had to be willing to make the changes. Honesty, open-mindedness, and willingness. If you have them, you got a shot at beating anything.

"I look back, and without question, the worst things that ever happened to me led me to the best stuff life has to offer. My addictions and mental illness have both been tremendous blessings. When I came out on the other side of all that pain, I was more awake and alive. Some folks say heaven is just a new pair of glasses.

"Now it ain't that way for everyone, and I understand that, Son. Some folks feel bad and take steps to change it. That's pain. Others just feel bad about feeling bad, and I call that suffering. My pride always wanted me to move into safety ruts and furnish 'em. Thank God I was able to swallow it, or it would've killed me. Pride truly is a deadly sin, and the misguided, mangled mind is the horse it rides around on.

"Life ain't easy for anyone. But it can be simple when we get out of the way. I've always looked at this life as a soul school, and class is never dismissed. That would be my unfinished business. I'm not done learning, you know? My soul's got room in the closet for more good stuff."

Slim shuffled over to the record pile and fished one out, placed it on the turntable, and gently set the needle down. The unmistakable guitar introduction of The Eagles' "Hotel Califorina" seemed to widen the room. A journey from innocence to experience. Could he have played it better?

"And life has a soundtrack. Some songs you like, and others you can't stand. Some songs are slow when you really feel like rocking. Others are upbeat when you feel like a slow sway. I think it's important to really listen to all of 'em, and to dance to whatever music you get.

"And silence. It took me fifty years to get to a point where I got quiet enough to hear the symphony of my soul. So many of us surround ourselves with noise, and we can't hear it playing. It's so important to get quiet and to breathe, Son.It's how I awaken to the majesty of my life, and it's such a shame to sleep through that, you know? So many do.

"Life is so precious, where smiles and laughter feel just as good to a pauper as they do a millionaire. To utterly love and rejoice the life we are given is our most sacrosanct task. Believe or don't believe in God, but we all possess the majesty and mystery of the ages deep within ourselves. How can one deny such a thing? Suffice it to say, I will spend whatever time I have left savoring every single moment I am gifted with. That's a promise, Son.

"I don't know what else I can share with you. I think the fat lady is ready to sing."

"Well, this has progressed way past any expectations I ever had. It was an honor and a privilege. I do not wish for it to be over, and I sure hope I see you again sometime."

"Maybe sometime, you can tell me your story. Everyone's got a story worth telling. I consider you to be a gentleman and a friend, and you are always welcome where my boots are sitting. Julie Marie would love to meet you, and she's a way better cook than I am a talker.

"And you wanna know something else? I'll be damned if I didn't figure out she's my special purpose. The love we share feeds the love I am able to have for others. It gets no better than. Sharing my life with that woman has given me a direct view into the very eyes of God. I finally see what He has wanted me to see all along—that love and service of others is the point of all of this. Giving, Son, with no thought of returns. The sanctity of life. Our holy and mighty mission.

"Shake my hand and take care of yourself. And when you tell folks about what we talked about here…when you tell my story…stick with the meat, Son."

"Now all I have to do is find my special purpose."

"A part of you knows what it is, Son. You just gotta get quiet enough for it to tell it to you. Ask for His guidance in the morning, and then go move around and see what happens. When you hit a wall, turn left. Doors will open. Teachers will appear. You'll get the guidance you need if you can keep that damn noggin' of yours open. We're responsible for the footwork and He'll take care of the results. And above all else, get grateful for what you got. Jump on that gratitude train and ride it until it runs outta tracks. Gratitude waters the garden of peace, Son. It truly does.

"There are plenty of folks sitting on the big fence, playing it safe. Don't be one of 'em. Pick your side and stand on it proudly. Especially when it comes to spiritual matters. There's no more important decision we make in life than that one. And nobody can make it for us. I walked without God a damn long time and I'll tell you this, I'm making up for it now.

"The world is full of naysayers. Be the king lobster. Surround yourself with folks who share in your vision. Spend time with those who fill you, not those who deplete you.

"And try to remember we're just here to learn. Soul school is in session, and we're supposed to learn how to keep it at one serious, you know? Grab a hold of that woman of yours and learn it all together. And remember, you ain't supposed to fix her. She's your partner, not your project. You're a team. And when times get tough, and they will, feed the faith, 'cause it gets hungry. Do all that and you'll be fine, Son."

"Thanks, Slim. I promise to give our love the very best I have to offer. I will never forget this night, and I can't thank you enough for allowing it to happen. I guess I shall shut this off and…"

Slim gripped my arm so tightly a yelp came out of my mouth. Minutes went by as we stared at each other in silence. Had I done something wrong? My eyes searched his face for a hint of what was to come. His eyes welled with tears and his grip became even tighter.

"Don't turn that off! Not just yet. I…need to tell you something. Damn it all to hell. I'm done running from this. Done pretending it didn't happen. It was the worst thing I ever did."

"What's that, Slim?"

Slim swallowed hard, appeared to shrink before my eyes. The story. He was going to tell me the story. I almost stopped him, but thankfully I kept my mouth shut and waited.

"She was a beautiful woman. Just starting out. So full of the good things. Hell, I can't even say her name…Su-san. Her name was Susan. We met after a gig and hit it off. We had a lot of the same interests, like dope and booze, so we decided to go back to her place. We got to talking about this and that, and next thing I know, she wanted me to introduce her to heroin. I told her it was too damn deep to step into. She wouldn't have any of it. She looked deep into my eyes, and I was a goner. I'd have given her anything I had."

Slim held his head in his hands as if to hold it together, and his breathing was down to gasps. He told the rest of his story to the wooden floor. I leaned my head to catch sight of his face, hidden by an apparent torture.

"We had a bunch of drinks and smoked some hash. I really liked her, and we ended up having sex, and that was real nice. We drank more. Smoked more. I tried to tell her some stories to get her mind off of the heroin. I put it off as long as I could, hoping she'd forget about it and we'd sleep it off.

"But then, she held my face in her hands. Her smile shattered my resolve.

"God forgive me…I fixed her a needle of dope. Man, it was safe dope, you know? I knew it like I knew my name. I'd done it hundreds of times myself, and I would never have given her too much. I was so damned careful. I swear to God I was.

"She…um…didn't make it, Son. Susan died in my arms. Something went wrong, and her heart just stopped. I did the best CPR I could for as long as I could, but she was gone. I didn't know what to do. I panicked and dialed 9-1-1, wiped down all my prints, and, God forgive me, I got the hell outta there and never looked back."

"Slim, I am so sorry. If I had any idea, I never would have continued to pursue it. I don't know what to say."

"There's nothing to say, Son. I've worked hard to hide it from myself, and I'm tired of carrying it. It gets heavier every year. I've thought about contacting her family, you know, to tell 'em how sorry I am for all of it. I dunno. I just want to do what's right, and I ain't afraid of any trouble it might bring me."

"You certainly have nothing to fear legally after all this time."

"I can't worry about that. I want justice for her, and I'll face down whatever I gotta face down. I dream about her still. I always tell her how sorry I am, and she always smiles and tells me it's okay.

"I've replayed it in my mind a thousand times, and I'd give anything to trade places with her. My disease killed her. That's the damn truth. I should've stayed there with her. Should've been a man and stood up to what I did. I just…can't fix it. I'd do anything…if I could just…take it all back… I'd gladly trade…I…can't…"

"You and I both know you did not kill that girl," I firmly stated. "She had quite obviously made up her mind to try the drug, and if you had not introduced her to it, it would have been someone else. Please, forgive yourself and be free of it. You are a good man, and you were so very young when it happened. You have suffered enough in this life, Slim. You must let it go and forgive yourself.

"I appreciate it, Son, I really do, but I'm a long piece away from forgiveness. I know I didn't mean to kill Susan, but I was responsible. I've faced down a lot of demons and made a truckload of amends in this life. This one's been stuck under my saddle for a damn long time, and it's time to dig it out. I know what I need to do. I'll get there. It's time. Time."

"You certainly had no intention to harm her, Slim. It was an accident that happened between two consenting adults. No more than that."

"Yeah, well, I've held it inside like a damn deep breath for so long, I don't know how I'd feel if it was gone. I don't even know if I wanna let it go. I dunno. I'm just ashamed."

"You have nothing to be ashamed of. Damn it, Slim. It's time to let it all go and be free of it. I'm quite certain that is what she'd want. Change your mind. You've hit the wall. Turn left."

"Yes, I have, and yes I will. My faith tells me God has already forgiven me. All I can do is to try to trust that. I'll tell ya, I wasn't prepared to put any of this out in the air like I did. Now that it's out, it seems bigger than it's ever been, but I feel like I'm breathing better about it. I'll pray for Susan tonight. I'll ask her to help me do the right thing for her. I'll face down whatever I gotta face down.

"I'm really tired, Son. Let's put this to bed."

"I'll say a prayer that you find a peaceful piece to put in your puzzle."

"You can go ahead and turn that recorder off. I've got nothing left, and I feel like I've been electrocuted. It's too bad we gotta end on this note, but it is what it is, I guess. Like I said before, life has a soundtrack, and we're ending this with a really sad song, but it's the one that's playing and that's gonna have to be good enough for me. We sure covered some ground though, didn't we?"

"We covered more ground than I've ever covered with anyone, I will tell you that."

"I can't believe how much came back to me. I honestly figured we'd talk a couple hours or so, and that'd be it. Good thing I got over my shyness."

Slim slapped me on the back, and we embraced. I held him tighter than my arms were able to. Tears drained down his face and onto my shoulder. I felt them soak through my shirt. I loved that. "You did a marvelous job. I'm thrilled you decided to do this."

"I can't imagine the dreams I'm gonna have tonight after opening so many drawers. Hell, I'm half scared to go to bed."

"Peaceful dreams are right around the corner for you, Mr. Slim Chance. I have a feeling this process will give you more peace than either of us are aware of."

"I hope you're right, Son, I surely do. I'm gonna call my Hunky Bunky and tell her how much I love her, and then hit the sack. I'll get back to you on those short stories and poems of mine. I ain't sure about it, but I'm leaning towards letting you read 'em. Just don't criticize my writing. I'm a damn sensitive artist. Make sure you leave your contact information with my secretary on your way out, and I'll call you if I need bail money. You have yourself a good day unless you've made other plans...and, Steven?"

"Yes, Sir?"

"If you only believe half of what you hear, it'll be much easier to remember, and don't let the lobsters get you down."

I laughed, but I was already grieving the end of one of the greatest nights of my life.

"I won't, Slim. I truly won't."

I walked down the path to my vehicle as slowly as I could. The sun felt like a friend on my face and I was not in the least bit tired or worn out. I was absolutely energized. Engorged with a feeling of wellbeing. The colors of all objects surrounding me somehow seemed new to me. A vibrancy I could not understand nor define. I glanced back at the cabin as I opened my car door. Mixed emotions rushed through and around me, finally settling upon an unbridled smile. I held the tape machine close to my chest as I started my car, as if to guard it somehow. I knew, without question, my life would never be the same. One night. Nine hours. A snapshot of a lifetime.

Show me what you love, and I'll tell you who you are. How could I have known at the time it was all about to change for me? That I was about to be introduced to someone I'd truly never really met before—me.

As I drove away from the cabin, I could not help but laugh and thank God for the magic and mystery of it all. For the love of my lady, and the hope now spread out before us. For that night in a Dayton diner, and an opportunity to ride along on The Slim Chance Tour.

About the Author

Shawn Michael Bitz grew up in the Black Hills of South Dakota and played music professionally for twenty-two years. His band, Abby SomeOne, released five studio albums and continues to record new material. He's also worked in the mental health field for over twenty-five years.

Shawn is the son of internationally acclaimed comedian Gary Mule Deer. He lives in Rapid City, South Dakota with his wife, Julia, and their three dogs. He is the author of *Butterfly Pit Crew* and is currently working on his third novel. Find him on Facebook at @ShawnMichaelBitz and at cabruce@hotmail.com.